A Follow Your Heart Novel

Love Scattered in the Wind

Linda Phillips

I just want to thank God for imagination, and the boatload of it He gave to me. If He can use a donkey to speak, He can use me to write imaginative stories.
Thanks, Lord.

Chapter One

"**F**ollow your heart, even if love takes you to the stars in the heavens or down into the depths of the sea. Enter new realms."

"So, sweet girl, fairy tales do come true."

"Are they real, Mommy?"

"Yes, dear. Didn't we just read about one?" She winked at her daughter.

The mother closed her child's favorite book, *Ember Pines*, and laid it on the nightstand. She handed a fluffy horse named Skyfire to her daughter. The little girl cuddled it and lay down on the pillow. Mom kissed the top of her head, tucked her in and turned the nite light on before leaving the room, stopping to listen to the creak of the door stop and not click close before heading down the stairs.

Outside the girl's window, an enormous pair of neon green eyes watched from the sky. Serpents slithered and hissed inside the iris, glaring inside the room. The little girl had fallen asleep already. A scorching ray blasted out of the ungodly eyes and burnt holes through the book. Then the eyes vanished.

$\sim$

Stench, darkness and fear. Impossible. The inhabitants of the province were in denial. They just couldn't shake the presence of an eerie blanket of evil covering the land that replaced their always sunny and cheerful dispositions. Dreary overcast skies replaced their always fragrant and blue skies. Concerned eyes searched the sky. Some dwellers rubbed their arms up and down as though they felt a cold chill, except in their dominion, the temperature is never cold or never hot.

Ember Pines was too happy to notice evil lurking. She was oblivious to all of the fear and dismal miens of every person far and wide. She twirled with hands over her heart, eyes closed lightly and a smile of pure joy. Nothing could alter her mood. Her valiant swain surprised her with a very romantic proposal. She was one hundred percent shocked by the engagement ring that held a diamazitieen rock found only in their region. It was a natural stone that looked like a diamond swirling with different colors and glitter. Handsome and dazzling Ari took her breath away and the rare gem was a representation of the passion she felt for him and he for her.

The proposal took the whole commonwealth by surprise. Her very dear friend, Addley, ran out of the house in tears at the news. Even though the lurking presence of something very wicked struck fear in the inhabitants' hearts, they were still abounding with joy at the news and nobody noticed Addley run out of the house.

Later that day, Ember finally floated back to the ground from her in-the-clouds state of mind noticing her dear friend was missing. "Sharley, where is Addley?"

"Gosh! I have no idea. Never saw her leave."

"Mmmm," Ember thought patting her lips with the index finger. "I know. She was so excited that she ran home to share the news with her family. That's it."

"If you say so," Sharley replied in a snarky tone.

"Why do you say it like that? As if she wouldn't be happy for me."

Sharley scratched her cheek. "Maybe I should have brought

this to your attention before. I didn't want to start something if perhaps I misinterpreted her actions."

Ember leaned towards her. "Just what are you deliberately not saying?"

Sharley held her hands out. "Okay. I'll tell you but don't get mad at me. I always felt Addley was jealous of your relationship with Ari. Before you came here, she hung around him like they were super glued together. Numerous—and I do mean numerous —times I caught her staring at him. You know, puppy dog eyes. Haven't you ever noticed?"

"No! Never! She's one of my best friends. I don't believe for a minute she would betray our friendship. Not a minute."

"Or she pretended to be your friend in order to stay close to Ari."

"No! Sharley! How could you say such things?" Ember's tone changed as she eyed Sharley. "I can tell that you believe what you're saying."

Sharley sighed. "Just consider this a warning. I guess you haven't noticed Addley's been leaving a lot and nobody knows where she goes. Not even her parents. I believe she's getting involved with something wicked. When she returns, her eyes are extremely dark, and she talks like she's in some kind of trance. Come on. Tell me you haven't noticed. If that's not enough, everyone is commenting about an evil presence lingering. Everyone."

Ember crossed her arms and squared her shoulders. With a defiant tone she expressed, "I refuse to believe that. She's one of my best friends. Surely, I would have noticed the changes you're talking about."

"EMBER, you've been with Ari day and night learning about your future roles, I just realized that, so you probably haven't been around her very much to notice. You haven't been around any of us very much, come to think of it. One day when you first arrived here, Sharley confided in me that she wished you never came, that you were taking away her time with Ari. You ruined her plans to marry Ari one day."

"None of this makes sense. She can't be in love with Ari

because at birth our mate is preordained. Ari and I can't help how we feel about each other, because when we were old enough to feel these love emotions, it was going to happen, and it did happen. She cannot be in love with him, I tell you. She is ordained by the bonds of heaven to her betrothed. Do you understand what I'm trying to say?"

"Of course I do. But, in her situation she allowed bad *juju* to influence her instead of the bonds gifted to her from God. Maybe she's too far gone for the preordained relationship."

Ember stared straight ahead not speaking. Then a thought hit her. "Has something like this ever happened before?"

"Not that I'm aware of...but wait! That must be how it starts."

Ember's eyebrows sunk with questions.

"What I mean is, once one of our people chooses evil, such as those who have become Eryndomnites, they lose the preordained bond with their mate. You've witnessed this with your own eyes."

Her head dropped. Softly she replied, "You're absolutely right. Once they accept King Eryn's mark, they no longer belong to themselves. Their minds begin to change and then their body contorts to something horrible and evil. Even the stench they give off is nauseating."

"Sharley, this is too heartbreaking. I need to think. What to do. What to do," she kept repeating while pacing back and forth, slapping her hands together nervously.

"Em, please forgive me. I didn't mean to ruin your happy mood. I just want you to be aware. Truthfully, I have noticed an evilness floating in the air." Her body shimmied after saying that and she squeezed her arms tightly around herself.

"You truly are my best friend. I can see how hard this was for you. As though you are the one betraying friendship," Ember admitted.

"Yeah, it was pretty painful to say, especially since Addley has always been one of my best friends," she replied choking on her words. Ember looked warmly at her and gently patted her hand.

"Maybe I could have stopped Addley from choosing evil if I

would have spoken up. I stopped hanging around her because she was acting so different, so freaky, actually." She choked up. "I'm so ashamed of myself. I need to get home. Please, keep your eyes and ears open. Pay attention and be safe. Promise me," Sharley begged. That overwhelming feeling was strong.

"I promise." They hugged and Sharley walked out. But she kept thinking about their conversation. Ember was more worried about Addley than believing her. She had always been a faithful friend. Anger rose in her cheeks. With a slightly puckered mouth, she turned back around, stopped and stared at Ember with glaring eyes. Being friends is a two-way street. Sharley strolled out and let the door slam on the way out.

Shocked by the sudden change in her mannerisms, Ember stared at the door.

Chapter Two

As Sharley walked home with arms wrapped around herself, teardrops sparkling down her cheeks, she tried squeezing the goosebumps to make them stop. And what was that gosh awful smell? She couldn't shake off the anger, not to mention fear engulfing her mind and body. Her cheeks puffed out and she held her breath because of the pounding of her heart. It was so loud that she couldn't hear anything else. Her eyes shifted back and forth. "Pay attention and be safe," she repeated softly to herself.

~

Lying on her stomach, knees crossed, swinging her legs, Ember extended her hand as she admired the spectacular ring. It glowed and sparkled shining out about eight feet in diameter. Neighing and a fretful snorting shook her out of the glorious trance. She jumped off the bed and ran to the window. "Skyfire, what's wrong?"

He jumped up on two legs and pawed at the air, snorting and repeating the action.

"I'm coming. Stay there."

She ran down the long, spiral, vine staircase. It sparkled with real and natural gold accents. Trying to reach up to his massive neck, she whispered in gentle, calming words. Then she laid her head against his muscular thigh that she could barely reach. He whinnied. "Come on. Let's take a walk. Something has you spooked, too, I see."

He kneeled so she could climb on his back. Her hand gently stroked his mane. Just her touch could calm him down. He would die to save her. That much she knew. Thankfully it never came down to that. The way he was acting now proved something was amiss.

After calming Skyfire down and settling him in the stable, she got ready for bed. Nightly she dreamt of Ari, always waking up in a gleeful mood. But not tonight. She tossed and turned.

Sweat beaded up on her forehead and above the lips. A blood-curdling scream echoed through the house. Flora, her mother, ran to her room so fast that she tripped on a rug, causing her to fall on top of Ember's legs. Ember jumped up wide-eyed, dazed from being awakened suddenly.

"I'm sorry. Did I hurt you?"

"No. What are you doing here, Mother?"

"Your scream scared the living daylights out of me. Is everything okay?"

Ember scratched her head. "Must have been a nightmare. I'm feeling rather fearful, I have to admit." She slunk down under the covers.

"Do you remember any part of the dream?"

Ember thought for a moment. "The only thing I can recall is seeing a huge pair of wicked eyes watching me."

"I'm sure it's nothing, but in the morning, I will speak with your grandparents. To be honest, I felt chary all day, but the proposal distracted me. What a magical moment." Her thoughts lingered with a smile. "But there is still a definite feeling of evil growing stronger by the minute; do you feel it?" Flora glanced around the ceiling, walls and out the window.

"Mother, now I'm scared. Can I sleep with you and Poppa?"

"Aren't you a little too old for that?"

"Well, Sharley felt the same thing as you're feeling now."

"Oh, my. That's enough for me to take this warning seriously.

In that case, I will sleep right here tonight. I'll send a message to your father and have him send word throughout the kingdom to be on the lookout. We'll all keep you safe."

"Thank you, Mother."

Ember and Flora creaked open the bedroom door in the morning. At first, she and Flora jumped seeing someone lying under blankets on the floor outside of her room, but his branchy strands of hair stuck out and Flora recognized him immediately. An affectionate smile formed. She jiggled his arm under the blanket.

"Arwood, wake up."

"What! What's going on?"

"Didn't mean to wake you, great protector," she said with a snigger.

"I didn't mean to fall asleep. When I heard your message, I came immediately and decided to hang outside of Ember's room. My eyes got too heavy, I suspect, and closed without my knowledge," he added in a confused tone. Both Flora and Ember smiled with adoring love knowing he tried to be protective.

After breakfast, Ember decided to find Addley. She didn't have to look very far.

"Ember. Ember. Wait up."

"There you are. I was looking for you. Why did you leave without saying anything yesterday?"

"Yeah, about that. My mum sent me a message to come right home. There was so much excitement over the proposal, I just couldn't interrupt. But now I think congratulations are in order." She embraced Ember and produced a sincere smile. Ember studied her face trying to decipher whether she detected insincerity or not. Why couldn't she see what Sharley could see?

"I was wondering, what about you? Have you met your preordained? You have never mentioned anyone."

"Nope. I must be a lost cause."

"That's impossible. It's predestined for each of us."

"Looks like God forgot about me. Oh well. I'm really happy for you, though."

"Do you mean it, Add?"

"Sure. Why wouldn't I?"

"No reason. Just asking."

"I'll even prove I'm happy."

"Maybe another time. Ari is probably worrying about me by now. I need to get going." Addley scrunched her lips tightly. Ember wasn't paying attention.

"Catch you later," Addley blurted with a quick smile.

Chapter Three

Ember glanced back in her direction because Skyfire was jerking his head and snorting at Addley.

"Hey-hey-hey! It's okay. What has you so riled up?" She backed up and twirled around. "See, I'm perfectly fine. Now, quit making a kerfuffle." His muzzle snuggled up to her. She kissed him gently and affectionately. He knelt down and she jumped on his back. They were gone in a flash with a streak of fire and smoke trailing.

Ari and Ember spent the day together, studying, reading, and applying what they have learned in real-life situations. But something was disconcerting. He was uncharacteristically quiet throughout the day. She watched him with caution, not knowing when would be a good time to question him. He kept turning his head back and forth, slowly, face serious, eyes slanting.

"Are you having second thoughts about the proposal?"

"What? Huh?"

Her shoulders slumped. "You don't want to marry me anymore. You are in love with Addley; aren't you?"

He threw his hands up. "That is utterly ridiculous." His eyes lingered on hers. It was obvious with blurry eyes that she was upset. Softly, he placed both hands on her shoulders. With warm eyes and a tender voice, he acknowledged, "My only regret is that I didn't propose sooner. Never, and I mean NEVER question my love for you. I fall asleep at night seeing your beautiful face in my mind and I wake up with your beautiful face in my mind. I am so crazy in love with you that I get embarrassed wondering if I'm being too mushy.

"And Addley, what is that nonsense all about?"

"Why do you act so quiet and disinterested today?"

"Didn't realize I was doing that. I'm sorry. I can't pinpoint the reason, but something feels wrong. And that disgusting odor. That just doesn't happen around here. It can't happen around here." Aggravated, he swished tree branches back and forth. "It's bothering me that I can't figure out why I feel this way. But why would you think I am in love with Addley?" His whole face wrinkled with a displeased expression.

"It's just that you seem to like being around her. A lot."

"Ember, she means nothing to me except in friendship. I love her like a friend and nothing more. Romantic feelings are for you and you alone. Can't you tell how crazy I am about you?" With serious eyes, he held her hands.

"Forgive me for acting like a silly child. There's been something weird happening lately. I guess I'm just feeling insecure. I know better now."

Relieved he replied, "Good. That makes me feel better. But what are you talking about, something weird going on?"

"Let's just say you're not the first one to say something is amiss. People are mentioning an evilness lurking about. I was so spooked last night, my mother stayed with me in my room and my papa slept outside my door. I can't figure out why I can't detect the evil."

He smiled. "I didn't detect it until today. I think we were both too happy yesterday to notice. The thought of spending our lives together makes it impossible for my heart to be anything but happy."

She rubbed his arm. "Me, too."

Rubbing his jaw, Ember waited patiently until he was ready to speak. "Now that I think about it, it would probably be best if you stayed at my house so I can protect you."

Her mouth dropped. "Are you kidding? That would cause quite a stir. No way. It's not worth the scandal."

"Ember! I live with my parents and tons of staff. Your room would be so far from mine, we would need vehicle assistance to get together. Everyone knows that."

"Or wings," she said with a winsome expression.

He grabbed her hands. "You are so darn cute. But truthfully, the last time I felt this uneasiness was when the Eryndomnites attacked."

"That's a spooky thought. Well, I should really go home. My family and Skyfire will be near me. He has been acting strange, also, I have to admit."

"Okay, if that's the only way to keep you safe, I'll take you home. But I'm not leaving until I speak with your grandparents."

"Ari, they're not here right now. They left on some business trip; you know one of their things. Some thing or another. My parents and plenty of staff are there. I'll be safe."

He blew out a sigh of frustration. "Okay, but if something happens to you, I'll never forgive myself and you'll have to live with that fact, young lady."

"I will be tortured by your words. Now that I am officially scared out of my wits, it's probably a good idea to head home."

From behind them a person yelled. "Hi guys."

They turned to see Addley heading towards them. Ari smiled. Ember analyzed his face wanting to believe he really saw Addley as a friend. Then she turned and watched Addley approach them, Addley's eyes constantly on Ari and a smile as bright as the sun. She shifted her stance feeling a tint of jealousy. Feeling guilty how she disbelieved Sharley, she instantly felt shame.

"Hello back," Ari returned with a grin.

"I was on my way to visit you."

"Me?" Ari asked since she was looking at him.

Acting like her body felt a chill, she stuttered. "Uh...I... No. I meant Amber."

"My name is Ember."

"Sorry. I don't know what came over me."

I do. Guilt. Not believing her story now, Ember interjected. "Why were you coming to see me?" Her tone was unwelcoming. To the point it caused Ari to stare at her with questions.

Feeling unsure of her answer, Addley shrugged her shoulders. "I just wanted to see you. That's all."

"I'm sure Ember would love to see you, right?" he asked nudging Ember.

With eyes of scorn staring at Ari, she replied. "Sure. As a matter of fact, Ari was just leaving."

Stunned and speechless, his expression froze while looking in Ember's eyes.

"He doesn't have to leave on my account. We all have spent much time together, so what's the big deal now?"

"No big deal," Ember replied coolly. "He has things to do."

"Ember?" he said with a thrown-off look.

"Go ahead and leave. We'll be fine." She whistled and Skyfire was there within seconds. It was amazing how fast he would show up. He snorted and became instantly enraged as he trotted past Addley. She backed up.

"It's funny how he reacted like this to you earlier. And apropos of the earlier incident, clearly this needs looking into," she said looking at Addley.

"I don't understand why."

"Me neither. He only acts this way if he thinks I'm in danger. Why would he react this way from being around you?" she asked looking sternly at Addley.

"Ember. May I speak with you privately?" Ari asked in concern. Addley puckered her lips, twiddled her fingers and swayed.

Ari and Ember stood beneath a white weeping cherry tree in full bloom. The dangling branches covered Ember's hair and took on the appearance of a veil. A mind could easily transport to wedding vows. Addley's face scorned with jealousy thinking about the upcoming wedding.

Ari placed his hands on her shoulders. Staring into her eyes he asked, "Why are you treating Addley like that?"

"Like what?" she huffed back.

"Like that. Like the way you just sounded to me. I don't understand."

"Are you taking her side? You are treading on very dangerous ground right now."

"What has gotten into you? Really? What just happened?"

"You taking her side, for one thing."

"I'm not taking anyone's side. We three have hung out together for years. Now all of a sudden you are questioning motives between us. Why? I would like an honest answer."

"Are you in love with her?" She said it quietly not wanting Addley to hear.

He lifted his hands and let them fall to his side. "What?" His brows squished together. "What has gotten into you? Didn't I just explain to you that you are my only romantic interest? I love you Em, not Addley. I love Addley like a friend and that is all. Nothing more. Ever!"

"Sometimes it feels as if you are happier to see her than you should be. And she certainly can't take her eyes off of you."

"Has someone been putting thoughts in your mind? How could you even think I or she would betray you? It will never happen. You're stuck with me whether you like it or not. I don't love Addley. I don't think about her, dream about her, have romantic feelings for her; nothing. But I have all of them for you. I always will."

"I'm sorry. I don't know what's come over me. Let's go back and I'll change my attitude."

He kissed her cheek for an extended amount of time, looked lovingly into her eyes and took her hand. Addley puckered her lips tightly but released the tightness as soon as they turned to walk back to her.

"I'm sorry, Addley. I've been under a great deal of stress."

Her smile looked genuine. "That's okay. I'm sure you have a lot on your plate. I understand."

Skyfire stood on two legs, raising them up and down, scratching angrily at the dirt. It was as if Ari's eyes were finally opened to see it for himself.

"It is strange how Skyfire is reacting to you, Addley," he confessed.

"I can't imagine why." She stuck her hand out towards Skyfire. "Come on boy, come here."

He neighed and snorted and kicked up his hooves. She fell backwards. Using her feet as props, sitting on the ground, she pushed her body back.

Ember went to him. She placed a hand on his face and spoke gently. "What's wrong with my boy? Everything is okay. You go on home. Go on. I'll be right there. That's my boy."

Skyfire walked off, but he stopped and looked back several times. Ember nodded her head in a soothing manner to make him feel better.

Ari helped Addley up. The slapping sound of wiping dirt off her clothes was loud. A face that was unhappy formed.

"Now, where were we?" she asked incredulously.

"You okay? I don't know what's gotten into Skyfire."

"I'm fine. Maybe he needs to get away for a while," Addley spurted with frustration.

"He will never leave my side. But what you stated is worth thinking about. Maybe I should take him away for a while."

"I beg to differ," Ari said surprised.

"Not right now, silly."

"Look, I'll walk Ember home so you can go and do whatever it was you need to do. I'll keep her safe. Come to think of it, I have a surprise for her."

"What kind of a surprise?" Ember asked curiously.

Addley shook the index finger her way. "Un-un-un. It's a surprise."

"Anything I have to do can wait. With Skyfire gone, I don't feel it's safe to let Ember walk back with just you."

Addley's eyes glared, offended that he didn't care about her safety. "What about her safety? Or any of the other people in the province? It's always about Ember. Ember this; Ember that," she mumbled under her breath in disgust.

"Oh, come on. It's not too far. We'll be fine," Addley assured him.

"Ember, what do you think? I'm still not sold on your safety."

She looked at Addley and back at Ari. "Go ahead and leave. We'll be fine. Go on."

He asked Addley, "Have you noticed an evil presence?"

"Don't be silly. Evil can't get in here. We have too many firewalls. Now, go on."

Ember's body shuddered. She hugged herself and glanced around. Nobody seemed to notice that behind the trees up in the sky, hidden from the clouds, was a pair of evil eyes staring down at them. An uneasiness developed among them causing short tempers, distrust and angry dispositions. Ember and Ari didn't understand why they felt such fear, so their cautious eyes scanned the horizon.

Ari looked at Ember. "Okay. But remember, if something happens to you, I'll never be able to forgive myself."

Addley grabbed Ember's arm and started pulling her. "Oh, give me a break."

Ari stood back and watched them walk off until they were out of sight. Addley kept checking to see if he was following.

"You know, you're acting a little strange today. You don't seem like yourself one bit," Addley informed her.

"I apologized. Remember? I have a lot on my plate right now."

Ember had watched Addley closely around Ari. She tried to find some sort of animosity or insincerity in her actions, especially towards her. But she wasn't convinced it was all in her mind. Addley wasn't acting like herself.

As they walked, Addley blurted out, "I almost forgot."

Her quick reaction shook Ember up. "What? What is so important?"

"My surprise for you. Do you mind stopping at Treelin's house? Just for a minute?"

"Not a good idea. Ari will flip out if I don't go straight home."

She snidely replied, "Well, what Ari doesn't know won't hurt him." Her defiant smile should have registered with Ember, but already feeling ashamed of her reactions, Ember chose to ignore the fiery warning.

"Where does he live? I don't remember."

"Just down this pathway. Come on Ember. I can't wait for you to see my surprise."

Now extra curious, because she loved surprises, she gave in. "We better make it fast; okay?"

Addley sighed with relief. "Sure thing."

"I'll bet you never knew that Treelin has a crush on you."

"Really? He must not be ready for his predestined mate, or he wouldn't be feeling that way. You know, like me and Ari."

"Yes. I'm aware," Addley replied almost sarcastically.

Addley grabbed the unusual door knocker and banged it. The eyes of the door knocker squinted, and the mouth formed a wicked smile. The door opened.

Treelin smiled widely. Then he noticed Ember standing behind her. His eyes lit up with excitement. "Who have we here?"

Ember peeked her head out from standing behind Addley. "Hello there."

"What a wonderful surprise. I wasn't expecting you." Addley winked at him. He avoided any reaction that would make Ember suspicious. First, he picked up Ember's hand, staring in her eyes, he kissed it. A shaky smile formed on her face.

He looked at her hand. "What is this I see? Say it isn't so."

"Oh, that. Yup, Ari proposed."

"That lucky dog," he said convincingly.

Her face changed to an awkward reddish color. "I'd say I'm the lucky dog."

"Blah, blah, blah. Let's get inside already," Addley urged, disgust on her face.

For some strange reason, Ember jumped as the door slammed behind her. Looking back and forth at Treelin and Addley's forced smile, goosebumps traveled up her body. She gulped.

"Treelin, are you forgetting something?" Addley reprimanded him with puckered lips.

"What? What?" he asked, not taking his eager eyes off of

Ember. "Oh, that. I'll be right back." Addley turned her face towards him and crumpled her mouth, face of pure scorn. As fake as ever, she smiled at Ember. Grabbing her hands, bouncing up and down, she said with excitement, "You are going to love our surprise."

But Ember wasn't feeling the excitement. Her head turned and scanned the room. She was beginning to feel that same uneasiness everyone else talked about. "I'm sorry. Something is wrong. I've got to get going." As she turned to run, her body froze in place. Breaths became erratic. Treelin walked up with a platter that held three goblets. His smile was ear to ear. Addley laughed behind her back.

"Ta da! Here is your surprise." Addley picked up one of the goblets, turned and handed it to Ember.

Oddly, Ember was able to move now. Nervous, she glanced around.

"Ember, we've been working months on this just for you. You don't want to hurt our feelings, do you? Please, taste the heaven."

Many colors swirled in the drink. It caused her to stare. She sniffed it. "Oh, wow! That smells amazing. What's in here?"

"It's your own special drink. We concocted it just for you. My best friend."

Enchanted by its magical appearance, hypnotizing her and causing a swirling in her eyes, Ember looked up and said, "Let's make a toast."

"What a good idea." They all raised their goblets.

"To friendship." Ember watched them as she brought the goblet to her mouth. They pushed their goblets up. When she took a sip, Addley added more to the toast.

"To love."

"This taste is so incredible, there must be angels floating about flavoring our mouths."

"Or demons," Addley added with a wicked laugh.

Shaking her head, Ember replied, "What? Why would you say something so bizarre?" She fell back, almost losing her balance. Eyes widened. "What's in here?" Holding the goblet forward with a shaky hand, she looked at Addley. "Why are your eyes black?"

Addley and Treelin broke out in a diabolical laugh. "I'll take that. He's mine. You're out of the picture," Addley proudly announced holding her hand out staring at Ember's engagement ring.

"What did you do?" slurred out of Ember's mouth. Feeling ashamed about how she disbelieved Sharley, shame rose on her face as she fell unconscious, the goblet clanking on the floor to a roll as the contents dribbled on the floor.

Just before she passed out, she heard a very evil laugh from behind her.

"Oh darn. I hope her head doesn't bruise badly." Addley laughed hysterically.

"You are absolutely ignoble. Thanks for the good time." Treelin doubled over in laughter. "I could never be in love with a goody two-shoes. I'm in love with you, Add. You don't love Ari, silly. You're in love with me; you just don't know it."

"Get to the portal now! Before it's too late," words echoed from the sky outside. It shook both of them out of their state of laughter.

The people of the whole territory ran for cover against the tornadic wind gusts. They hid in caves, and any spot that would protect them. They had no idea what was happening, because in their land, nature elements are always in harmonic order. This was the first time, for some folks, that they faced fear. Screams and crying echoed through the wind gusts.

That wasn't the only fear, though. An emotional fear that a love so sweet and precious was scattered in the wind. For reasons that were unidentified, tears fell down the faces of the inhabitants. Something so painful just took place, and they knew in their hearts that a great love had just been torn apart.

At Ari's home, as the wind died down, he stood with a stare. His eyes watered but he couldn't understand why. He swallowed hard. His mother walked over and laid a hand on his shoulder. Softly, she asked, "Ari, what is it? Your countenance is scaring me."

His hand rested on his heart, and with rainy eyes he mumbled in a trance, "Love scattered in the wind." He snapped out of it and spoke louder. "I feel it deep inside my heart. Whose love? Ember and my love? Don't you smell that putrid odor? That's not normal. Something evil is lurking. I have to go. I have to make sure she's okay."

Like the raging wind, he took off in search of his love.

Chapter Four

Tyrus McKendry drove down his long dirt driveway. Dust spread like a cloud. It was close to dusk.

He pulled up to the ranch-style house. One he had remodeled, made bigger, and designed to look like a rancher's house. Several barns were built on the property and separated to hold a variety of livestock. It didn't look anything like the place he bought from the former owners. They would never recognize it now. Grabbing two bags of groceries before slamming the door closed and not locking the truck, he headed for the front door. Something caught his attention from the corner of his eye.

He glanced over to see a glow coming from around the corner of his house. "What in the world is that? I bet that outside light fell," he scolded himself. "Should have fixed it."

Walking casually, his body tensed up as he approached. The glow became brighter and looked cautiously different from any light glow he had ever seen. He tipped his head up and inhaled the most pleasing and comforting fragrance; a scent he had never smelled in his life. A smile produced and he tried to distinguish what could possibly make that perfumatory fragrance. Softly, he spoke out loud. "Warm cashmere woven with sunbeams and marshmallows." Where did that come from? He gave his head a quick shake and moved forward. Taking deliberate one-step-at-a-time movements in order to not make any sounds, he stuck his head out around the corner. Not sure what to expect, he proceeded forward with caution. Raising his head higher, he could now see the area in question and his mouth dropped and his eyes widened.

Forgetting he was carrying groceries, some cans dropped to the ground and thumped over and over as they rolled to a stop. Cussing under his breath, he jumped back. He heard her stir. *Why is a glow coming from her? Could it be something toxic like radiation*, he questioned himself.

He leaned in closer, and that intoxicating scent was coming from her. In the background, a dust tornado rotated, and instantly Tyrus felt a need to weep. He noticed the moonbeams reflecting from the dust tornado, plus he heard the whooshing of air. He rubbed the dirt from his eyes and stared at it in complete shock. Two green neon lights swirled in the rotation just before disappearing.

He looked down and noticed the girl, or young lady, he couldn't quite tell, was covered in dust and had a sparkly glow. He gently touched her shoulder. With just eye movement, she glanced around the surroundings. Tyrus came into view. Her eyes froze on him. In a state of panic, she sat up, and using hands and feet, she pushed herself back next to a shrub in a cowering manner. The gown she had on was slipping down the shoulders. She kept pulling it back up and resumed her frightful position.

With a soft tone Tyrus spoke. "I'm not going to hurt you, young lady. Are you hurt? Lost? Do you need help?"

Arched eyebrows and a scrunched-up face, she just stared.

He set the groceries down and very slowly extended his arm towards her. "Could I help you up?"

An "Hhhh" gasp very quietly escaped her throat as she grew more fearful, pushing herself firmly against the shrub, and pulling her crossed arms together.

Waving his hands down, he said, "It's okay. I won't touch you," and he backed up. "I'll bring you some water." At the pace of a turtle, he reached for the cans and placed them back into the grocery bags. He turned and walked back towards the front door. She followed him with her eyes. When he moved out of sight, she jumped up and peeked around the corner. She could hear the screen door rattle as it closed. At this point, any sound terrified her. She jumped.

She looked around, eyes blurred. Wanting desperately to weep, she couldn't reason why, and she wrapped her arms around herself and stared with sorrowful eyes, tears streaming down her cheek. Not knowing what to do, she sat back down against the shrub. Her mind kept drawing a blank. Feeling defeated, her head fell on top of her arms that laid across her knees. Tears kept stinging the back of her eyes, blinking constantly as a method of relieving the burning sensation. Feeling the gritty sandy feeling all over her, she wiped the sand off of her arms, confused, and she rubbed the texture of sand between her fingers. Not even conscious of it, while thinking she picked up a twig and started swirling it in the dirt. A small section of the dirt changed colors as tears dropped.

Tyrus walked to the bedroom window and peered out trying not to be seen. His head dropped. He didn't know what to do. If it were a farm animal, then yes, knowing what to do would come easily to him. But a young lady who seems lost, frightened, and untrusting, this posed a real challenge for him. He wiped his hand down his face and neck. Eyes popped wide open. Staring up at the ceiling, with his crossed arms, he continuously slapped his hands against his arms.

"Whenever I was scared, my parents would fix me a glass of chocolate milk. It worked every time."

He gave his head a quick nod and smiled, then moved to the kitchen. The spoon clinked against the glass as the chocolate swirled and became a rich brown color. "I may just have to make myself a glass when I come back, Mr. Rabbit," he said admiring the picture on the container.

Very slowly he turned the corner. She naturally jumped from the surprise of not hearing him walk up. His lips formed a warm smile as he extended the glass towards her. She didn't budge, so he took a small sip, licked his lips and placed the glass on the ground just feet away. "This is too delicious to let it sit and go bad. I'm heading back in the house. I'll be back later with some food. I know all young adults love macaroni and cheese, so I'll make you some. My, but you are a tiny thing."

While the macaroni boiled on the stove, he went to peek out the curtain. A relieved smile appeared. She drank it down, some dribbling down her face and staining the white gown. She placed the glass back where he left it for her previously.

The drape swished as he walked back to the kitchen. "Well, that's a start. But how do I get her to trust me? She needs shelter." The sky rumbled in the distance.

Checking the conditions of the sky, the screen door rattled behind him, alerting Ember that he was coming back. Her body tensed. But that adorable nose lifted and sniffed. Something smelled good and her face produced curious expectations as he rounded the corner.

Always trying to make her feel at ease, Tyrus laid the hot bowl with a kitchen towel underneath it on the ground and collected the empty glass. He touched the bowl to alert her that it was hot, waving his hand and repeating, "Hot-hot-hot." If she burnt herself, it could easily cost trust issues with her.

Before he left, he pointed to the sky. The rumbling was louder, and cloud coverage was making it pitch dark out. "Please, come inside when you're done. Looks like a wicked storm approaching." He waved to the house hoping she understood. The wind was picking up as he walked away.

This time she got right up and grabbed the bowl and towel, touching the tines of the fork with a confused mien. She copied him and touched the bowl. Shaking her index finger, she put it in her mouth to cool it off. The wind began to cool down the macaroni. She tasted it and savored the bite. Her expression showed, "What is this stuff?" She devoured the food in no time. A mild mist of rain touched her, and she looked up to the sky. Understanding the need to seek shelter, she stood up, grabbed the bowl and ran to the front porch. The door was not latched, so she peered inside.

He walked out in time to see her peeking in the door. "Come inside. Please." Holding the kettle, he pointed to her bowl and asked if she would like more? Still no answer, he turned and went back to the kitchen.

She painstakingly slowly followed the scent. Looking around at the inside of his house, she made a confused expression. He wouldn't understand, but everything that she looked at was new to her, not anything like in her world.

He looked her over and realized she didn't look normal. Delicate ivory skin, she was absolutely beautiful, and her hair actually looked like gold streaked through it. Real gold, like the mineral. He reached his hand out and asked, "Could I touch your hair?"

One eye slanted and she, with extreme caution, nodded yes. He drew his hand back in surprise. "Wow!" He stood back and looked at her hair again. She was as enchanting as a storybook princess, except her hair was rather messy. It reminded him of a lion's mane. Something above her cheekbone started glittering and swirling. He was speechless. Next, he glanced in her eyes and his imagination went crazy. Never had he seen brown eyes speckled with gold so brilliant, deep and rich. Even her fingernails looked off, more animalistic than he wanted to believe.

She watched him rub his jaw back and forth forcefully while his face revealed hinky thoughts. *Make contact with this alien being*, he kidded himself. But how? A strategy was rolling around inside his brain and the light bulb came on.

Pointing to himself he said, "I'm Tyrus. Tyrus," he repeated. Then he pointed to her.

Her shoulders shrugged.

"Can you speak?"

Silence.

"Do you know your name?"

Her head tilted. He pointed to himself again. "Tyrus," he said elevating the volume.

"T-y-r-u-s," she almost spelled out in the way she pronounced it.

He nodded, "Yes, yes. What's your name?" he asked pointing to her.

She raised her hands and shrugged her shoulders.

"You don't know your name?" Her head shook.

"Do you know where you are?"

Her head shook no.

"Do you remember anything?"

Sadly, casting her eyes down, she shook her head no. This time her eyes blurred with noticeable fluid.

Just to be certain, he repeated his name. "I'm Tyrus. Do you understand that is my name?"

Her head nodded. Invisible sweat vanished from his relieved thoughts. She moved strands of hair from her eye, and that is when he noticed the bump and bruise mixture.

"Don't you worry, little one. You can stay here until we figure out what's going on. Looks like you have an injury. I should clean it up and medicate it for you. Tomorrow I'll call my neighbor over for help. You'll really like her. Are you okay with that?"

Clearly uncertain, she barely nodded yes.

"Good. I'm going to run you a bubble bath and find something for you to wear. Give me a second and I'll fix it while you eat more macaroni and cheese."

The storm was clearly rolling in. Lightning struck close by, and thunder blasted like a bomb.

She jumped to her feet and gasped. Where she was from, it never thundered and never had a lightning bolt struck. A gust of wind and rain streamed in through the windows. "It's okay. Let me close the windows and we'll be safe," he nodded while stomping window to window. Every time it thundered, she jumped and squeezed herself. He grabbed a blanket and placed it on her. It worked for scared animals; maybe it will work for her, too. Funny, but it was just what the doctor ordered. She pulled the blanket over her head, pulled the bowl of macaroni inside of it and felt secure. He shook his head and proceeded upstairs to fill the tub. In about ten minutes the water pipes quieted down, and thunder moved on. She pulled the blanket down.

Tapping fast down the stairs, Tyrus turned the corner. "Bath is ready. Follow me."

Her movements were like that of a cat. Her feet made no noise. Walking up behind him, she stood there looking into the bathroom with undeniable questions on her face.

"I thought you might like a bubble bath. My wife used to keep these suds around for when her niece came over. Which was a lot while she was..." clearing his throat overwrought with grief "...still alive."

Ember caught the sound of his voice and looked up curiously at him.

"There's a towel and some clothes that will be too big for you, but we'll figure all that out tomorrow. Go ahead. I'll clean up dishes and see what we have for dessert," he added wiggling his eyebrows.

When she walked in, he gently closed the door. At the bottom of the steps, he stopped and listened. The splash sounded like a dolphin dove in the water. Splash after splash, he could hear the swishing of water and the different volumes of a thump as it hit the floor and walls. "Great. I better get the mop."

Before he turned the corner, he leaned his head towards the stairs. His face lit up. She was giggling and humming.

After wiping the last dish, he turned to walk into the living room. She stood there silently. A nervous laugh escaped his mouth. "That's much better. Do you feel better?"

"Yes, much. Thank you."

"Have a seat and let me take a look at that bump. I'll fix you right up." He was gentle and dabbed some ointment on it and covered it with a bandage. "There. That should do until I have a doctor take a look.

"Let me turn TV on for you while I check on the horses."

"Come."

"You want to come with me?"

Her nod reminded him of a horse nodding.

"I'll let you wear my wife's boots but walk slowly so you don't trip. They'll be way too big."

When she walked, she had to hold up each side of the pants to keep from falling to the floor.

"Stay right there." He skipped off and returned with a piece of rope. He inserted the rope in the belt loops and tied it tight to hold her pants up. "You are a little thing. Try walking again."

She walked in a circle. He was pleased his experiment

worked. He wrapped his late wife's coat around her and put a jean jacket on himself. They walked to the stable, both wrapping their arms tightly around their waists and pulling the collar up tighter to their necks. As soon as they walked up to the opening of the stable, the horses ran right to them. They whinnied with excitement and kept moving between each other to get close to Ember.

"I've never seen anything like this," he said perplexed, looking at her strangely. "They seem to know you or like you...or both."

Nudging her with their muzzle, she climbed up on the oak two by four planks, then rubbed and kissed each one of them. Then she jumped down and unlatched the gate. Before Tyrus could stop her, she was inside.

"Stop..." He didn't know what name to call her. He stood in the doorway and the horses acted gentle and rubbed up to her. They weren't biting each other nor chasing each other like normal. One of the horses knelt down and she climbed on top of it. The palomino pranced around the stable with his head high and tail held up proudly. Funny, his healthy gold coat was almost the same color as her hair, except for the very shiny gold streaks. Tyrus watched gob smacked. She looked over at him and laughed with glee.

What he just witnessed was strange, but remarkable. Never had he witnessed this exchange between the horses and anyone. Watching her closely, he noticed when she was happy that a glow would beam around her. Where it came from, he didn't know. It was nothing like a flashlight beam. It had glitter in it. He scratched his head. After coaxing her out of the stalls, she helped him feed the horses.

Making sure each horse was fed, she kissed them all goodnight. Tyrus had to gently pull her arm away from them.

Holding the front door open for her, he asked. "Why do you suppose the horses react to you the way they do? I've never seen them react like that with anyone. Not even me. Can you explain it?"

She squished her lips together and shook her head no. "I love animals. I guess they know I love them." Her English was some-what shattered but pronounceable. Voice was sweet as honey.

"Well, they sure love you. I have one more question. Why do you glow sometimes?"

"Huh?"

"That glow that comes out of you at times. What causes it?"

Her hands went up, along with her shoulders. "I do not know."

The screen door rattled as it closed, and this time he shut the front door all the way.

"I'll make up a bed for you. There are some cookies in the cookie jar. Go help yourself while I do this."

"Huh," her face formed.

"You like cookies; right?"

"Cookies?"

"You don't know what a cookie is? What planet are you from, young one?" He sniggered.

Tyrus walked past her and held the kitchen door open so it wouldn't swing back and trap her between swings. He brought the cookie jar to the table and took the lid off. Then he poured a glass of milk. The chair screeched on the floor. "You sit here and eat while I get your bed ready." She complied. He turned around to check on her and she was in cookie heaven.

The kitchen door swung back and forth as Tyrus stood by the table. He looked into the cookie jar to find it empty. "You ate all of the wafer cookies?" his face showed incredulously.

Not certain he was upset, she nodded yes as her head shrunk down.

"How does someone so little eat all of that?"

Her shoulders shrugged.

He tucked her in bed, pulling the warm, fluffy blanket up to her chin. The sheets and pillowcases didn't match, nor did the furniture in the bedroom, and none of that mattered one iota to her. "Thank you," she commented with a warm smile. Turning on a nite light, he said, "Good night, Little One."

"Night, Tyrus."

He watched her eyes closely while closing the door. Worry

rose fast. He glanced over and saw a teddy bear. "I almost forgot. Here," handing her the teddy bear, "Mr. Teddy would like to sleep with you." She grabbed and hugged it.

"Thank you."

He left the door cracked, walked downstairs and closed his bedroom door. His head fell into his hands. *What is it about her? She's special. I mean really special. And when she is happy, it looks like a magical kingdom swirls in her very unusual birthmark.*

Boots clunked on the floor. Pieces of mud and sand spread on the floor around them. His shirt and jeans were piled on the floor next to his bed. The light clicked off and there was nothing but silence.

Chapter Five

The next morning Tyrus flipped pancakes and stirred scrambled eggs while it was still dark outside.

His feet tapped quietly up the stairs to her bedroom. The door was pushed open all the way, blanket and pillow missing. There was enough moonlight shining into the room that allowed him the ability to see.

She was gone.

He stomped down the stairs and pounded on the bathroom door. Nothing.

He called for her. Nothing.

A thought came to his mind. Grabbing his jacket, he ran out the front door that was badly in need of paint. Dust particles spread as the screen door rattled close. Before entering the stables, he stopped and walked extra slow so as to not startle her, if she was even there.

The horses stood in a circular fashion, giving the perception they were guarding something. One of them let out a quiet neighing sound, a mild alert to the others. He bent down and looked between their legs. His head fell forward. She was covered up with the blanket sleeping on the straw. He stood back up and scratched his head.

Next, he gently cleared his throat. She stirred. He cleared it louder. Her eyes blinked open. Arms stretching, she yawned. Just her head lifted as she looked around. She spotted him. No movement; no words. Complete silence.

"Good morning, young lady."

A pleasant smile formed. "Morning." Her head fell back down, and the horses nuzzled their kisses on her face. She broke out in giggles and began glowing. She giggled so much that she didn't realize her body levitated just barely. He choked on his saliva, which got her attention, and she automatically fell like a feather back on top of the hay.

Trying to catch his breath, still gasping between coughs, she sat up and watched him with concern. "You okay?"

Waving his hand down forcefully, he said between coughs, "Just give me a minute."

Finally able to catch his breath he asked, "Would you be interested in pancakes, eggs and hot chocolate?"

She recalled the word he used last night with chocolate milk, and how tasty it was. Her head nodded up and down, and again, almost as if she were a horse nodding.

She hopped up and the horses moved out of her way. He held the gate open, and she walked out.

Craziness began. The horses got anxious, kicking their hooves up in the air, standing on two legs, waving the front legs violently, as if defending themselves against a predator.

"Whoa, whoa there. We'll be back. Right?" she asked Tyrus.

"Yes, in about half an hour we'll come back to feed them."

"See?" she said looking at them.

But they took off and bucked fiercely around the stable. Tyrus looked around to see if perhaps a predator was hiding nearby. Just then a shadow in the sky darted by. His head looked up and his eyes squinted. Whatever it was didn't have the shape of any type of fowl, and whatever it was, was huge. The horses immediately settled down.

With slanted eyes, furrowed brows, he asked her, "Did you see anything strange?"

She just shook her head no, but her eyes blinked continuously, and she rubbed her arms.

As they walked to the house, a sense of fright washed over

him. While looking up at the sky, he gently pushed her forward. He wanted to get them in the house safe and sound.

As they sat down for breakfast, he asked her one question and one question only. Her answer would lead to more questions, especially about floating. But, if it caused her anxiety, he would end any questions right away. Why cause her concern if she didn't know anything.

"Do you know anything about your life? Where you came from? Your family? Anything?"

Her head dropped and sad eyes looked back up at him. "Nothing. I know nothing."

He patted her hand. "No worries. We'll figure it out."

He chuckled under his breath. She had whipped cream on the tip of her nose and upper lip area, and she was totally unaware. "My dear, you have a whipped cream mustache."

One side of her mouth lifted up. He rubbed his nose and upper lip area with a napkin and pointed to her to do it. She copied his movement.

"My neighbor, Virginia, is a really fine lady. She plans to take you into town and get you some clothes. Are you okay with that?"

Her head dropped and she shrugged her shoulders.

"She's really nice. It just wouldn't be appropriate for me to take a young girl clothes shopping. Do you understand?"

With a questionable face she nodded yes. "But we feed the horses."

"Of course we'll feed the horses first."

She smiled ear to ear.

"Let's clean up the dishes first. I'm leaving these plates in the oven for my ranch staff. They'll be up soon."

While they washed and wiped the dishes, cleaned off the table and appliances, something was eating away at Tyrus. He stared at the sink for moments before Ember bent her head up to look at his face. He saw her from the corner of his eye and looked at her.

"I've been thinking about this all night. So, I tried my best to search the internet for an answer. Would you be okay with me calling you Tania until we find out your real name?" It was pronounced *Toh nee ah*. "It's a Russian name that means "mystery," and your name and life is a mystery to us both. What do you think?"

She gave a quick nod and slowly repeated the name. "T-a-n-i-a.

Ember knew just how to feed the horses without any instruction. Tyrus sat back amazed once again and watched her work harder than any ranch hand that ever worked for him. After feeding the horses, she cleaned each and every stall. When he tried to help, she protested loudly, so he just leaned on the fence to observe her.

A cute squirrel scooted through the stalls up to Ember. She bent down and picked it up, kissed its forehead and rubbed its coarse fur. Tyrus' mouth almost hit the top board of the fence he was leaning on. He sat there in serious contemplation about her. Why the animals were comfortable with her, not natural in any way. How she knows just how to deal with each one she meets. The sunrays beamed in the stall reflecting the amazing shiny gold glitters in her hair. And her scent. It was natural too, and his thoughts always went to warm cashmere woven with sunbeams and marshmallows. That hit him as odd. He would never think of those things in describing a scent.

Tyrus was thrown off balance by the vigorous snorting and barking. He looked over just as his two dogs ran through the stall up to Ember. The squirrel scolded them and scampered away. They jumped up on her, and she said some very strange, but enchanting words. They stood next to her with eyes looking up. She kissed and rubbed them. Tyrus tried calling them away, but it was like they didn't hear him. She said more words that he had never heard before. They ran straight to him.

"Tania." She didn't look over at him. Louder. "Tania."

Realizing now that he was talking to her, she raised her chin and rested it on the pitchfork handle. The handle grip was too high to rest on.

"What do those words mean that you said to the dogs?"

She raised her shoulders up slowly.

"You don't know?"

Her head shook.

"How could you speak those words if you don't know what they mean?"

Even slower her shoulders lifted up. Her eyes squinted.

"It's okay. Don't you worry."

Tyrus watched the birthmark above her left cheekbone start to swirl and glitter. The gold in her hair seemed to sparkle brighter and the specks of gold in her eyes twinkled like stars. So glued to her, he didn't notice the horses flipping out in the stalls or see the shadow in the sky dart by.

Chapter Six

"Mornin' Tyrus."

"Mornin' guys."

"Whoa! Who do we have here?" Garrett asked all twinkly eyed.

"Her name is Tania." Both guys squinted their eyes and dropped their mouths, but Tyrus spoke before they asked questions.

"I found her lying on the ground on the side of the house. She has no memory. When she trusts us enough, I am going to bring the doc over and have him run some tests. Right now, she's too scared and won't handle it well. We need to be gentle with her. Do you understand?"

"Yeah, boss. Sure."

"There is something so mystical about her. I want to say she is a character out of one of my little sister's storybooks," Jacob noted.

Garrett leaned his head forward. "Good golly. That almost looks like gold in her hair. Hey, we struck gold." He laughed out loud at his words.

"I will remind you to be gentle and do NOT ask her any questions about her life. None. She doesn't have an answer anyway."

"It's obvious, boss, she is not from around here," Jacob remarked mystified.

"Or Earth," Garrett said in a trance watching her.

"What's even more mysterious is how I found her this morning. The horses formed a circle around her in the stall as she slept on the hay in the middle of them. Every animal that comes in contact with her is drawn to her in a magical way. I can't explain it."

"I have an idea. Let's test that theory," Jacob suggested.

"Let's hear it," Tyrus replied.

"Think about it. There is one very touchy animal we tend to daily. Let's take her over by Mr. Horns and see how he reacts to her. I guarantee she won't have a magical way with him."

"I don't know, Jacob," Tyrus replied mildly shaking his head.

"Oh, come on. We'll stand right next to her and keep her safe."

Rubbing his chin he answered, "Why not?"

"Tania, would you come here, please." After two attempts she looked up still not used to being called Tania. He waved her over. Her face turned a nervous mess.

"It's okay. These guys work for me," he said patting their shoulder.

She inched closer, taking her sweet time. The horses sensed her fear and started bucking around the stall. She spoke words to them, and they calmed immediately. All three men looked back and forth at each other.

"Tania, please meet Jacob and Garrett." They tipped their hats.

"Would you want to meet our bull?" Garrett asked with excitement.

She nodded.

"Stay near me, because this bull is very fierce." She walked close to Tyrus, while the two guys stared at her in wonderment.

They stood next to the fence. Jacob yelled for Mr. Horns to come over. He ignored him and kept eating the straw. She bent down and looked between the fence boards. "Mr. Horns," her sweet voice said like a mild gust of wind. The bull turned his massive head and saw her. He turned completely around and ran right to her, hooves stomping the ground sounding like an animal stampede. She smiled brightly. With a gentle moan, he brushed up against the fence. Tyrus was in pure shock and didn't realize Ember climbed up the fence and became face to face with the bull.

Finally realizing the situation, he yelled in a panicked voice. "Tania, get down! He has a very mean temper. Tania!"

She and the bull ignored all concerns. She rubbed his snout and he licked her hand. One of the guys walked right up to them and the bull snorted his anger and pawed the ground. The bull was a hundred percent agitated.

Ember spoke quietly to Mr. Horns, again, in a voice no one understood, not even her. The bull stood perfectly still and rubbed up against the fence. The guys were too flabbergasted to speak. Everything about her from looks to mannerisms was so mysterious.

"Can I touch your hair?" Garrett asked as he raised his hand towards her.

She backed away.

"No! You can't touch her. Period. I won't let them touch you. You two feed the dogs and your breakfast is in the oven. Scat."

They walked off and kept turning around. "And clean up your messes. Then get to work. No dillydallying."

"Yes, sir," they both responded.

Chapter Seven

Dirt and gravel dusted the air and clattered to the ground as a truck slid to a stop. "She always drives too fast. I'll have a talk with her before you leave," Tyrus commented with a nudge to get Ember walking.

"Good morning, good morning," Virginia spouted like a ray of sunshine. "Aren't you the most adorable little thing." Ember took a step backwards.

"Uh, Tania is really shy. Really shy."

"Oh, I beg your pardon. I come on a little strong. Been told that many a time." She laughed. "Let me remedy that right now." Softly she said, "Hi. My name is Virginia. I live down the road a couple of miles. My place is a little worn down, but I am working on some remodels." Looking at Ember's disinterested face she added, "Not that you would care about that. So, what do you need my help with, Ty?" She positioned her body in a comfortable stance and waited for his reply.

"I need you to find her some clothes."

Nibbling on her finger as she looked at Ember, she spoke. "This may be a little difficult. I can tell you are not a child, but your size is extra tiny. If I had to guess, I would guess your age to be anywhere from eighteen to twenty-five."

"That's a pretty big gap," Tyrus replied.

"I'm usually really good with age, but not this time. This is my best estimate. As far as finding clothes for her, don't worry. I know just where to take her.

"First, let me make sure I pronounce your name correctly. It's *Toh nee ah*, right?"

"Yes, that's it," Tyrus answered for Ember, who was too shy to speak.

"Well then, shall we go?"

Tyrus reached in his pocket and handed her a wad of cash. "Get you both some lunch, too."

"Why thank you kindly," Virginia responded.

"Let me help you get in Virginia's truck." He walked Ember to the door and helped to lift her up, her eyes glued to his. He winked and nodded. "Ms. Virginia here is my good friend. She'll keep you safe, plus show you a good time. Get ready to laugh."

As hard as she tried, her smile faded.

They drove away and he watched them drive down the cloudy driveway. When winter comes around, the ground will be solid, and dust won't blow out like a windstorm. He walked towards the stables picturing Ember with Virginia. Did he do the right thing? Was this move too fast?

Virginia was a very nice lady. She was very comfortable to be around and very caring. If you didn't laugh at her corny jokes, your joke button must be defective. Nobody could resist, because her facial expressions is what made them so funny. She was semi attractive, a little overweight and usually dressed very casual. He liked her a lot. Both of them lost their spouses years ago. They struck up a friendship quickly.

Tyrus was a mild-mannered man. You would think being ex-military would have made his personality stronger, but retirement softened him tremendously. He was very passionate about his beliefs and ready to take a stand, but he would have to be pushed in that direction. His hair was a mixture of gray and black, mostly gray. A face etched with wrinkles that showed difficulties in life. But those eyes were warm and kind. That is what would attract women the most.

Bouncing up and down from all the potholes and rocks in the road, Virginia couldn't help herself and said, "Maybe I should tie you down with weights or something. I fear you may fly right out of this truck."

Ember shot her a don't-you-dare look and Virginia corrected herself immediately.

"Don't worry, I would never. No one would ever come to think of it. You seem awfully tense. Anything I can do to change that?" Virginia asked.

She shrugged her shoulders, the usual correspondence.

"I know. We'll get some ice cream. Do you like ice cream?"

And again, the shrug.

"My favorite is chocolate chip or java chip or mint chocolate chip." She licked her lips.

The mention of chocolate warmed Ember's eyes.

In an attempt to make small conversation, Virginia remarked, "That Tyrus is a good, good man."

Ember smiled and nodded her approval.

"My church has a thrift shop. I'm sure the ladies can help us find something for you to wear. Is that okay with you?"

Nodding, she replied, "Yes," soft as a mild breeze.

"Is that your real hair color?"

Ember shrugged her shoulders.

"Oh, that's right. Tyrus informed me of your situation. Tyrus and I have been friends a long time. His wife and I were best friends." Tearing up she added, "When she died, it tore him up. And me. She was a wonderful woman. You may be just what the Lord had in mind to bring some life back into him. He's been so lost without her. But you, you seem to make him smile. It is rare to see that man smile. I will be forever grateful to you for that."

With eyes of gratitude mixed with sadness, Ember responded, "Thank you. That is so sad. Tyrus never mentioned anything about her."

"That's because he can't. It's just too painful."

Ember teared up.

Virginia very carefully patted her knee. "You may be the miracle Tyrus needs to bring love and some cheer back into his life. The Lord knows why you're here. It will all work out and help you and Tyrus in the process."

She smiled genuinely at Virginia.

With much difficulty, they found some outfits for Ember. She wore a child's jean dress and boots, looking absolutely darling. They stopped at a diner, and she ordered grilled cheese and chips. Of course, a chocolate malt with loads of whipped cream was a piece of art in Ember's opinion. The straw slurped continuously in her mouth. By now she was at ease with Virginia.

Three young men walked by and stopped to address Ms. Virginia. Two of them wore cowboy hats and the other one had golden blonde hair that hung down about two inches from his chin. "Good day, Ms. Virginia," he said politely. Ember was too shy to look up at them. The three young men couldn't take their eyes off of Ember, Virginia noticed.

"You did a nice job on my lawn, Aaron."

He smiled.

"Boys, please meet Tania." She introduced them as Ember timidly looked at each one. She put her head down but looked back at Aaron, just staring. Her heart flip flopped for some reason.

"Tania, why don't you come to our young adult's group at church tomorrow night? You will enjoy it. I'd even pick you up. Looks like you have a head injury. Does it hurt?" The other two young men nudged Aaron in the back and jabbered behind him. She didn't answer.

Feeling her discomfort, Virginia added. "She is staying at Tyrus' place. I'll discuss it with him and see if she wants to come with us."

"Okay, Ms. Virginia. I'm new here, too, but the people at the church took me right in and I made friends fast. Well, we'll see you later, Tania." Aaron stared at her the whole time until he walked out the door.

Her head was down, but she managed a quick glance and smile.

"What do you say we stop at the bakery and pick up a coconut cream pie for Tyrus, his favorite? He drives over here once in a while with a craving, because they make the best pie around. Maybe we'll throw in some chocolate chip cookies."

Ember blinked several times and her eyes grew bright at that remark.

A trail of dirt spread across the driveway as they drove to the house. Tyrus heard and ran out the front door, that old, flimsy screen door flapping back and forth.

He held his arms down and out. "My, aren't you a picture? Look how cute you look."

Ember twirled around with excitement. She looked at both of them and said, "Thank you for everything." With almost tearful eyes, she said again, "Thank you both."

He messed up her hair in fun. "Don't mention it."

Virginia opened the backseat door to her truck. "Tania, don't forget the surprise."

She took a quick breath, dropped her mouth with an excited smile and ran to the truck.

Like she was holding an infant, she walked up to Tyrus holding the pie. He slapped his hands to his mouth. "Why thank you. My very favorite pie. Let's go have a piece right now."

They walked in the door and Virginia carried the bag with clothes. "Oh! Tania, I almost forgot. I bought you a surprise. For the life of me I couldn't pass it up. It's just that it suits you so well."

Ember almost hopped around in anticipation. Virginia pulled it out of the bag and held it up. The fairy costume shimmered with beautiful colors. She was in awe of how beautiful it was. Ember held it up to her and turned it around so she could see the back. The wings opened when she did that. She stared and stared and stared. Her face had excitement, but her brows creased as she rubbed the wings with her fingers. Then her eyes blinked constantly.

In complete surprise she clutched her hair in both hands and squeezed tight, then ran for the bedroom dropping the costume onto the floor. As tiny as she is, it sounded like a cat running up the stairs.

Blood drained out of Virginia's face. "I don't understand. She seemed to like the costume."

"Until she saw the wings. Something about the wings. It's as

43

though she fought for a memory that wouldn't come together," Tyrus said with an encouraging tone.

"Maybe she dressed as a fairy one year for a costume party."

"Yeah. I'm sure once she starts to regain her memory, a lot of these outbursts will happen. Don't take it personally. It wasn't against you. Her initial response was happy," he assured her.

"You're probably right. I think she's had enough excitement for one day. Before I forget, though, Aaron invited her to the young adult's group at church tomorrow night. I told him I'd check with you first. She seemed interested in him. Let me know what you think later after speaking with her about it."

"Sounds good. Thanks for taking her shopping. I really appreciate it." He couldn't help but smile affectionately at her.

Now he had to plan a strategy to get Ember to talk to him. He might need Special Forces for this task, flashing back to his team in the military with a fond smile. Just before he headed upstairs, a shadow blocked out the sun temporarily. He looked up and rubbed the rising goosebumps on his skin.

Chapter Eight

Chaos and panic gripped the shire. Ari searched high and low for Ember. Other search teams ventured out into unsafe territory. Skyfire galloped in rage, running out of control. Nobody would dare walk up to him and nobody was stupid enough to try. When it came to Ember's protection and safety, he took his job seriously. Not knowing where she was turned him into a raging beast.

Ari paced the floors of his home while his parents, her parents and grandparents strategized. Grasping his hair on both sides of his face, his words just shot out of his mouth. "How is this even possible? It's my fault. All my fault. I should have insisted on walking her back home, but no, I trusted Addley."

His mother walked up to him, laid a hand on his shoulder and spoke softly. "Son, blaming yourself will not help us find her. We need to think clearly. Please focus, for her sake."

He couldn't look her parents or grandparents in the eyes. "You see," he referred back to his mother's comment, "it's very easy to blame myself. If I would have followed my gut feeling, I wouldn't have let her out of my sight. If...if...if..."

"Ari, not even Skyfire was able to prevent this from happening. I feel right here," Ember's grandfather said placing a hand over his heart, "she's safe and sound. I didn't say out of danger, but for now, safe. I suggest we all meet with the elders and take this request to the highest authority."

"Yes, you're right. That's exactly what we need to do."

Ember's grandfather waved his hand around, "Come all. Join me."

The evil that lingered increased fear. Were they smelling a dead carcass of an animal or of a person? No, the smell was far worse. Perhaps rotting fruit and vegetables. No, the smell was far worse. Also, a constant burning odor hung in the air.

Ari's condition was fragile. He slipped to the floor, bent his face down and sobbed. It tore everyone up. The joy the kingdom felt over the proposal was not supposed to end like this. There wasn't a smile to be seen or a laugh to be heard.

His dad bent down, fighting back the tears. He loved Ember as if she were his own daughter. "Son, we will find her. It's my promise to you, and you know I always keep my promises."

With the back of his hands Ari wiped an excessive amount of tears away. "Father, there's no way you can make a promise like that. Don't say such things." He reached up and squeezed his shoulder. "Thanks anyway. I know this is hard on you, too. We must not give up. With the Lord, we will have more help. He'll guide us. I believe that, Father."

A tear dropped. "Son, I couldn't be more proud of you. You're right." He stood up and faced everyone. "Ari's right," he yelled out with confidence, almost shouting. "The Lord will guide us to her. She is very special to Him. She will be safe. Don't lose hope. We should all know better than to accept defeat."

Without speaking, they all agreed and returned to order. "Now, then, on with organizing a plan," Ember's grandfather ordered.

A soft breeze played a harmonic melody through the leaves as it passed by, spreading soft, aromatic fragrances replacing the lingering stench that brought peace to their thoughts.

They retreated back to the secret war room to engage in further prayers and a stratagem of Biblical proportions. They knew in their hearts that they were dealing with something very evil that was connected to Ember's disappearance.

~

Sharley walked down a secret path that she and Ember shared. A place they could get away from it all and forget the demanding duties Ember had no choice but to be involved in. She loved every minute of her future duties, so it wasn't for that reason she needed an escape. Everyone needs time to relax and just do nothing.

A person could not enter this spot without feeling awe. A gurgling creek emptied into a pond that was surrounded with beautiful willow trees, flower trees, mammoth-sized trees, wildflowers, and water the bluest of blue colors. It sparkled like diamonds. The pond had just the right amount of cattails and lily pads.

Who needs a painting when you have this to look at, she couldn't help but think. Wings flittered in a kaleidoscope of colors. Some of the boulders surrounding the pond took on a form that resembled a chaise lounge. They were covered with moss. She and Ember would lie on them for hours. She plopped her tiny body down and closed her eyes as a beautiful breeze tickled her. It picked up the fragrance of the flowers and showered her with the pleasing scent.

But today, even she couldn't allow all of this to make her feel better or relieve the mounting tension.

No one in the prefecture ever experienced a headache. Her fingers rubbed the temporal muscles back and forth. She broke out in tears. They glittered down her ivory cheeks. Trying to contain the wall of tears forming, she broke out in a cough, choking on those tears. She had warned Ember, but to no avail. Did she do enough? No. She should have met with Ember's parents, grandparents and Ari. This is all her fault.

"Lord above, forgive me for not taking my concerns to the appropriate people. It's my fault. Ember wouldn't believe me about the concerns I had for Addley. But, I didn't have proof, just a gut feeling. I would have been ignored or made fun of, but so what. If I had, maybe Ember would be here right now. It's time for me to face the consequences. Please, Lord, let Ember be okay. I promise I will always share my concerns with everyone instead of worrying about looking silly. Just bring her home."

Rising slowly, shoulders slumped, she headed for Ember's home. On the way, a rumbling wind stirred up again. *What is this that is happening?* Her mouth dropped and her heart pumped faster. Powerful and frightening gusts of wind blew her up in the air. The miasma was nauseating. Their land was a sanctuary from natural disasters. *How can this be happening?*

She grabbed a branch from one of the mammoth trees and climbed inside of it. It sheltered her. The other tree branches blew around violently, and the trunk of the tree swayed. This was terrifying and something she had never experienced before. She silently prayed and held onto the trunk of the tree with her life. She couldn't use a hand to cover her nose and mouth area, because her life depended on the grip she had on the tree. The odor was like walking into a hole of decaying corpses. She didn't understand what was happening. Nobody did.

The next thing she heard was hooves pounding the ground. Snorts and ferocious horse neighing spewed out of Skyfire's mouth. The smell of smoke drifted away. She climbed down and plopped on his back. This was the first time anyone other than Ember was allowed to ride him. She didn't know how to handle her thoughts, but she didn't have to. He took off like a jet traveling at the speed of sound. Before she knew it, they were at Ember's place.

Ari walked out just in time to marvel at their entrance. His mouth dropped. "How...how in the world are you riding on Skyfire's back?"

"I'm just as shocked. He just saved my life. Let me get down and I'll explain it all to you and to everyone inside."

The magnificent horse knelt down, and she hopped off. She turned back to him and rubbed his muzzle. So enamored by this once in a lifetime opportunity, she planted a soft kiss on his muzzle. As she turned, something in his eyes caused her to look back at him. Her eyes narrowed with affection, and her tiny hands rubbed his massive neck. *Are his eyes tearing up?*

She walked with Ari but kept looking back at Skyfire. He

stood erect and proud, but those eyes almost made her burst out in a river of tears. As they entered the war room, her first time ever, she looked around in complete apprehension but in veneration. The fast-paced shuffling of their feet alerted everyone to their entrance.

The elders and Ember's family, along with Ari's family, stood to their feet in uncertainty. Very few people were allowed in this sacred area, and Ari was well aware of that. Valeska, Ember's grandmother, demanded answers. "Ari, why do you disregard our sacred rules by bringing her here?"

"She has information that may help lead us to Ember. Please, we have to hear her out. And furthermore, Skyfire allowed her to ride him here. That, alone, should tell you a whole lot."

"He let you ride him?" Arwood, Ember's dad, asked in complete shock. "I received a message that you were in trouble and sent Skyfire, but I never expected him to allow you to ride on his back. Sorry everyone. We were so involved, I forgot to mention it."

"Yes, he did let her ride on top of him. I couldn't believe it either," Ari commented.

"I won't take up much of your time. My information may or may not be helpful, but Skyfire seems to think it will help; otherwise, why would he bring me here?"

"My dear loved ones, let's skip all formalities and hear what she has to say," Ember's grandfather suggested.

"Of course. Of course," Valeska replied.

"Please proceed," Flora, Ember's mother, said with blurry, pleading eyes.

"After the proposal yesterday, we all were floating on clouds, but when I noticed Addley left without saying a word or congratulating Ember, it caused a warning to go off in my head."

"How so?" Ari asked confused.

"Addley is her friend, so that's what makes this difficult."

"Addley? What does she have to do with anything?" His impatience was growing.

With a solemn face, Sharley continued but turned her face to the others because of the irate vibe coming from Ari. "I told

Ember that she had been leaving the area a lot, even for days at a time. When she comes back her eyes are dark, and honestly, scary. Ember was concerned how Addley left without congratulating her. I explained that before she came here to live, Ari and Addley hung out. A lot. Inseparable. I could tell she was madly in love with him."

"That's just plain lunacy. We've always been best friends. I don't like where you're going with this. I have never and never would cheat on Ember," Ari spewed.

Fuming, face growing red, she added, "That's precisely why I held it in so long. Look at your reaction, and Ember had the same reaction. To take it a step further, Addley is the last person to see Ember."

Flora spoke up gently. "But dear, it's impossible for her to be in love with Ari. Embers marriage to Ari was ordained at birth. Addley has someone she is predestined to marry, but obviously she is not ready for that revealing. So, it's just not possible."

"Hold on. Just hold on everyone. If you think about it, something like this has happened before," Ember's grandfather informed them.

Valeska slapped her hand over her opened mouth. "That's very true. Malvoil never recovered and accepted the mark of the Eryndomnites. She turned wicked. So, in that case, this could happen. God will wipe His hands of her and allow her to face the horrible consequences."

"I have witnessed firsthand how she looks at you, Ari. I've seen jealousy and hate in her eyes. A scorn in her expression when she sees you and Ember together. She was livid when Ember was brought here. I feel ashamed talking about her, because she is a good friend, and I didn't want to believe that of her. Plus, it was my word against hers, so that is why I never pursued telling anyone. But now I have a gut feeling that she is behind Ember's disappearance, I admit with shame."

Ari swiped a hand through his full, golden head of hair. "I can't believe it. I refuse to believe it. She's always been my friend —and Ember's too. You're wrong, Sharley."

Hands on her hips, head tilted forward, Sharley replied, "I am not wrong. She pretended to be Ember's friend so she could be near you," she shouted back and stood up straight.

"I get it now. You are just trying to stir up trouble for Addley because you're jealous of their friendship. Since you were good friends with Addley, you must realize how you're stabbing her in the back with these accusations. What a horrible friend you are."

Sharley threw her head down and shook it back and forth. Grinding her teeth she looked back up. "That's a big, FAT lie. Ember and my friendship is solid. I didn't want to believe it of Addley, but lately I couldn't help but notice the change in her. It's not like I was making it up in my head. She's a traitor. I can't believe you are sticking up for that traitor. You both should be thrown into prison."

"Okay you two, that's enough," Ember's grandfather said sternly. "When is the last time either of you saw Ember and Addley together?"

Ari cleared his throat and spoke. "Yesterday. She said she would walk Ember home."

"Did anything strange happen during that time?"

He looked up at the sky and thought about the gathering. "Something was strange. I'm not in any way acknowledging that Addley is guilty."

"Oh brother," Sharley spoke. "Maybe you and Addley have gone to the dark side together. Traitor."

Melisande, Ari's mother, jumped in. "Let's quit the accusations and just state the facts, please."

Ari and Sharley glared at each other, then he looked over at the rest of them. "Skyfire turned into a raging beast attempting to attack Addley. I don't know why, but Ember had to calm him down and send him home."

"Are you certain his reaction was towards Addley?" Flora asked.

"Yes, a hundred percent."

Ember's grandfather got up and paced. When he returned his face was pale. "It's not looking good for Addley, Ari. To add fuel to the fire, the fact Skyfire felt comfortable enough to allow Sharley to ride on him, makes Sharely's information seem substantial. And as we all know, none of us, nobody, saw Addley bring Ember home."

"All right. I guess we need to consider Addley as a suspect," he caved hesitantly.

"And with motive," Sharley offered with a sense of shame. He glared at her, still uncomfortable with the idea that one of his best friends is responsible for such betrayal.

"Thanks for sharing Sharley. We'll be in touch."

All her emotions piling up inside of her, she remembered the hateful stare she gave Ember as she left her. Her head bent and she covered her shameful face as teardrops poured out. She ran away refusing to be comforted.

"Poor girl. This is what we'll do," Ember's grandfather announced. "Ari will go to Addley's house and bring her back here. He will convince her that we are seeking her help as Ember's friend. You'll take her to the enclosed, solid rock room where we will be waiting. She won't be able to use any magical methods to evade our questions. We cannot let on about our suspicions. Besides, a person is innocent until proven guilty.

"Furthermore, Ari, you have to keep this secret and forget about your friendship until this is resolved. Ember is our urgency, not your friendship with Addley."

A face that held shame for what he has to do, he answered defeated, "Yes, sir." He bowed his head out of respect and left. As he did, a very dark shadow covered the sky. There has never been a time the territory has ever experienced any kind of darkness, except during the war with the wicked Eryndomnites. Ari was too saddened by what he had to do to notice. But everyone else looked up, faces of fearful wonder.

Chapter Nine

Ember came down the stairs the next morning dressed in jean shorts and a t-shirt. For being in Alaska, it was quite warm outside.

"There you are. I thought I'd find you outside in the stables fast asleep."

"Actually, I did sleep there. I got up early and cleaned the stalls, then jumped in the shower. Should we feed the horses, or is it way too early for that?"

"Right after breakfast. It's not even daylight yet. You know, most young adults like to sleep in late. Don't you want to do that?"

"Oh, gosh, no. There's too much to do and too much to see," she said twirling.

Tyrus stood amazed as trails of glitter shot out of her. He didn't know if bringing this to her attention would upset her, so he kept it inside. It was hard for him, but he already cherished this breath of fresh air and wouldn't do anything that would compromise her safety—or his reputation. What would anyone think if he told them such balderdash?

"How about some bacon and eggs?"

Slamming her hand on her heart, she replied forcefully, "No! How could you even ask such a thing?" She dropped her head and covered her face. He could see tears splash through her fingers. She cried softly, but yet, it was a whole lot of tears that sparkled like she swallowed a bottle of glitter. He watched in amazement.

Sensing she couldn't eat meat because of her love for animals, he offered a compromise. "I have a better idea. How about Cream of Wheat and toast?"

Sniffling, she removed her hands and looked up with a face that melted his heart. She nodded yes.

This teeny, tiny young lady has captured his heart. Even when she was upset, she showed a kindness. They sat down at the table and ate. At first it burnt her tongue, and she waved her hand back and forth to cool it off. Then she blew it and took another bite. A smile crept in slowly and turned wide. It was so satisfying. She ate fresh berries like candy.

After cleaning up the kitchen, they walked out into the living room. Tyrus eyed her with suspicion before speaking. "Are you ready for a physician to give you a checkup? I'm sure you want to find out things about your life. I can't say if he can help you or not, but I think we should give it a try. After we feed the horses."

She shrugged her shoulders. "I don't know. What's a physician?"

"You don't know what a doctor is? Or physician?" He didn't want to confuse her.

She shrugged her shoulders and shook her head back and forth.

"A person who checks your body out, listens to your heart, looks at your eyes and mouth, and just examines you. I think it is a good idea. Virginia will come over and be with you every step of the checkup. Being a man, I wouldn't feel comfortable being in the room during an exam. I promise you that the doctor only wants to examine you to be sure there are no injuries causing your memory loss.

"Oh, I just remembered. I know of this nice woman doctor. That should make you more comfortable."

Part of her top lip lifted, and she got this look on her face. Swinging her head gently, she answered. "I'm not sure."

"How about this: if you feel uncomfortable at any time, we'll ask the doctor to stop. Tania, I really feel it is wise to have an exam done. I want to help you and that is what a doctor does. I can't imagine what your parents are feeling right now."

A frown formed. "Okay," she barely whispered.

"Great. We'll go feed the horses and get ready."

That brightened her day.

"You know what I was thinking?"

Her shoulders pushed up.

"We'll have oatmeal for dinner with toast and jam. It's breakfast, but so what. What do you think?"

"What is oatmeal?"

"I'm glad you asked," he answered in a light-hearted manner. "Just what the name says. It is oats cooked into meal, just like Cream of Wheat. But we'll add brown sugar." His tongue immediately licked his lips. "My favorite breakfast of all time." He pushed three fingers to his mouth, made a smacking sound, and snapped the fingers out.

She couldn't help but giggle. "Sounds flavorful."

They fed the horses and dogs. Kisses and hugs were granted to each and every one of them. A frantic sound of feet running made them look up. Garrett came running at full speed and skidded right in front of them. Tyrus stared without talking.

Panting, Garrett tried to say what was on his mind. "One of the...calves is injured. It doesn't look too good." He bent over and took in big breaths.

"Is it in walking distance or should I drive?"

"Maybe you should drive," Garrett answered not saying what he was thinking. Tyrus understood.

A dreaded exercise program was necessary. He groaned at the thought but knew in his heart that getting older would require it.

"We'll be right back, Tania."

"No! I'm coming."

"That's not a good idea," Garrett couldn't help but say out loud. "We may have to shoot it and put it out of its misery." Tyrus gritted his teeth. Garrett noticed.

Throwing his hands up, he said, "What? I'm just trying to prevent her from having to see it."

"I'm coming with you. You will not shoot the calf."

"Tania, if the calf is dying, it's the humane thing to do. We don't ever want to do that," Garrett tried convincing her.

"Get in the truck. Let's go!" she yelled.

They drove to the spot. Even before he turned the truck off, Ember was out the door and ran straight to Jacob where the calf rested. She bent down next to the calf and laid a hand over its heart.

She closed her eyes, and with a voice and words no one understood, she continued. A glow surrounded her body and the calf's. Jacob literally couldn't move. Just as Tyrus and Garrett walked up, the calf stood up, licked Ember in the face and trotted off to find its worried mother, who was watching in the near distance. She licked her baby all over.

"How did you do that?" Jacob asked stunned.

"Do what?"

"How did you heal that calf?"

"I don't know. I don't know."

"What about that glow?"

"What glow?" her wrinkled face asked.

"You don't know that you were glowing?"

Her face wrinkled again. An eyebrow raised up. "What are you talking about?"

"Never mind. Jacob, Garrett, get back to work, please," Tyrus admonished.

Jacob started to argue but Tyrus cut him off.

Tyrus gently swung his head. "Just go back to work." They left but kept looking back at Ember. Chattering endlessly.

Tyrus laid a hand on Ember's shoulder and looked softly into her eyes. "Can you heal animals?"

She held her palms up. "I...I don't know."

"Do you know what it means to glow?"

"No."

"Then never mind. The calf is good as new, you're happy, so let's get home and make that call."

Virginia and the doctor led her into one of the bedrooms. It had a quilt on the bed, lacy pillowcases and was really charming. Ember looked at the dresser and saw a picture of Tyrus' wife.

"Who is she?"

"That was Tyrus' wife," Virginia answered with a quiver to her voice. Ember looked at her eyes and had the same reaction. Tearful eyes appeared.

Out of the blue, Ember gasped. "Hhhh!"

"My child, what's wrong?"

"I know her, Ms. Virginia. I know her."

"How curious. Does anything come to mind?"

"No. Just that I recognize her picture."

"All I can tell you is that she loved animals just like you do. Animals were comfortable around her. She was always treating an injured animal."

Index finger to her lips, Ember just sighed in thought.

"Well, I think we should get started," Doctor Warner said.

Ember tensed up but allowed the doctor to examine her. The doctor listened to her heart and pulse. She jumped back in shock. Ember looked at her with terror in her face.

"I'm sorry dear. I think a mosquito or something bit me." She and Virginia laughed.

After the exam, they walked out into the living room. "Tyrus, if you don't mind, I'll go over the examination results with you in the bedroom." She smiled at Ember. "Looks like you're in good shape. We'll find out why you lost your memory. Maybe we'll take a scan of your brain."

Ember jumped up and clung onto Virginia with shaky hands. "Dear, it's okay. A scan is a procedure that takes a picture inside of your head, and it doesn't hurt you at all. I promise. She wants to find out if there could possibly be anything obscuring your temporal lobes." She heard the doctor describe it that way. Slowly and hesitantly, Ember released her grip. Virginia patted her back for encouragement.

In the room the doctor shared her fascination. "Tyrus, I have never, ever heard a heartbeat or pulse like that. My curiosity wants to explore, but that will only make a spectacle out of her."

"Yeah, that's not going to happen. Are you able to tell what age she is?"

"Being so tiny, that makes it difficult. I would say between twenty and twenty-five."

"No kidding. What about her glowing? What could cause that?"

"What?" the doctor chuckled out.

"Sometimes a glow surrounds her or sometimes glitter."

"What else. She's a fairy."

They laughed for a few good minutes, and it felt good.

"Seriously, doc, do you think she is a victim of radiation poisoning or something?"

"It's hard to tell. I tell you what. Bring her to the office complex tomorrow and I'll find out. Better bring Virginia with you."

"Sure. We'll be there around nine. Thanks for everything doc. Please send me a bill."

"Huh, you better believe it."

After making Ember feel safe, Tyrus informed her they would be going to the young adult group tonight. He and Virginia would join the adults in church, and she could make some new friends. It was obvious she was leery about it, but he knew she would be okay.

Virginia scooted home and Tyrus went to his recliner for a much needed nap. Ember started up the stairs but turned back and went into the room where the examination took place while Tyrus reclined in his chair. She lifted the picture of Tyrus' wife and stared for minutes, but her thoughts wouldn't come together. So many unanswered questions.

Chapter Ten

Tyrus arose from his nap. First, he released the recliner to a sitting position and sat up. He wasn't very coherent yet, so he leaned his head down to rub the sleep out of his eyes. Grabbing his boots sitting next to the door, he strolled upstairs to check on Ember. She was watching some comedy. She glanced over at him and covered her mouth with a giggle.

"And just what is so funny?"

She messed the top of her hair, and he followed by feeling his own hair. It clicked now. "I'll comb it shortly. I'm going to make us some oatmeal so we can get ready to go to church. Think you can put on a pair of jeans and a nice shirt?"

"Okay." She jumped up and ran to the dresser. She had put her hair in a ponytail that looked cute as could be and went into the kitchen. Walking up to the stove, she looked at the oatmeal he was stirring. Toast popped up from the toaster. She grabbed the slices and spread butter on them. A plate of toast was set on the table between them.

"Go ahead and have a seat. This is really hot, so you'll need to sit back so I can put some in your bowl. Wait for me and I'll show you what to do. Take a couple spoons of brown sugar and mix it in the oatmeal." He poured milk in the bowl and in their glasses. He spread jelly on his toast, and she did the same.

"Wait 'til you taste this raspberry jam. It must have come

down from heaven with the manna the Israelites ate in the wilderness. But first we better give thanks, or my wife would be livid with me."

After giving thanks, they dove in. Ember took a spoonful and quickly spit it out. Waving her hand, "Hot, hot, hot." She chugged down some milk. She had an irate look on her face as she frowned at him.

"I'm sorry. I thought I told you it was hot. Poor some more milk in the bowl. That should help."

She stirred and steam rose up. Holding the spoon up to her lips, she blew on it before putting it in her mouth. "Mmmm," she moaned. "This is good."

The kitchen was spotless, and they were ready to head out. He handed her a Bible, and she hugged it between her arms. They stopped and picked up Virginia and off they went to the church in the valley. It was painted white with a white steeple. They stopped and spoke to several congregation members on the way in, then they walked her to the young adult group area. They were playing basketball outside, but he knew she would feel out of place, so he took her straight to the room.

He introduced her to Mike, the young adult's pastor. She took a seat and Tyrus pulled Mike aside.

"She has lost her memory. I found her lying on the ground at the side of my house. She has an issue with trust, as you can imagine, and doesn't do well with loud, boisterous activity."

"Oh boy, that poses a problem with these overactive kids."

"If she gets in a panic, please bring her out to me immediately. I call her Tania. Don't tell anyone about her circumstances. It won't help her with all the questions they'll ask."

Mike's wife sat with Ember. He called everyone in from outside. Aaron's eyes landed on Ember. He sat down next to her. "Glad you made it."

Her smile was quick and ended quickly.

"So, you're staying with Mr. Tyrus. For how long?"

She shrugged her shoulders. Something about him fascinated her. She kept looking at him.

He was a really nice-looking young man, but that wasn't it.

She watched him as though she thought she knew him. In reality, he looked identical to Ari, but her memory wouldn't allow that realization to come to the surface.

"Do you like it here so far?"

"Yes. Tyrus is a nice man."

"I'm new here, so I haven't met him. Miss Virginia told me about him. How old are you?"

"I don't know."

"You don't know...?" His mouth dropped.

Mrs. Klondike broke into the conversation, seeing the discomfort Ember was feeling. "Aaron, no more questions. Pastor Mike is getting ready to speak."

"Yes, Ma'am."

All through the evening, Ember caught him staring at her and he caught her staring at him. She was a bottle of nerves but for some odd reason, probably subconsciously relating him to Ari, she felt comfortable around him. But she couldn't figure out why. At the end of the evening, Aaron walked her to the truck where they waited for Tyrus. He carried a cola.

"What is that?" she asked pointing to the soda.

"Cola. Want a drink?"

"Yes, please." The carbonation tickled her nose. She drank and drank some more. "Mmm. That is so tasty."

"You act like you've never had soda before."

"I haven't."

"That's literally impossible."

She shrugged her shoulders.

"Do you mind if I pay you a visit?"

"No. I won't mind."

He broke out in a smile. "Good. It may be tomorrow or the next day. I need to help my dad with the cattle," he lied.

Tyrus walked up and patted Aaron's shoulder. "Thanks for staying with her until I got here."

"Sure."

"Well, we need to get home." Ember crawled in the truck, and they were gone in a flash. They all discussed the mid-week message and a few questions about the young adult group.

"Aaron's nice," popped out of her mouth from nowhere.

"Yes, he is."

"And quite a good-looking young man. And quite a respectable young man," Virginia added.

Ember sat in the back seat with her head in her hands. She kept picturing Aaron in her mind. His name was almost familiar to her and his looks. But why? It's obvious she isn't from around here because nobody knew who she was, so why does something about him make her feel comfortable and draw questions? He was new to the area also.

Just as they turned onto the driveway to Virginia's house, a huge shadow flew over them. Tyrus slammed on the brakes and dust flew out like he was in a desert. "Did you see that?"

"What was that?" Virginia asked.

He opened the door, stood on the floorboard and looked up in the sky. "I have no idea, but it certainly wasn't a bird, owl, eagle or plane."

"Underdog, perhaps?" Virginia spouted in laughter.

He sat back in the seat and closed the door. They all looked ahead. "What is that reflection in the sky over there?" Ember said pointing.

"Am I drunk?" Virginia looked at him cross. "I swear it looks like really, big eyes. It's shaped like eyes." Then it disappeared.

"All right. I'm a little freaked out," Virginia stuttered.

"Why don't you come home with us? Just to be safe."

"Can't. All my chickens, horses, cattle and pigs are counting on me, not to mention my cats and dogs. I'll be fine. Really."

"Okay, but call if you need me."

"Nah. Winchester will keep me company." Tyrus snorted at her humorous choice of words for a shotgun and how she named it after the make and model. Actually, he did the same with his. She waved goodbye and walked into the house without a care in the world.

Hopping out of the truck at the ranch and walking inside, he stared around the sky. Ember grabbed his hand.

"You scared?" he asked.

She nodded yes with eyes of worry.

He walked to the closet and pulled out his shotgun. "No worry, little one. Remington here will protect us. But you stay away from it. No going outside tonight. It may be dangerous. I can't take a chance with your safety until we know what is out there."

They turned the TV on and munched on cookies with milk. Tyrus sat in a daze. He never believed the folklore of old, but now something pressed against his disbelieving mind. *Surely that couldn't be a Thunderbird. I never heard the thunderous flapping of its wings.*

Chapter Eleven

The next morning Tyrus ran straight up the stairs when he woke up. He wanted to make sure Ember hadn't snuck out in the night to visit the horses. He gently cracked her door open. It was still dark, and clouds kept the moonshine from coming in the windows.

"I'm here," a squeaky voice informed him.

"Thank the Lord. Go back to sleep, little one."

Today they would wait for daylight before doing their chores and feeding the livestock. Blueberry muffins and cereal were set in the middle of the table, along with a container of milk. The percolator gurgled and cast off the most enticing coffee aroma. He poured a cup, checked his texts and sat in silence. Holding the cup up to his mouth, he stopped and listened. A very tiny tapping came from the living room. He waited for a minute and the door to the kitchen swung back and forth making a rackety announcement as Ember walked through it.

He took a sip and put the cup down. "Good morning sunshine."

Her smile was bright as the sun itself. "Morning."

"Fix yourself some cereal and have a muffin. Then we'll feed the crew outside and clean all of the stalls."

She rubbed her hands together. "Good idea."

"For the life of me I can't help but wonder if you're not half cat."

One brow raised up.

"I have never heard such a soft walk in my life. It's almost as if your feet don't actually touch the ground. You are full of magnificent mystery, little one."

Her laugh was precious. She couldn't help but feel affection for him and the way he called her little one, even though she was no child. They worked all day in the outdoors, except at lunch where they ate a peanut butter and jelly sandwich with chips. Lemonade was becoming her favorite drink of choice.

A repeat performance from yesterday happened. Tyrus felt like he was experiencing Groundhog Day. "What is wrong this time, Garrett?"

Garrett gasped for breath. "Hop in the truck and I'll show you."

They all ran for the truck. Garrett held his hand out. "No! You can't come this time. One of our calves has been killed. It's kind of gross to see."

The sound coming from her mouth sounded like frequent short breaths. "I'll be okay. I need to see what happened. I just do." Even she couldn't understand why animals meant so much to her, but she cherished each and every one of them.

"All right. Come on," Tyrus replied while coaxing her forward.

They arrived at the scene. They could hear moans from the cows. Something was upsetting them. As they walked closer to Jacob, Ember threw a hand over her mouth and squeezed her eyes shut. "You're right. There is nothing I can do for the poor thing now," the words muffled out of her mouth. She ran back to the truck.

"What do you think? Wolves? Grizzlies? Coyotes?"

"To be honest, if I was superstitious, I would say the Thunderbird," Jacob answered feeling foolish.

Hearing his guess, with a forcefulness Tyrus wiped a hand down his face and rubbed his neck. He examined the body. Its neck was twisted around its body and had a mark as if hit by lightning. He felt just as foolish as Jacob felt.

"Looks like I'll need to consider hiring some guys to watch the herds at night." Both guys nodded in agreement.

Ember and Tyrus ran back to the stables and checked on the horses, bull and dogs. A rushing and pounding of paws was heading their way. The horses bucked violently. The bull scraped the ground with his hooves and snorted violently. Dogs tried climbing out of the fence.

In complete panic Tyrus ordered her to get in the house. They ran but the grizzly beat them to it. His eyes stared hatefully at Ember. Tyrus jumped in front of her. The grizzly stood on two legs and growled with raging anger. It knocked Tyrus out of his way, landing him on the ground with a claw mark that bled through his pants.

It moved back down on four legs and bared its teeth, a sooty, disgusting substance dripped from its teeth while moving towards her. She spoke in an unknown language encouraging the grizzly to calm down. It grew wild with rage. It acted possessed. Before it made a move, the bull crashed through the fence, horses jumped over the gate, and other animals ran to them from the forest. The grizzly backed up and snarled at the animals. They prepared to attack but it ran away. The malodor it left was nauseating and not a familiar scent in any form or shape, except when they found a decaying body of an animal. They could relate the smell to that.

The forest animals and Tyrus' own livestock ran around Ember, rubbing up against her, creating sympathetic sounds that Tyrus was stunned by. He lied there in complete shock.

How is it possible wild and tame animals worked in harmony to save her life? Why did the grizzly want to harm her alone and ignore Tyrus? Every animal that comes in contact with her automatically adores her. What is going on? He had no answers to those questions. Ears standing tall on all sizes and shapes of animals, the forest bunch ran back to the forest as Jacob and Garrett drove up. They walked up as though they were in a trance.

Inside the house, Tyrus sat on his comfy recliner. Ember sat on the couch. Nothing was said for a moment. Thankfully the claw scratch wasn't deep. They cleaned and medicated the area before applying a bandage. He intertwined his fingers and laid his arms on his lap.

"Tania, I need some answers. Is it possible you can help me with that?"

Sorrowful eyes looking down at the bandage on his leg, grateful it was only on the surface of the skin, gazed hopelessly at him.

"You are becoming really special to me. Like my own daughter." Her lips fought to rise. "What I just witnessed outside—and several other instances—doesn't make any sense. Wild animals come to your rescue. My livestock break out of their stall to save you. Sometimes a glow forms around you and sometimes bursts of glitter trail behind you. Not to mention that birthmark glitters and swirls at times, and I even saw you elevate slightly. Who are you? Where are you from?"

Tears forming puddles in her eyes, she jumped up. She threw her arms out. "I told you; I don't know. I don't know anything." Sobbing hysterically, she almost floated up the stairs to her room, another unexplainable event. He dropped his head and rubbed the temples back and forth. Is he perhaps going insane? No. Jacob and Garrett witnessed the same thing.

"Father up above, forgive me for not talking with you since my wife's death. I ask your forgiveness. Truly there were times I hated You and refused to speak with You. I know now that You didn't take my wife by accident, and I know how happy she is in heaven. It's just my selfishness of missing her, Lord.

"Right now, there is a scared little girl crying her eyes out. She doesn't have any memory. My heart aches for her. I'm beginning to love her like my own daughter. She is such a good, kind, caring person. Sometimes she looks more like a child than an adult, which makes her extra special. Something strange is going on, Lord. I'm beginning to fear for her life. Something supernatural is after her, I fear. Protect her and send armies of angels.

"Why does she have such a bond with animals? What are the

strange happenings all about? She needs her memory and needs to know who she is. She is so much better than any person I have ever known. Something really special. Please help, Lord."

A gentle hand laid on top of his. He jerked up. Her loving eyes connected to his. "It will all be okay. I heard you say that you hated God for taking your wife. No, no! Never hate God and never blame Him.

"Don't be mad at God. We all have an appointed time set. He may be holy, righteous and fearfully powerful, but His love is like puppy dog kisses, butterfly joys and every flower of the field in the world blended together."

"Hold on," he said straightening his body. "You have no memory, but yet you know everything about Him. Are you an angel?"

"I am not an angel. At least I don't think I am."

"I do. There is a special purpose for you, but what is the question. I believe you are of importance wherever you're from and that someone evil is out to destroy you and get you out of the picture. Unfortunately for them, but fortunate for us, they failed. I'm sure God made sure of that. You're needed in His plans."

They both went to bed feeling a whole lot better about things.

Chapter Twelve

Ember and Tyrus were outside most of the day. Virginia came over with a picnic lunch and they sat under a huge black spruce tree. She laid a delectable choice of fruit, veggies, honey and peanut butter sandwiches, chips, and the moistest brownies in the whole wide world on a blanket. Tyrus had praised her for the brownies many a time. He poured three glasses of lemonade. They laughed and chatted about everything under the sun.

Ember watched the interaction between Tyrus and Virginia. She couldn't help but notice the smile on their faces as they spoke to each other. And she couldn't help but wonder why they haven't dated and eventually married. There was a connection. A real connection.

As she watched them, she felt something cold and wet on her leg. She bent her head down to see a vole. She picked it up and kissed its head and fed it berries. She was in constant giggles.

Not hearing anymore conversation between Tyrus and Virginia, she glanced over, still giggling and playing with the vole. They were staring at her. Frozen in time. She said something that sounded like it should come out of heaven, almost like her soft voice got caught in the wind. The vole crawled back into a hole.

Virginia and Tyrus still stared. "Hey guys, something wrong?" She leaned towards them.

"Tyrus, why are you staring at me like that?

"Tyrus!"

He shook his head and said, "Don't you notice how wild critters are affectionate with you? Have you ever seen them come near anyone else?"

"I don't know. I guess not." She couldn't see it, but the birthmark above her left cheek swirled.

"How odd. That birthmark looks like a shape of a lioness." Virginia moved closer to Ember's face to examine it.

"Everything is just fine, little one." He noticed how concern showed in her face. His plan was to make her feel at ease. "We are taking you for some tests tomorrow morning. They canceled it for today, but we rescheduled. I'm sure we'll figure out soon what happened to you."

An old Chevy truck jiggled and rumbled down the drive. They all looked over. Aaron waved as he passed them and parked up near the house. Ember's face lit up and a smile broke out. He jumped out and ran up to them.

"Hi everybody," he said with a cheerful voice. He looked specifically at Ember and smiled ear to ear.

"Why don't you join us," Tyrus asked.

"Thank you. I believe I will. Oh no, Ms. Virginia, are those your brownies? I may have just moved here, but I remember how good they were when you gave me some after mowing your lawn."

"They most certainly are."

He licked his lips a few times. He sat so close to Ember that their knees touched. Barely able to look him in the face, she would smile and then become serious; smile and then become serious. She just didn't know how to act around him. For a few seconds, her eyes kept blinking, almost out of control. Her mind drifted away and they could all tell she was deep in thought. Then she snapped out of it, as though the thoughts vanished right away. While he chowed down on lunch, she observed his golden hair, sort of messy, about two inches below his chin. He was tan, and she couldn't help but notice that his body was fit and trim. He had told her that he was a quarterback for four years in high school, which was another lie. But that wasn't it. Something about him made her want to weep. She had to look away before the tear dam opened up.

"Tania, we'll clean this up. Why don't you two take a walk and get to know each other.

Aaron, why don't you take her down to the river?"

"Yes, sir." He stood up and grabbed her tiny hand to help pull her up. "Are you okay with this?"

She nodded yes.

Something was burning her skin. She whistled in air from the pain. He let her hand drop. "You okay?"

"My hand started burning like it was on fire."

"That's weird. Hold it up and let me take a look."

She held it at a distance, not quite certain why she was skeptical of him now. "I don't see a thing."

Invisibly, a deep red stain disappeared slowly.

They walked. He bent down and picked up stones from time to time and threw them out far. She could hear the rushing of water, and as they got closer, she could hear the water crash against the riverbank and recede, just to do it over and over again.

"Where are you from?" he asked.

"I don't know."

He stopped walking and looked at her with questions. "You don't know how old you are, and now you don't know where you're from. I don't understand," he lied.

"I don't know because I have no memory."

"Say what? So, you don't know who you are, where you're from, how old you are; nothing?" Oddly, his eyes lit up at her remark.

"Nothing."

"Hmm. How did you end up with Tyrus?"

"He found me."

"Then if you don't know your name, why does he call you Tania?"

"He wanted to give me a name. He said Tania means mystery.

71

That's how I got it. I am having tests done tomorrow. Hopefully they will bring answers to the mystery."

"Wow! That must be scary for you."

She really appreciated that he understood. Her lips formed a sincere, grateful smile.

"How old are you?" she asked.

"Twenty-two. I took some time off before going to college so I could help my parents with their farm. This Fall I will be heading to college.

"What is college?"

"You don't know?" Truthfully, he didn't know either. He had heard other boys and girls talk about it at the young adult's group.

Her head dropped and her eyes fogged up. "Nothing. I know nothing."

Aaron looked at her with sympathy. He grabbed her hand and tenderly exclaimed, "I'll help you remember. Would you mind if I come with you tomorrow?"

Her eyes popped open. Scrunching up her face, her hand started burning again. He noticed and pulled his away. "If I didn't know better, I'd think you were allergic to me. Not very comforting to my ego."

"Sorry. Maybe the doctor can figure it out. You want to come to the doctor's office with me?" She was puzzled why he would want to spend time at a doctor's office if he didn't have to.

"We're almost here." He started to grab her hand but stopped, then pushed large weeds and foliage down for her to pass by. They tugged through brush and boulders. Incredible beauty stood before them. A river was lined with huge boulders, along with a constant rhythm of water splashing up against them. They found an opening between the boulders where they could walk right up to the riverbank. Ember was all giddy and ignored the diminishing burn sensation. He pointed to the waterfall that emptied into the river. Her mouth dropped and she placed her hands over her heart smiling.

"Aaron, I love it. I just love it."

"For some odd reason that I can't explain, I knew you would love it." But he could explain.

They sat on some boulders and dangled their feet in the water. She leaned back and used arms to prop up her body.

"Aaron, I have to tell you something."

He leaned back, propped up by his arms, too. "Yeah, go ahead."

"You look so familiar to me. Something about the way you look and something about the sound of your name, but I can't remember. Did I know you before?"

"You mean, did you know me before you lost your memory?" She nodded. "Sorry, but I've never met you ever or anytime previous to the diner. I would remember. There is something unique and special about you. Well, nobody would be able to forget you. Not to mention that birthmark on your face. It has a magical quality." He laughed out loud at his statement. She laughed, too. He kept telling her lies, but she had no way of knowing that. He knew everything there was to know about her.

He would watch her when he thought she wouldn't notice. His thoughts were constant and expression serious. Even though it appeared they couldn't be an item, since he couldn't even touch her without causing pain, something about her captivated him in a way he never expected. Never wanted.

A family of otters swam right up to them. "Whoa, back up slowly. They may be cute, but they can be fierce. Come on, Tania, back up." His feet were pushing him back slowly.

"No. They won't hurt us."

He watched as they climbed up the bank and snuggled around her. She giggled, rubbed their sleek fur, kissed the tops of their heads, and was completely at ease with them. They seemed to catch his scent and began to show distress.

Not feeling confident in himself, he just stuttered, "Uh, Tania, we should get going."

She kissed each head and hopped up, waving to them as they swam away.

"That was strange. I'm not used to seeing wild animals act

like that with any person. They have to be tamed first." Another lie.

"I love animals, and they love me."

They followed the trail back, and Aaron avoided holding her hand. He was falling for her, and mad at himself for feeling that way. But she didn't reciprocate the feelings. He could tell she liked him, but he realized that her subconscious was trying to remember Ari. He already passed "go" heading straight for jail, a jail that locked up his heart. How is it even possible to feel this way? It didn't make sense. And it wasn't in the plans.

They stopped and looked at various things, Ember always bending down to smell a wildflower or fascinated by something. Aaron stood tall and still, pushing her behind him, he whispered, "Be still. Look at the wild horses."

Her mouth lowered slowly. They watched and started their way, but when Aaron started moving, they backed up and started neighing a warning. He looked over at her. She was frozen and had an odd look on her face. He could picture her mind swirling with thoughts the way she stared. It was as if she were alone in the wooded area watching the horses.

"Tania, are you okay? Do you remember something? Tania?"

She walked out in front of him. "Shhh. Just watch."

A beautiful white stallion walked to the front of the herd and took command. He raised up on his hind legs and snorted while pounding the ground. Ember wasn't used to any animal acting scared around her. She looked over at Aaron and saw him walking slowly, step by step closer to them. Now it made sense.

"Shhh. Stop. You're scaring them."

He did what she said. If things weren't weird enough, the stallion with a most beautiful long mane walked up to her. Any movement Aaron made would cause the horse to buck around and snort. He made himself be still. It was an awestruck moment watching the horse nudge her. She rubbed him, hugged his enormous neck and spoke soft words that he understood, but words she had no idea what they meant or where they came from.

Aaron still stood like an iceberg. The only movement was a

blinking of his eyes now and then. Ember spoke again and the stallion led the herd deep into the forest.

He walked over to her with his eyes still on the herd as they left. "What was that all about?

How do you do that?"

When he looked over at Ember, she was silently heaving tears of grief. Her hands covered her eyes, but the deluge of tears slipped right through her fingers.

"Tania, what's wrong?" He placed his hands gently on her shoulders and removed them fast as she shrunk down. She wouldn't look up at him or remove hands from her face.

"Did I do something? Did the horse harm you?"

She shook her head no, but the silent heaves of tears were now audible. Body lethargic from crying, she dropped to the ground, still crying. Aaron did not know what to do at this point. He stood next to her and gave her a moment.

Like a windshield wiper, she constantly wiped the tears from her face with a serious case of the sniffles. Finally, she stopped. The saddest eyes he ever saw stared at the ground.

"You have to tell me what's wrong. Please."

She coughed. "Something about that horse. I can't remember what it is. Something about that HORSE," she yelled. Selfishly, he knew just what it was about.

"Hey there. Don't be so hard on yourself. You're probably trying to bring out a memory. I bet you have a horse just like him. You'll remember. Just give it some time. We'll all help you through this. Tyrus is probably worried about you. We should get going."

He stood back as she pulled herself up off the ground and they walked back in silence with him stealing sympathetic looks at her. And that, he couldn't understand. He liked wild and spunky girls. She was always sweet and innocent. A goody-two-shoes.

When they got back, they entered the house. Aaron spoke like he was riding the fastest roller coaster on the planet. Tyrus attempted to slow him down many a time. After Aaron finished the story, he looked into everyone's unmoved eyes.

"Aren't you the least bit curious if I'm fabricating a story to you?" he asked with his palms held out.

"Nothing I've never seen before," Tyrus mentioned nonchalantly. "By the way, did you two step on a dead carcass or something? Phooey." He waved his hand back and forth around his face.

"Well, I gotta go. See you later." He was gone in a flash. Ember and Tyrus looked at each other peculiarly.

Within five minutes, the door blew open and crashed against the wall, scaring everyone in the room.

"What's wrong, Jacob?"

"Something really weird just flew over my head. It was HUGE and oddly enough looked like eyes."

"Eyes?" Tyrus repeated as his face wrinkled.

"Yes, eyes."

They all went out the door, but whatever it was departed. Tyrus patted Jacob's shoulders. "Don't worry, son, it wasn't a hallucination. I've seen something like that before."

"So have I," Virginia added.

"Well, I haven't," Jacob said mystified.

"We don't know what it is son. As silly as it sounds, I've been wondering if there's any truth to the Thunderbird folklore."

"Heh-heh-heh," Jacob pretended to laugh nervously.

"It's about time for me to head to the bunkhouse. Garrett is taking a shower. Maybe I just need sleep."

"Sure, go on home, son."

He left scanning the sky this way and that way.

"Is it okay if Aaron comes with us tomorrow?" Ember asked.

"Huh? Why?" Tyrus asked.

"Told him about the tests; that's all."

"Okay. More the merrier, I hear they say."

He squeezed Ember's hand, and she went to the kitchen in search of cookies, cookies and more cookies. Virginia decided to leave, and Jacob took off on the 4-wheeler to check on Garrett. At this point, everyone was mentally worn down.

Chapter Thirteen

E mber sat on her bed deep in thought. She squeezed both sides of her head to stop the voices.

Who is talking? How are they talking in her mind? Is she going crazy? The window snapped and a huge shadow soared inside her room. It darkened the room. Ember scanned the room trying to adjust her eyes to the sudden darkness. A very angry hissing sound started low and intensified in volume. Her scream came instantly.

Tyrus ran into her room just as the shadow retracted out the window. He pulled her in tightly to him. "What was that, little one?"

Her terrified eyes looked into his. "I don't know. Something flew in my room and then I heard hissing. What could it be?"

Not even thinking, he swung his head around. "I have no idea. From now on you will sleep in my room with the door open. I'll sleep on the couch. That way I'll be near you at all times. This is getting weird. Really weird."

She didn't answer. Couldn't answer. It was weird to her as well. They grabbed her things and made new sleeping arrangements. Neither of them was interested in eating dinner or watching TV.

Chapter Fourteen

A ri's stomach was in knots. Now he felt like a traitor. A traitor to one of his best friends. She couldn't be guilty of such evil. Could she? He kept running his hand through his hair on the top of his head. Several of his best friends met him on the path.

"Where are you heading?" Arledge asked. "Looking for Ember?"

"No. I'm heading over to Addley's. And, yes, I mean, always looking for Ember. Any news? Anything?" His eyes were pleading.

"No, sorry. Nothing."

Ari kept walking. As he headed up the steps, Treelin dodged out of Addley's house.

"Sorry. Have a nice day," Treelin spouted running hastily away. Ari looked at him with a quirky expression.

Taking a deep breath, he knocked on the door. As it opened, a smile that was almost the whole length of her face appeared. She bent down and kissed his cheek. "What a nice surprise." He had stepped down a few steps before she opened the door.

"Really? Why is that?"

"You never stop by my home. Never."

"Oh. I didn't realize that. You know, duties, duties and more duties. Hey, I didn't know you and Treelin were such good friends. He took off like a rocket ship."

"Since you are spending all your time with Ember, I needed a friend. What else could I do?" she said rubbing his hand. "Come on in."

"Do you think we could take a walk instead?"

She looked curious but agreed. Taking his hand, they walked down the steps together. She had taken his hand several times before, but this time it bothered him. He pulled it away and acted like he was adjusting his belt. She cocked an eye watching his expressions carefully. Actually, he felt a mild burning sensation.

"Is something wrong?"

"You mean like Ember missing? Something like that?" He said briskly.

"No—I mean, yes, exactly. Is that what has you acting like such a grump?" she asked with a flirtatious smile. As though he would think she was being adorable.

"You seem like you're in a good mood." Tapping his finger against his lips he added, "Come to think of it, you're the only one who isn't bothered by her absence. How do you explain that?"

Pressing her hands to her heart, showing hurt in her expression, she answered, "How could you imply such a thing? Just because I'm not sniveling like everyone else doesn't mean I don't care. It's nice to see my friend here. That's all."

"Why aren't you out looking for her?"

"Why aren't you?" she countered back.

"I haven't stopped looking. Actually, I was hoping you could fill in the blanks from the time you last saw her. Wait a minute, come on inside, now that we're at my home, I'll get us both something to drink before we discuss it."

Her footsteps slowed down. Is she smelling a rat? He never came to her house before. He seems more nervous than she's ever seen him be, and just why is he bringing her inside his home without Ember present? That would cause a scandal. Something doesn't add up.

"My, you have a skeptical face. I meant to tell you that my parents and Ember's parents wanted to find out if you know anything else about Ember's disappearance. Since you were the last person to see her, they are hoping something will click in your memory and give us something else to go on."

Starting to feel trapped, she answered briskly before they walked inside. "I don't know. My mum is waiting for me. I forgot to tell her where I was going. She'll be frightened. I must go back immediately."

He grabbed her hand and began pulling her inside. "Don't be silly. One of our messengers will run right over there. This way we can spend some time together like we used to do." He had to say something to catch her off guard. Suddenly his friendship with her didn't feel right. But he couldn't let on about his suspicions. Possibly before, he was blinded by her loyal friendship. There are no romantic feelings. None. It does hurt, though, to think a good friend could betray him and Ember. He prayed that wasn't the case. And oddly, his hand tingled but not in a romantic style.

The ensnarement faded and she glowed at his proclamation of their friendship, which meant a whole lot more to her than it did to him.

In a room designed to ward off any transmissions, Ari pulled her inside with her hand in the crook of his arm. She was smiling as though all was perfect in the world. Ember's grandfather saw her and reacted immediately according to plan. "Ah, my dear, please come forward."

Putting on a show to ease her mind, they all hopped up and embraced her, making her feel right at home. Ember's dad offered her a chair. Behind her back, they rubbed the burning sensation scorching their skin.

She sat down, crossing her ankles and laid her hands on her lap. Smiles were permanent.

Behind her, Ari felt an uneasiness inside. His hands moved out in a clutch form. His dad noticed and quickly went to his side, moving Ari's hands back down to his side. Ari pressed down on his stomach to alleviate a queasiness developing in his stomach.

Only a handful of the people in their land were privy to the secrets of this room. It had a way of seeing the truth in people. Sort of like an invisible lie detector but worked on only the accused. The accused didn't have the advantage of knowing what was really going on, like they did. Ari's mom placed a comforting hand on his shoulder. Not often did Ari lose his temper, but being in love consumed him, so losing his cool was unavoidable. In order to pry out information from Addley, he had to pretend to be her friend. His emotions ran hot with anger to cool with denial.

Ember's grandfather began. "Addley, my dear," he used jovial tones, "so you were the last person to see Ember. Would you be a gem and describe the time you were with her up until the time you walked her home." He smiled.

She described the day just as before. Except this time her voice was full of cheer. When nothing new was added, there was one more test.

"Well, thank you for your cooperation, dear. Nothing is different from your first statement. Let's walk her out and get some much deserved fresh air," Ember's grandmother suggested.

The plan was to have a stableman walk Skyfire by as they came outside. Flora nodded to the posted stable hand, and he ran out to the stable quickly.

"It was such a pleasure to see you again," Grandfather Berthold said.

She bowed out of respect. "Ari, will you walk me home?"

Before he answered, Skyfire went berserk, bucking, snorting, kicking up dirt, neighing his warning. And, pulling the stable staff behind him like he was a kite. He was so strong that he broke loose from the stableman's grip. A potent smell of smoke trailed behind him as he approached Addley, pulling himself up on his hind legs. She fell to the ground and cowered with an arm covering her face. Snorts and smoky odors came out of his nostrils. He was enraged.

"Ari, stop him?" his father urged.

He jumped in front of Addley. "Whoa boy, calm down. That's right, calm down." He grabbed the rope and held him tightly. Skyfire was still agitated and wanted desperately to get to Addley. Thankfully Ari's strength was powerful enough to get control back and he led Skyfire out to the stables. The stableman was now able to grab control of the rope and take him back the rest of the way.

Ari ran back just as Addley stood up swiping her hands together to get the dirt off. Her face was fearful and angry. Keeping up appearances, he commented. "Whew, that was a challenge. That horse is stronger than a hurricane. You okay, Addley?"

"I guess," she huffed.

"Sorry, dear, but Ari won't be able to walk you home. We have teaching and training on the schedule for today. I'm sure you understand that. However, I could get one of our helpers to walk you home if you like," Melisande, Ari's mother, exclaimed.

"No thanks," she replied with a fake smile.

"Be safe dear, Valeska and Berthold added with a quizzical glint in their eyes.

The two families walked back inside the secret room and pushed a button to close the entrance. An entrance that looked like part of the wall.

Pacing in circles, Flora spit the words out. "We all saw Skyfire's reaction. Addley is involved with Ember's disappearance."

Berthold walked up and took her hands and stared into her weeping eyes. "Daughter, we have to conduct this search with much caution. You know from experience that the Eryndomnites can trick us. Then, we'll never find out the truth. This is hard on all of us."

He looked over at Ari, who was squinting his eyes with force. Not only was he upset about the disappearance of Ember, but now he is convinced that one of his best friends is behind it. It was tearing him up inside. As hard as he fought it, the rivers opened up and rushed out from his eyes.

Dillon walked up to his son, crushed for what he was going

through and no way to comfort him. Placing a warm hand on Ari's shoulder, Dillon faced Ember's grandfather. "I think it is safe to assume Addley needs around the clock surveillance. She needs to be followed. May God be with us."

Berthold patted Dillon's worried shoulder, "I couldn't agree more. We have to keep in mind that Ember may have been kidnapped by the Eryndomnites. They won't kill her immediately, but in time I'm sure that will change. We need to extend our search to unsafe territory, as fearful as that sounds. Let's put our brains together and come up with a safe and strategic plan for both."

Everyone pulled themselves together for Ember's sake. A plan was coming together.

Chapter Fifteen

Tests were complete. Tyrus, Virginia and Aaron sat in the waiting room, fidgeting, pacing, and not able to carry on a conversation. A nurse opened a door and requested Tyrus follow her. He stuck his shaky fingers in his pockets and followed, casting a worried look back at Virginia and Aaron. They nodded their support.

"Thank you, Nurse Jane. That will be all, Doctor Wilson said, filling in for Doctor Warner.

"Now, I have a nurse sitting with Tania in the other room. I wanted to speak with you alone first." That statement caused his eyebrows to rise up.

"Nothing to worry about. She has no outward injuries but give me a day or two for the lab work results and scans." He raked his goatee. "Something was a little strange that my mind couldn't conceptualize. Her blood pressure and pulse are in ranges I've never seen before. I used different cuffs and devices to recheck. You know, to be certain it wasn't a faulty device, but they all came out the same way."

"What are you saying?" Tyrus asked confused.

"I don't know." He held his hands up. "I need more research and consultations with other doctors to find an answer."

"Are you thinking something is fatal with her? Incurable?"

"No. No. I'm saying she doesn't seem human."

His shocked face didn't need to ask any questions.

"Tyrus, she must be from another planet. Maybe she fell from heaven, as sweet and gentle as she is," he remarked nervously.

Both men rubbed their approaching headache.

"I will give this complete attention and call you in the second I get the results and consultation transcription."

He squeezed Tyrus' shoulder and helped him stand up. They both nodded their farewells without speaking. "I almost forgot," the doctor shared before Tyrus was out the door. "I'll get the nurse to bring Tania out. Please don't say anything to cause her worry."

"I won't. I could never say anything to upset her. She is becoming quite special to me." The doctor shook his head as though he understood completely what he meant. The small amount of time he spent with her brought an immediate fondness and likeability.

Tyrus drove them to an ice cream fountain. All the answers to their questions were "we have to wait for the test results." Nobody was satisfied with the answer, so the next best thing to disappointment is ice cream. The mood lifted. A chunky woman wearing a pin-striped apron and a big smile arrived at their table. She sat the banana split next to Tyrus, strawberry sundae next to Virginia, hot fudge sundae for Aaron and a chocolate malt and piece of creamsicle ice cream cake for Ember. She was a trooper and deserved to be overfilled with as much ice cream that her stomach could hold.

When they returned to Tyrus' house, Virginia went straight to the kitchen and decided to prepare dinner. It would take time to cook in the crockpot. Then she'd run home and take care of her animals and freshen up.

Tyrus waved to her as she drove off. "See you tonight." He shuffled his feet to the stables. Aaron and Ember went for a walk, not hand in hand.

Ember felt a little uneasy about the situation. To her best recollection, he was just being a friend, supportive. She went along with it. But did she have some sort of mental hang up about him touching her? Tyrus and Virginia's touch never burned. Neither did the pinches and play fighting with the guys.

The weather was perfect. In the mid-60s with a soft breeze. If she were allowed, Ember would spend all her time outside. She always arose before Tyrus in the morning and cleaned the stables. That had to be a clue to Tyrus that she couldn't be a human, especially a young adult. Normally, they have to be pushed to get up that early and, yet, to clean the stalls. He felt guilty, but she acted as though she truly loved doing it.

Aaron looked down at her hands and then at her face. "I like being with you," he said.

"I like being with you, too," she replied.

"What I mean is, I like you a lot."

Her eyebrows pulled together. "I like you a lot, too."

"Maybe I'm not wording this right. You seem confused." They stopped walking and he started to take both of her hands but pulled back before feeling the humiliation of how his touch was painful to her. "Would you want to be my girlfriend?"

Her foot swung around. "What is a girlfriend?"

He nervously twiddled his fingers. "It's sort of like I belong to you, and you belong to me. We don't date anyone else. Just you and me."

Her face blushed. "You mean like marriage?"

"No, no. I mean—I don't know what I mean."

His hands reached for hers again and he stared into her eyes. The sun's rays beamed over her hair and strands of gold sparkled. It just mesmerized him. Even from where they came from, Ember stood out in a crowd. No one else had gold in their hair or specks of gold in their eyes like she did. He bent down and kissed her lips, then applied more pressure, trying to get her to understand what he was trying to express.

But that didn't work. She backed away. Her face showed anger and pain. "That doesn't feel right, and it burned badly. Tyrus and Virginia don't do that."

This was getting ridiculous, and he was doubly offended. "Because they're just friends. They're not boyfriend and girlfriend. Just friends." He had no idea that his touch actually burned. It was news to him.

"WE are friends, not boyfriend and girlfriend."

His expression dropped at her words. Not what he wanted to hear. Maybe he was pushing her too fast. They've only been friends for a few days. What was he thinking? He knew exactly what he was thinking, and he was failing. Badly.

"I'm sorry. I didn't mean to make you uncomfortable. Let's just head back. Okay?" His voice had a tone of being fed up.

She nodded. In her mind, it just didn't feel right to be his girlfriend, or whatever it meant. She knew it meant more than she could understand, but something kept tugging at her mind that it wouldn't be right. It was so frustrating not knowing what it could be or if she'll ever remember. A long sigh escaped. He looked over and she gave him a forced smile, then walked home with her head lowered.

Aaron kissed her cheek really hard. His eyes were glaring above her. Then he drove home. She sat on the top plank of the fence where the horses entered into the stable. Head in hands, elbows propped on the knees, she drifted to thoughts. "I like Aaron so much, but not like that. But why not? He's so handsome, so kind, so strong and confident. I like those characteristics—I think." She was talking to herself. "But something is wrong. Something won't let me like him like that. And Tyrus, he is just like a father, poppa to me."

The horse in the wild came to her mind.

"What is it about that horse, that beautiful horse? I just wanted to jump on its back and gallop into the sunset. Why can't I remember? Why?" Something soft nudged her forehead. She looked up to see one of the horses. She smiled sincerely and rubbed its muzzle, laid her face against the horse and felt secure at the moment. "You know what else, Montana? I feel inside like there's love in my heart for someone, but it's like these leaves scattering in the wind. I feel an emptiness like it's love scattering in the wind, and I feel like I have to pull these leaves which represent love back to me," she said as she swiped at the wind.

"This is so frustrating and so sad." She laid her head on Montana's muzzle.

"I thought I'd find you here."

She popped up and looked at Tyrus. "Virginia is back and soup and home-baked bread is ready. Come on down from there, little one."

She took his extended hand and climbed down, blowing kisses at the horses as they walked off.

"Where is Aaron? I hoped he would stick around for dinner."

"Nope. He left."

Tyrus analyzed her features. "Everything okay?"

With a slight nod, she said, "Yes."

He wasn't going to pester her with any more conflicting questions. Her face said enough, and she deserved that privacy.

After dinner and cleanup, they all sat out on the wrap-around porch. She sat on the porch swing, and they creaked back and forth on the old, tattered rocking chairs. Part of his house was old and untouched during the renovations, but that's what gave it its charm. A loud neighing and stomping caught their attention. They ran out to the stable. In the back of the stable, a very large shadow snuck off through the sky. Tyrus pushed his arms back to guard both women from going any farther.

"What is it?" Virginia asked nervously.

"Tania, I don't think you should look at this."

It was too late. Her head was peeking around him, and she saw the damage to the stable boards and the large, red writing on the wall. "LEAVE IT ALONE OR SHE DIES."

Virginia and Tyrus' eyes met for seconds. They turned to look at Ember. She stood motionless and speechless. Softly, his calloused hand squeezed her shoulder. "You're safe. I promise."

But her face didn't believe him. The horses didn't believe him either as they stormed over to her, trying to break down the fence to get to her.

"Tania, we need to calm the horses down. They see how upset you are, and they are going to get hurt if we don't get control of them. Please, Tania."

With warm eyes she thanked him. "Yes, we don't want them hurt. It's okay. Everything is okay."

She climbed up the fence and pet each one and cooed them with soft, loving words. Once they settled down, they walked into the stable to investigate the damage. Tyrus felt the red paint. He smelled it. His eyes met Virginia's again. She got the connection. It was blood. From who? From what? Ember was brushing the horses and speaking softly to them.

"How did someone get in here to do this? There is no ladder. How was this done?" Tyrus had to grab a ladder out of the storage room to touch the blood, and he could tell the ladder hadn't been removed. It was in the exact spot he had previously left it. Who in the world was tall enough to reach that area on the stable wall? The cellphone went to his ear and his good ole friend, Sheriff Lippincott, headed their way.

Chapter Sixteen

The sheriff arrived, and the forensics team followed within forty-five minutes. Tyrus' ranch was out in the middle of nowhere and anybody needing immediate attention would not survive waiting for emergency services. A risk he was willing to take for solitude, peace and quiet.

It was a long night. Forensics had all their samples and evidence secured and logged. Now they had to wait on the results.

A heated discussion between friends, Sheriff Lippincott and Tyrus, took place by the stable. Virginia had taken Ember inside to prepare dinner.

"Harry, stop. No, she will run away if we take her somewhere else. She doesn't have a memory, and this is the place where she feels safe."

The sheriff tilted his head. Critical eyes peered into Tyrus' fuming eyes.

"I get it. Just how safe is she here; right?" Tyrus responded sympathetically. "Virginia will stay with us and we will carry our shotguns wherever we go. Besides, some really weird things happened that you won't understand, because I don't understand either." The sheriff stood up straight at that remark eager to hear the explanation.

"This little girl—well, I guess she's a young lady. She's so small that I can't help but think of her as a child. Anyway, every animal that comes in contact with her protects her. No matter how wild or how big or small an animal is, they love and defend her. It's absolutely amazing to watch."

"For real?"

"In all my sixty years, I have never seen anything like it."

"You don't say."

Discussion about their lives and current events progressed while feeding the livestock.

"I'll let you know what we find out. Be patient. We're going to Seward for their help," the sheriff informed Tyrus. His phone chimed. "Huh. Looks like they're having difficulty identifying the blood source. The good thing is they are mystified by the results, so with that interest, they'll make it a priority. Using their words, it seems the water, salts and proteins of the plasma are whackadoodle. Weird. We'll get to the bottom of this. Try not to worry."

"Really? Is that advice from the sheriff or a friend?"

"Both. Do some prayin' and let the good Lord above protect you all. That's the best advice I can give you."

"Now that's advice I will accept. Thanks, Harry."

"You bet. Be in touch with you soon."

"I'll be waiting."

Tyrus strolled inside. His face had a fake calmness. She lost her memory and now someone is trying to kill her. What more could she take. He needed her to feel safe, and by golly, she will.

A nice vegetable soup was brewing, biscuits baking and apple cobbler in the making. He sniffed the air and walked into the kitchen just in time to hear a crunch as Ember bit down on a slice of apple.

"Am I in aroma heaven? It smells awfully good in here."

"Well, awfully and good clash. Maybe it just smells heavenly," Virginia countered back.

Ember chuckled.

"I beg to differ. It smells so good that I will most certainly put on weight and that's awful."

Virginia waved a hand down and went back to preparation.

Ember helped by setting the table. "Will the boys be joining us?" Ember asked. She was referring to Jacob and Garrett. They lived in a bunkhouse near the back of the fenceline.

"Let me give them a buzz."

"A buzz?" she asked.

"A call."

"Oh, I see."

He walked out of the kitchen to place the call. He didn't want Ember to hear the conversation. After about five minutes he poked his head inside the kitchen. "Yup, they're on the way."

"Oh, good. Those boys work hard. They deserve a hot meal," Virginia said in passing.

The guys were informed not to discuss what had happened. Since they were far out in one of the pastures mending fence, they were unaware of what had taken place. They stopped at the stable on their way in to see for themselves. Both of their bodies slightly squiggled. Inside the house Jacob had mentioned that he saw a huge shadow in the sky around that time. It was Tyrus' turn to shiver.

"Ring, ring," Virginia said to inform the guys that dinner was ready pretending to ring a bell. "Un-un-un. Wash those hands before you even think about sitting down at the table," she remarked from behind closed doors. The guys looked at each other with part of their lips pushing upward. Drat! How did she know?

Ember always sat next to Tyrus. She was much more comfortable with the guys now. To the point of treating each other like brothers and sisters. They even pulled her hair in fun and teased her. She gave it right back. In the midst of fear, they all laughed throughout the dinner.

Tyrus was a firm believer that laughter is the best medicine. It helped the special ops group he was a part of through many a tough time back in the day.

"Aaron, huh?" Garrett teased Tania.

"We're friends. What are you trying to say?" she asked.

"You know, Tania and Aaron up in the tree. K—"

"Just stop right there, Garrett," Tyrus snarled.

Ember looked at him and jutted her nose up in the air. Take that.

Tyrus chuckled under his breath. He liked the family vibe very much. Never in his wildest dreams did he have any idea that having her around could bring out such fatherly instincts, but he was enjoying the heck out of it. After everyone pitched in with dishes and cleanup, they resumed in the living room and watched an old movie. The smell of popcorn hung in every crack of the house. They munched away. Tyrus and Virginia chatted back and forth. It really was like one big family.

Ember looked around at each face. This is now her family. Even though the guys annoyed her, she felt secure and safe with all of them and was learning to love them. Her eyes sparkled with relief and fondness. God was good.

At that very moment, an eerie darkness creeped across the moonlight and then vanished, causing everyone to glance at the window. Nobody spoke. Nobody wanted to ruin the mood, especially for Ember. She eyed all of them to see what their reaction was in regard to the eerie feeling that came and left. She couldn't identify any of them as being worried, so she settled back against the couch and watched the movie.

Jacob wasn't convinced he felt safe and secure. He walked casually to the window and looked out. Ember watched every move and expression he made. Thankfully, she couldn't see the front of his face. His head looked in all directions. He looked straight out over the sky and froze. Two huge eyes were staring back at him. Two huge, evil eyes! Without turning around, Jacob said, "Hey Tyrus. Come look at this beautiful view."

The recliner squeaked as he got up. He walked to the window, searched Jacob's face and looked in that direction. He gulped and froze. They carefully looked at each other and turned back. Clouds drifting by covered the scary image. They were careful not to let Ember see the fear.

When Tyrus sat down, his focus returned to watching the movie. Ember stared at him for a moment. Feeling all was fine, she continued to watch the movie. Once he knew she wasn't analyzing his face, he slowly turned towards Virginia. His eyes were wide, frozen in place. Virginia stared back at him and her body trembled. She clutched the shotgun and drew it in closer to her body.

Chapter Seventeen

While Tyrus and Ember cleaned stalls, his phone rang. He lifted it to his ear and walked far enough away from Ember to speak but stayed close enough to get to her if something went wrong.

"What did you find out, doc? Can't you just tell me over the phone? I see. Okay. Let me get Virginia to stay with her and I'll be right there." He put the phone away and looked up at Ember. She was working diligently. "Almost done in there?"

"Yes. It's all nice and tidy for my friends."

"I have an errand to run. I'm going to drop you off at Virginia's." A quick thought hit him. "Better yet, I'll give her a call and drop you two off at the soda shop while I run some errands in town. How's that?" He felt safer knowing she was close by. Town was almost an hour-and-a-half away. Nothing else in between.

"Soda fountain treats? You don't have to ask me twice."

"Think you could clean up quickly?"

"Of course. When ice cream's involved, keep out of my way. Hey, wanna ask the guys to come with us?"

He rubbed his chin deep in thought. It was Ember they were after, not the animals, so they should be safe. "How kind of you to include them. I think they would love a break. Let me call them."

Like Ember, he didn't have to ask them twice. Inside the truck country songs blasted out of the radio. Whenever Tyrus turned his head, Garrett would reach over and turn up the volume. Ember laughed at the back and forth. She held her stomach laughing the time Garrett reached over and Tyrus grabbed his hand saying, "You touch it again and I'll break your hand." He was smiling when he said it but serious just the same. The calmness and seriousness on Tyrus' face made her bust out laughing more.

Garrett, on the other hand, knew that expression and knew it well. He never touched the volume again. Tyrus was the dad these two guys never had. He cared deeply for them and treated them as sons.

The respect was mutual.

The guys ran into the shop while Tyrus shook his head and provided Virginia with instructions. "We'll discuss the results once we're alone tonight. I think I'll have you all stop and help me feed and take care of my critters. I'll gather my belongings and stay at your place tonight. If that's okay," she commented.

"Absolutely okay." He drove off looking affectionately at her. She waved.

"If I didn't know better, I think you and Tyrus were preordained to be together," Ember remarked.

"Preordained? That sounds so old-fangled."

"Huh?"

"Never mind. We are good friends. That's all."

"Very good friends," Ember commented with a brow raised.

Virginia glanced at her with a shocked expression. She warmly moved her towards the shop door.

Tyrus walked into the doctor's office. The receptionist told him to take a seat and that the doctor was quite busy. Fidgeting like he was on a sugar high, Tyrus finally jumped up and walked back and forth by the window.

"Come on in, Tyrus. The doctor will see you now." He followed her while pulling his hands inside and outside of his back pockets.

"Thanks Hilda," the doctor remarked. "Please close the door on your way out."

"Sure."

"Let's have it, doc. No beatin' around the bush."

"Okayyyy. Have it your way." He placed the x-rays on the screen. "I just don't know what to make of this. I would say her insides—organs, whatnot—look more like a lion's than a human's."

"Say what?"

"Here. Notice this x-ray of a teenager and this is a lion's. Now you compare."

Tyrus examined them both. "Look at the diaphragm of a lion and compare it to a human. Now, this is Tania's x-ray. Which one is closest to hers?"

"Neither. She has organs the lion doesn't have but, yes, there are differences. I'm confused." He backed up and sat down.

"That's not all. The water, salts and proteins of her plasma are whackadoodle."

He jerked his head up. Those were the exact words the sheriff described about the blood smears on the stable walls. He sighed. "Doc, just lay it out for me, pease." He meant to say please but his nerves got the best of him.

"Okay. I see you are concerned. Frankly, so am I. I can't give you a satisfying answer. There's no way. She has a lot of human body functions, but she also has animal body functions. I can't explain it. Nobody can. Her heartbeat and pulse are pretty close to a normal human but also close to a lion's. Again, I can't explain it."

"My question is, can you?"

Tyrus' head plopped in his hand, elbow resting on the counter. His eyes drooped. Without raising his head he said, "I've heard her speak in a language I have never heard before. Being in the military, I have heard many languages, but nothing like the one she used. The problem with that is she doesn't even recognize it when she does use it.

"If that's not enough, at times this glow comes out of her, sparkly and stuff, which she doesn't seem to know about. I've seen her sleeping, and she barely levitated above the ground. And that birthmark is shaped like a lioness and swirls at times. You tell me!" he replied unable to make sense out of any of it.

"I'm not one to speculate such foolish things about fantasy or aliens, anything loony like that, but I'm at a loss here. Truthfully, for her, she seems in topnotch shape. How I know that I don't. It's a gut feeling."

"What do I do, Doc? How can we help her memory return?"

"Tyrus, this upsets me greatly to say, but there is nothing we can do. I have searched all over the world to find any such similarities in any patient but there are none. Zero to compare with."

"So, what you're saying is I will need to consider keeping her around permanently? Fingerprints don't match anywhere?"

"Yes, to your first question, and check with the police on your second question."

"Doc, you can't tell anyone. This could destroy her. And now, someone is trying to kill her. But get this: Jacob and I have both seen these huge, evil eyes in the sky. Both of us. And no, we didn't eat, drink or take anything to cause hallucinations."

The doctor stood there while goosebumps began at the tips of his toes and ended at the top of his head.

"Oh, how I wish I had good news for you, but I'm sorry that I can't help you. But, please, keep me updated on the progress. You might imagine that my curiosity is at peaked levels."

"More than you know, Doc. I'm not exactly bothered by the fact I will need to keep her with me permanently. I can't help but think of her as my daughter. I really enjoy her company."

"You don't have to tell me that. I could tell by the last visit how you feel about her, and I think she feels the same way about you. She spoke affectionately about you."

"Would it be possible for me to get copies of your results and x-rays?"

"Do you have a few minutes to wait?"

"Yes, of course."

"I'll have Hilda get right on it. We're short on staff today. A bug is going around."

"Thanks. For everything."

"Any time."

Tyrus joined them at the soda shop just as they were leaving. "Hold on. Where are you going?"

"We were going to show Tania around the town."

"Oh, well, please don't get lost," he chuckled looking at the few stores on the street. "Jacob, Garrett, do not let her out of your sight. I'm getting some ice cream."

Jacob threw out his thumb and index finger. "No problem."

Virginia and Tyrus sat at a table in a corner. Their voices remained low as they discussed the results. Her eyes needed help reducing in size at the information.

Tyrus was quiet on the drive home. Ember noticed. "You okay, Tyrus?"

"Huh?"

"Are you okay?" she asked again.

"Oh, yeah, sure. I'm fine."

The rest of the drive home music played while everyone just listened. They stopped to take care of Virginia's critters, help carry her belongings out to the truck and headed home. Like normal, Virginia went straight to the kitchen, put on a pot of coffee and began dinner preparation. Ember would get quite distraught if meat was served, so they had to find ways to make a fulfilling dinner for all of them.

Many mornings Tyrus would slip over to Virginia's for bacon and eggs while the guys stood watch. Ember none the wiser.

"Tania, would you mind calling the guys?"

"Sure I will."

She jumped off the couch and went looking for them. "Jacob, Garrett, supper is ready." No answer. So she looked around and lifted her head up as high as possible to scan the fields and didn't realize she had floated up. Tyrus came out at that moment and froze. "Vi...Vi...Virginia, come here quick."

Wiping her hands on a dishtowel, she walked out. "What is it?"

His finger pointed. She looked and froze, too. Ember floated back to the ground and took off through the pasture. The horses galloped alongside of her.

"How...how did she do that, Tyrus?"

His head shook back and forth. "I don't know." So low it was hard to hear, he repeated, "I don't know."

Virginia exhaled a large sigh.

That sound helped to shake Tyrus out of his hypnotic stare. "You can't ask her about it." Virginia started to speak up and he spoke in an almost demanding voice. "Not one word to her about it."

"Okay," she replied offensively.

Ember was almost to the creek when Jacob pulled in a trout. She screamed and he dropped the fish that flipped back and forth around the area.

"What's wrong?!"

She reached them. "You're killing it."

"Yeah...so?"

"You murderer."

He was speechless.

"Get that hook off of it now."

The fish seemed to take his last breath. She cried and picked it up, hugging it to her heart. A bright glow appeared, and the fish started flapping around. She smiled and placed it back in the water and watched it swim off.

Her head swerved around to see fish in a bucket, not moving. She heaved a sigh of anger. With gentleness she picked up each one until the glow from her hands and heart engulfed the fish and they flipped around. She did this to all three fish, not even realizing the healing power her touch had.

She breathed a sigh of relief.

"How did you do that?" Garrett could barely ask.

"Do what?"

"Bring them back to LIFE."

Her eyebrows rose. "I just hugged them and put them back in the water." She turned around and took off running. "Come on, dinner is ready."

They stared at each other for a brief moment and headed back with an empty bucket. The guys hung around until dinner was over before jumping on the 4-wheelers back to the bunkhouse.

Chapter Eighteen

Instead of the normal goofing around at dinner, everyone sat and ate quietly, constantly looking over at Ember, but for different reasons. Beaming a happy smile at them, she piled shredded cheese in her potato soup and didn't look up the rest of the meal. It was so tasty.

The other four snuck bits of bacon in the bowl, then covered it up with gobs of cheese before Ember noticed. Jacob and Garrett chuckled, but Ember thought nothing of it. Boys will be boys.

Virginia's phone rang. She excused herself and pulled the phone out of her purse, then went into the living room to talk. She walked back into the kitchen staring straight ahead.

Tyrus pushed himself up. "What is it?"

"It's Ms. Prissy. Arthur just delivered hay and found her lying dead in my driveway." Tears poured out with quiet sobs and coughs. Ember burst into tears as well.

"Don't worry. Just let Ember bring her back to life like she did the fishes," Garrett commented.

They all stopped and stared at him.

"What kind of foolish talk is that at a time like this?" Tyrus bellowed. Ember looked in shock.

"It's not foolish talk. We both saw it with our own eyes," Jacob added.

They all turned to look at Ember. She didn't understand what they meant, but Tyrus knew she was unaware of her abilities.

"Tania, please try," Virginia asked with pleading eyes.

"I don't know how to do that. I don't know what to do."

"Hold the goat next to your heart," Garrett corrected her.

"Please try," Virginia pleaded.

"I'll try, but I can't promise anything. I don't even think it's possible that I can do it, but I have to try. I love Ms. Prissy."

She sat completely motionless on the trip to Virginia's. What if she couldn't save the goat like the guys had insinuated? How could Virginia bear it? How could she bear it?

They pulled up and Virginia and Ember convulsed with tears. Tyrus put an arm around each of their shoulders and walked them slowly to the pet goat. Ember was so distraught, she fell down by the goat and held it in her arms just out of sadness, still crying intensely. And then... the glow formed around her and over the goat. Ms. Prissy made a bleating sound and wiggled in Ember's arms. The rest of the gang stood in amazement, not knowing how to react.

Ember sat back and stopped crying, wiping her tear-filled face with her shirt sleeve. She helped the goat up and it took off for Virginia after licking Ember's face a few times. Virginia's tears were happy. She hugged the wiggling goat and kissed its head.

"See. I told you," Garrett said with pride in himself.

"I have no idea how that happened. Maybe Ms. Prissy was just sleeping," Ember offered.

"No, dear. Arthur checked her and she wasn't breathing. He said she was dead."

Ember threw her hands up in the air. "I'm telling you; it has to be a coincidence. If I knew how to heal animals, why wouldn't I know about it?"

"Because you have no memory. Duh!" Jacob retaliated. She glared at him. It was like a brother and sister disagreement.

"Jacob, that's enough."

"But, Tyrus."

"Enough I said. Let's just enjoy this happy reunion. That's a much better idea than turning it into a battle."

"You're right," Ember commented and giggled as Ms. Prissy licked her face over and over again.

"Tyrus, I need to get a blood sample and see what happened to Ms. Prissy. Do you think you can help me?"

"Sure I can. You'll need to keep it on ice until you drop it off."

"I can do that. I think I'll stay here this evening to watch after my critters."

"Good idea. Jacob and Garrett, would you mind staying with her?"

"Sure. With all the goodies she bakes, we might eat her out of house and home though."

"Just see that you don't."

"Yes, sir," Garrett replied in an annoyed voice.

"Let's go to the barn and get a syringe, Tyrus."

"Sure thing, Virginia."

When they entered the barn, she gasped. He looked up. In big, red letters, up too high to reach for even the tallest person, it read. "One by one they die. Leave it ALONE."

His phone came out immediately. Hands went over her face.

"It happened again Harry. I mean Sheriff." Just because they were close friends, Tyrus didn't want to show any disrespect for his position. "We'll be waiting."

After collecting the evidence, Sheriff Lippincott shook Tyrus' hand with a sympathetic face. "I see what you mean. There is something so special about that young girl."

"She may be tiny, but she's not a girl."

"Sorry. But, hey, what's up with those glittery gold streaks in her hair?"

Tyrus shrugged his shoulders. "I don't know any more about her than I did before. It's all a mystery. A few really strange things happened, but I'll fill you in on that after the results come back. Give me a call when it's done, and I'll meet you somewhere private."

The sheriff's eyebrow lifted high. It made his face look crooked. Tyrus placed a hand over his smile so he didn't offend him.

Chapter Nineteen

The next morning Tyrus and Tania drove to Virginia's. A few minutes later dirt spread over the driveway. Aaron drove in. "My, he is one handsome fellow, Tania," Virginia expressed only to get raised eyebrows and a pushed up nose facing her.

"He's not my mate."

"How do you know that?"

Caught off guard, she thought. "I don't know. I just know."

"Hey. I went looking for you at your home last night and saw the cop cars as I passed Virginia's place. I didn't want to get in the way, so I figured it best to wait until the morning. I thought I'd check to see if you were here. Anyone hurt?" Aaron said to Ember.

"No. We're fine."

"What happened?"

"We're all fine," Tyrus said in a tone to leave it alone.

"Wanna take a walk, Ember?"

Ember looked curiously at him. Just as they took off, Jacob yelled. "Hey Aaron. Where did you say you moved here from?"

Nobody had heard of him around town. He made friends easily, but didn't talk much about personal things. "From the northeast."

"Where?" Jacob asked again.

He pretended not to hear and walked off with Ember. When he went to grab her hand, she pulled back. "Is something wrong?"

"No. I just don't want to hold hands."

His sizzling eyes looked straight ahead.

Her nose moved up and down. "What is that smell?"

"I don't smell anything." He wiped sweat from his forehead and noticed it had a grayish color. He hurried and wiped it off on his buttock.

"There's my good girl." Ember held her hands out for Ms. Prissy to run to her. Instead, her head went down, and she head butted Aaron. Ember didn't have time to react before the goat backed up and head butted him again. This time Ember stopped her. "What has gotten into you?" Ms. Prissy looked up and made a soft bleating sound.

"You okay?" she asked deeply concerned.

"Yes, I guess. A lot is going on. I'll come see you tomorrow." He walked off bull legged and in slow motion.

Garrett and Jacob zoomed past him on their 4-wheelers. They had gone home before staying with Virginia so they could hurry to work in the morning and not have to disturb her. "What was that all about?"

She scratched her head. "I don't know. Ms. Prissy does not like him for some reason. Hey, do you guys smell something disgusting? It's kind of fading away now."

"No, I don't," Jacob replied.

"Me neither," Garrett answered.

"That's weird." They headed back towards Tyrus. She couldn't quit thinking about Aaron. Her eyes stared ahead as thoughts swirled in her mind. As far as looks, yes, she was very attracted to him, but, never more than a friend. Her heart just didn't feel it. She sighed walking behind them. What is it about his appearance that makes her want to see him and hang out with him? It was driving her bonkers.

When he held her hand, she got a sick feeling in her stomach, and it always felt like her skin was burning. His eyes looked so distant. Why did she feel repulsed by his touch? Stranger yet, why did she desire to see him but not touch him?

"Tania!"

She looked forward.

"Tania!"

"Wh...What?"

"Where's your mind been? We've been calling for you to catch up," Garrett said annoyed.

Off she ran and passed them running into Virginia's house. Sitting on the kitchen table was a basket of homemade pastries and muffins. Ember's eyes popped open. The guys ran past her and started grabbing them.

"Put those back down and go wash your hands," Tyrus roared. "You, too, little one."

She snapped her fingers and skipped to the bathroom. When all three came back, they stood to attention awaiting the pretend green flag wave.

"Use your manners, sit down and be civil," Tyrus ordered the men who acted more like boys.

"Thanks, Ms. Virginia. These are the best ever," Ember said with a blissful face.

After consuming the basket full of manna from heaven, Tyrus and Ember headed home. One of the guys would sleep on the couch and the other in the guest bedroom at Virginia's. Of course, Jacob being older won the guest bedroom fair and square.

Ember looked around before they entered the house. "Could we please check on the horses, bull and dogs first?"

"Great idea. We'll keep the dogs in the house tonight."

All was well with the horses. She even gave them a kiss and treats before leaving. Mr. Horns rushed over, and she kissed his head and provided a treat to him as well. The dogs barked happily about spending the night in the house.

"Tyrus, why can't they stay in the house all the time?"

"Because I need them to keep watch of the livestock. You know yourself we can hear them bark even inside the barn."

"Then they could hear things from the house; right?"

"Right, but too late. This happened before and I didn't make it to the pasture on time. Coyotes killed some calves. Right now, I only have the bull and horses, plus the cattle, but I'm thinking of getting more cows."

"That is so sad. I understand now."

As they turned the corner, a shadow darted by, but they didn't see it. The dogs growled; teeth bared.

"I don't know what to do. If I take you with me, you could get hurt. If I leave you in the house while I check things out, I can't protect you in the house."

"I'll walk between these two. They'll protect me. Besides, the animals always come to my rescue, so I'll be safe; but you won't. In that case, I shall stay right next to you, Tyrus."

"Can't believe I'm going to admit this, but that makes a lot of sense. Why ole Mr. Horns would probably break through the fence to get to you."

"Good. That settles it."

He used the flashlight of his cellphone. The dogs stopped and small growls came out of their throats while they stared towards the forest. A shadow zipped into the trees before they could make it out.

"Whatever it was is gone," he said

"Wait! There it is again."

"Do you see something?" Tyrus asked.

"No. Don't you smell it? It's gagging me."

"Sorry, but I can't smell a thing. Are you certain about this?" Tyrus asked.

Her cheeks puffed out as she covered her mouth. "It's fading away. The smell is fading away."

"You smelled this before?"

"Yes, when I was walking with Aaron."

"Did he smell it?"

"No, just me again."

"Let me know when you smell it again."

She perked up. "You believe me?"

"Little one, you have given me no reason not to believe you. Of course I do."

He allowed the dogs to run around and exhaust the excitement bursting out of their precious bodies. They played before having to settle down for the night. Running across the floor, they skidded into the walls and their tails would not quit wagging. "Okay you stinkers," he joked, "calm down. Now." Ember picked up the few things that they knocked to the floor. She brought out a bowl of water and plenty of treats. When she plopped down on the floor against the couch, they plopped on each side of her, heads resting in her lap. She couldn't quit kissing their furry heads.

"That Aaron is a nice, young man."

"Yeah, sure."

"Do you like him? He seems to like you."

"As a friend. He will only be my friend," she said sternly.

"Message received."

Chapter Twenty

Ember slept in Tyrus' room downstairs with the door wide open. He slept on the couch. The early morning sun snuck under the curtains right into his eyes. He squinted and felt something in his hand. The shotgun rested there all night. He pushed himself up, ran fingers through his hair and walked over to check on Ember. She was sound asleep with the dogs lying on each side of her. *What a Kodak moment. Sheesh, where did that come from?* He couldn't help but ponder how that commercial was showing his age.

He took advantage of her sleeping, and with shotgun in hand went out to the stable. He grabbed the rake and cleaned out each stall, filling them with clean hay. He walked over to the fence and started to lay his arm on it for support when he noticed something slimy dripping from it. Head down next to the fence board, he stared in wonder. It had a sooty appearance. His gloved finger scraped a little and he examined it further. It was so close that the stench almost made him hurl.

The barking of dogs made him look towards the house. Ember and the dogs were running and playing on their way to the barn.

"Hey, that's my job," she announced.

"Well, I decided you need a break. Maybe you should just focus on housecleaning stuff instead."

"Yuuuck! I hate housecleaning. I'm an outdoors person. Did you feed them yet?"

"No, but look at this. Is this what you were smelling?"

She stared at the gook. A memory wanted to come out, but it just wouldn't. She squeezed her fists and gritted her teeth.

"Tania, do you know what this is?"

"Something in my brain says I should, but that's as far as I get. Yes. That is the stench I smelled."

"It smells like...death." A quiver ran through his veins at that moment. Ember twitched at the thought.

They hung around outside by all of the animals. She brushed the horses and sat up on the fence to brush Mr. Horns' soft hair. It was actually a good day. Virginia didn't feel comfortable leaving her farm animals alone after what happened yesterday. Jacob and Garrett worked out in the fields mending fences for Tyrus.

"Jacob, what is this stuff?"

He stared at it, swished it around with his gloved finger and coughed. Both of them covered their noses and mouth. "That's definitely from something dead. Yuck. It may be contaminated. I'll take a picture and show Tyrus later," he informed Garrett. "Let's get away from it."

Back at the ranch, grooming went on and Tyrus tinkered around the stable. It was the fall season, and the ground was getting hard. They wore insulated jackets and gloves every day. A truck drove down the driveway without much dust. Ember looked up to see Aaron waving. His smile was wide. He looked so much better than the other day. Actually, the other day he was not himself. Jumpy, tense and just different. Ember actually felt a twinge of caution around him that day.

Something about his golden hair, gorgeous face and good build ate away at her memory, as if she knew him previously. Dang, it was frustrating to her.

"How's my girl today?" His smile appeared genuine.

"Where were you yesterday? You said you would stop over." Why couldn't she take her eyes off of him? And why did she still feel uncomfortable? Why? She'd seen girls falling all over themselves trying to catch his attention, but his look was freaky, at times almost robotic looking. And he never noticed the cute girls.

Mr. Horns lost it when he came up. He bucked and scraped his hooves. Snorting was loud and challenging. He backed up. More and then some more. That didn't cause questions in her mind, because Mr. Horns wouldn't allow anyone but her near him. She sensed something wasn't right. But why, dang it? He's always nice and helpful. She shook off the cautious thoughts and jumped down from the fence after calming the bull down.

"You sure stir up a lot of trouble," she said in joking.

"Beats me as to why," he said holding his hands up.

"Oh! I found the source of that awful smell I was asking you about. Actually, Tyrus found it. Wanna see it?"

"Not really."

"Come on, chicken."

"Just for a second."

She brought him to it and he shook it off. "Yeah, what of it."

"Can't you smell the putrid odor? It's death in liquid form. Gross."

Sounding perturbed he said, "Like you know what it is. Let's go."

She eyed him curiously before walking away. "So, where were you yesterday?"

"Didn't feel well, so I stayed around the house."

"Do I get to meet your parents?"

"No!"

Her face formed wide eyes. "Why so touchy about it?"

"Was I? They're really busy right now, so it wouldn't be a good time."

"Some other time then."

"Let's sit on the swing. Okay?"

"Okay," she said hesitantly. Why? She had no idea. She sat on one side while he was on the other side of the swing. He moved closer and took her hand. "You don't mind, do you?"

Unexpectedly, she pulled it away. "I don't know why, but it just doesn't feel right to me to hold hands. I can't explain why."

He held them up and turned them back and forth. "What? Are they gross or something? Do they feel gross? What's the reason?!" he shouted.

That reaction surprised her. Not only her but Tyrus rounded the corner with concern on his face.

"What's the yelling about?" He stared at Aaron with sternness.

"Sorry, sir. I didn't mean to react like that."

Wrinkling her nose, covering it with her hand, she noted, "Ewe, there's that smell again."

"What smell? I don't smell a thing. Guess my time is up here. I'll get with you later this week." Aaron walked off before they could question him.

"Come on, little one. How about a toasted peanut butter sandwich?"

Still in thought, she said, "Yeah, sure."

Tyrus walked in while she watched Aaron drive away. Something caught her eye but faded from her memory fast.

Chapter Twenty-One

Virginia stopped over for a brief moment. Tyrus sat on the swing with her while Ember walked amongst the flowers. They seemed to dance in the breeze. Always listening, she could hear the swing creak back and forth. It was a comforting sound with all the weirdness happening. To Ember, silence was as disturbing as hearing the katzenjammer voices in her mind. She didn't like the quiet at all, and she didn't like the voices in her head. She never touched a drop of alcohol, but at times she felt like she was recovering from a hangover because of the nausea and headaches the voices produced. She only knew about hangovers from hearing Jacob and Garrett talk about them when Tyrus wasn't in hearing range.

"What is that hideous smell?" Virginia asked, squishing her face.

"I smell it too." He looked around and saw a sooty drop fall to the deck floor. This took some thinking, so he stared at the glob and replayed the day's events. It struck him hard. He felt ridiculous for even thinking this way, but Aaron sat right here where the glob lingered. Maybe he was still sick or had some kind of a disease. Coincidence or what? He decided not to share his thoughts.

"We need to get away from this terrible smell. Let's go out by Tania," he said.

Virginia bent down to pick some flowers and Ember let out a shriek.

"What? What's wrong?" she asked Tania.

"You can't pick them."

Pushing her head back, Virginia asked, "Why not?"

"I don't know why," she said staring forward with a crinkled-up face. Then she answered more to the point. "Because...because they're too pretty. This way we can sit out on the swing and admire them."

"That's fine, dear, but you didn't have to get all drama queen about it. Just a simple explanation would suffice."

"Don't mind me," she said in a sweet voice. In reality, she considered all of nature her friends but felt ridiculous telling them because she, herself, couldn't explain.

"Hey, my good buddy the sheriff is driving down the driveway," Tyrus informed them.

"That's my cue. I'll see you all later," Virginia stated.

Tyrus watched the sheriff's expression pulling up. His face was serious. *Oh boy. Here we go.*

Addley and Treelin walked nervously to the secret opening. Their heads looked back constantly to make sure no one was following. What brought on this nervousness all of a sudden? How many times had they walked this path throughout the years? Countless times. With a quick movement, they were out of anyone's sight. The secret door closed automatically behind them.

A message was sent immediately to Ari. He opened the folded paper. In disgust he balled the paper up and threw it down. Huffing and pacing brought instant attention from his parents.

"Son, what's wrong?" his mother asked,

"Addley escaped our watch. She and Treelin were walking a great distance, then disappeared. Just disappeared. I'm going to rush over where the watchmen are waiting for me."

"Someone needs to accompany you, son. And, to be honest, disappearing isn't all that strange around here."

"There's no time to discuss this. Sorry, but I'm out of here now."

Without waiting for his mother's response, he was gone in a flash. All she heard was a swishing sound.

Ari arrived at the location. One of the guys ran to him. "Here. Over here, sir."

He followed and stared at the goop dripping from the rocks. His head looked straight ahead. Thoughts whirled and whirled. "No! It can't be." The substance was toxic to their touch. They could not touch it without a devastating outcome. "Stand back."

They walked around looking for an opening, being very careful of where they walked. Ari sent a message to his parents and to Ember's family. It was an urgent request for them to come to his location with complete head-to-toe suits that would protect them from the toxic substance. They would bring along with them enough of the suits as was needed at the location.

Ari and his crew sat far away from the rocks awaiting the arrival of the rest of them. It looked like a small army arrived.

$\sim$

Inside the secret opening, an evil presence was felt. Huge eyes filled the whole area of the room. Addley and Treelin bowed to show respect, and truthfully, out of pure fright.

"The plan worked. The girl has no memory. Once you gain the affections of Ari, it will give us the advantage. I have waited a very long time for this. You two shall be rewarded.

"There is a tiny problem, though," she added with a threatening voice. "The girl keeps trying to regain her memory, but my power is too strong for that to happen. The man who took her in, however, is trying to find ways to help her recover them. I have arranged warnings to scare them off, but they keep disobeying MY THREATS. My next threat will be one they will heed. Take my word. As for the one spying on her progress," staring with menacing eyes at Treelin, "the fool here thinks he has feelings for her. Idiot," she grumbled, thrusting hateful eyes at them. "It would be quite foolish to mess up my plans," still glaring at them.

"As for the other girl, she hasn't been found yet. It may be too late for her if she isn't found soon. Such a pity." A terrifying laugh escaped.

"If these plans falter in any way, I will have to take extreme measures. Prepare the animals just in case. Our plan with the grizzly bear was foiled. If we have to, we'll release our army of animals."

Addley and Treelin just nodded, shaking physically. They were too scared to look in her eyes. A scourging heat passed through their bodies. Stench and a sooty substance began dripping from them.

"Imbeciles are standing right outside. They have no power to get through." Brimstone covered the rock walls. She laughed in hysterics. "Leave through the other secret entrance. Fix yourselves up, first. And, Addley, make sure Ari is under your magical powers quickly. Don't you let him slip away."

"I'm working on it. I promise."

"Now, leave and make it back home before you have been discovered. DO NOT LET ME DOWN. The consequences are very unpleasant."

Her eyes disappeared but the maniacal laugh echoed in the room. Addley and Treelin locked eyes before they had enough strength to move one muscle. The transcendent level of evil scared them greatly, to the point they appeared like stones.

Chapter Twenty-Two

The search was tedious and unsuccessful. Ari kicked rocks, smashed branches in two on his leg and held his emotions in far too long. His body collapsed to the ground, sobs heaving deep from his chest. Ember's mother ran to him, embracing him, crying herself in such despair. Arwood took in the scene and rivers of tears flowed out his eyes. How he, and how they missed Ember. She was like a cheery sunray sparkling love into their lives on a daily basis.

"How could Addley do this to her? How could she become evil? I don't get it," he screamed. Flora tried her best to comfort him, but how could she? She was in emotional turmoil herself. Nobody could muster up the strength. They were all drained.

His eyes stung from the mixing of sweat and tears. Blinking a few times, his eyes adjusted. That is when footprints appeared out of nowhere. He looked up to heaven and nodded his thanks. Nobody knew what was going on, but they stood back and watched Ari follow the tracks. They went right up to the mountain of boulders and stopped. He motioned everyone over.

"This is where the footprints end. There is a secret entrance that is probably only accessible to the Eryndomnites. Now that we know they are involved, God save her. How did they escape? How?"

Ember's grandfather placed a hand on his shoulder. "She's

alive and well. Don't ask me how I know, but I do. I believe the good Lord above is giving me this peace. Now, we have to plan a strategy against the Eryndomnites. My heart is heavy. The last battle was catastrophic. But we have something they don't have: The Lord God Almighty on our side. He helped us before. He'll do it again.

"We're all forgetting one really important fact." They all stared at Berthold in thought trying to figure out what they were missing.

"God loves all His creation, but Ember Pines has a special place in His heart. He loves that little thing. He will take care of her, and we will win this battle...again," his voice deflated towards the end.

The last battle was excruciating and exhausting. "Please don't think I am kicking us when we are down. That is not my intention, but we sort of stood back and let this happen again. Things were going so great and evil sort of creeped in unaware. We need to stand tall, fight and keep this from happening again. I blame myself for not being on my guard. After the last battle, you would think I had learned a lesson. For shame on me."

His heart was so heavy it felt like a bomb about to explode. Comfort was declined by one and all. He went to the highest authority on his knees, bearing a broken, contrite heart.

Dillon walked over to Ari. "What he said is true. We all failed. But, with God, we have an avenue to repent and redeem ourselves. Now is the hard part. You have to pretend to be interested in Addley for Ember's sake. You have to make her believe you without compromising yourself. Avoid affection and entrapment. Once you accept King Eryn's mark, it's all over and there is no coming back. Be strong, son. Be very strong. They are so deceptive that even the purest of hearts can be deceived and fall into their trap."

"Father, my heart physically hurts." He held a hand on his heavy heart with pleading eyes staring at his father. "My heart feels like a campfire as it sizzles out. The embers scatter in the wind to ignite no more. Is this a warning to me? Like Ember's love has scattered in the wind also? Don't you understand? I don't want to be with anyone other than Ember. If I don't find her, I will never love again."

And then, it was like a bolt of lightning struck him and his courage returned. "Well, my attitude isn't helping. That will change. I will find my love, no matter which way the wind takes her."

A boldness came over all of them. Ari pulled himself together and set his mind straight. He was ready to take Addley, Treelin and King Eryn's evil army down. They all went back to their homes to make plans. The kingdom would come together in the morning for instruction.

Wherever the soot dripped, it turned the vegetation, rocks, and everything it touched rotted and caused decaying. The smell of death lingered in their heavenly realm.

Chapter Twenty-Three

"What did you find, Harry? I hope that doesn't offend you. While you're visiting at my home, I just think it's more personal than calling you sheriff. When we're out in public, I will always refer to you as sheriff," Tyrus reasoned.

"Seriously, you even have to ask that?"

Tyrus shrugged his shoulders.

"Now, we need to go somewhere private for this talk."

Eyes wouldn't stop widening for Tyrus. He dragged his feet, and they went out to the stable. Ember and the guys hung around outside playing catch with a baseball and gloves.

"Let's hear it."

"Forensics came back with nothing. They were completely bumfuzzled. The blood doesn't compare to anything or any animal. What could it possibly be? Maybe it's not blood."

"Is that the results in your hand?" Tyrus asked.

"Yeah, why? Certainly, you can't read this lab stuff."

"No, but we can compare."

"To what?"

"Follow me in the house. Keep this info between us and don't let Tania see any concern in your face," Tyrus whispered. "We'll be out in a minute," he yelled to everyone.

Harry waved.

His hands nervously pulled open a drawer hiding a manila envelope. The papers rustled apprehensively as he pulled them out. "Come to the kitchen table. Lay the results down."

"Yeah, so?" Harry held his hands up.

"Compare the results and quit being a jerk."

"Just hold on there." Hands went to Harry's hips.

"Well, are you? You know, are you going to arrest me for the hundredth time?" Tyrus blurted.

Harry smirked at him and began comparing. His eyes lit up. He squinted at them and kept looking back and forth. He pulled his glasses off, stood up and looked straight ahead for a second. "Where did you get this and who does it belong to?"

"This is Tania's lab results. The doc discussed the results with me alone."

"This is weird. It may not be her blood, but it is the same type of sample as the smear on the barn wall. How can that be? This blood sample is not human. What I mean is it has human characteristics, but it is way different than a normal human's blood." He scratched his head. "How is this possible?"

"It's probably a good idea for you to discuss the results from Forensics with the doctor. You'll need a court order first, I'm sure you're aware of that."

Harry's lips folded down. "Of course I'm familiar with that. Geesh."

"Man, you're a Mr. Horns today."

"What'd you expect? Nobody knows what we're dealing with here. Aliens? Ghosts? What?!"

Tyrus patted his back.

"Hey, you said there is some weird stuff you would tell me about when I brought the results. Let's hear them."

"Ya know, we are friends. I would appreciate it if you would treat me as such instead of an annoying party of interest to your case."

"I'm sorry. I'm going on two days without sleep and at a loss for words. Now please, tell me what you were talking about."

"Sorry to hear that. I'll tell you if you promise to go straight home and sleep. Actually, I have a better idea. Virginia is bringing over apple pie and ice cream. The game is on tonight. Stay here and sleep upstairs in the guest bedroom. Tania's been sleeping in mine, and I've been sleeping on the couch. Come on Harry. It's not safe to drive in your condition."

"Let me call Emma and see if she's okay with that. You're right about it not being safe. My eyes drifted and I almost went over the edge. That was scary."

"I'll put on some decaf coffee so the caffeine doesn't keep you awake. Call Emma and we'll get back to the discussion."

The kitchen door swung open sounding like old West saloon bar doors. "She said to thank you, that she was worried about me driving home. She was just about to call you and ask if I could sleep here."

"That's great. I feel better. There. Coffee is on. Now have a seat and I'll fill you in on the crazy, weird events." First Tyrus described how he found Ember, but Tania to him, and how she had a glow around her body that actually came from her body. He could tell Harry was alert and questioning it in his mind.

Next, he told him about Tania's devotion to animals and that no matter how wild, big or small, they all adored her, to the point of protecting her. When he told Harry about the horses making a circle around her as she slept in the stable, Harry felt his eyes would roll out of his head.

This is the part that floored him. Tyrus explained how her body elevated a few times during sleep and how she floated up in the air without realizing she had done that.

"Boy, don't you be making stuff up," he said.

After catching his breath from laughing, Tyrus said, "I don't blame you for not believing it."

He continued. "Sometimes, she talks to the animals in a language that is enchanting, except she has no idea she does it.

"Wait for this one, if you think that's all fabricated. The boys and I have seen this with our own eyes: she has held dead animals up to her heart and they were healed. A glow encompasses her and the animal. They come back to life."

"Okay, where's the music?" Harry said with a stutter.

"What music?"

"The *Twilight Zone* music, that's what."

Virginia was true to her word and brought over homemade apple pie and ice cream. They all sat in the living room enjoying it while watching the game. Ember was bored and walked to the huge picture window Tyrus installed during his remodel. Her mind went to Aaron. His face features brought joy to her, but the rest of him brought concern. Her heart ached for the man she would marry someday, and there was a churning inside her soul that that someone was out there looking for her. An awareness. Why did Aaron stand out? Why was his face always on her mind? Hopefully one day she would find out the answer to her questions.

As she leaned against the window, a hand rested on her shoulder. "Follow your heart, even if love takes you to the stars in the heavens or down into the depths of the sea. Enter new realms. Just go wherever your heart leads, dear," Virginia commented.

"If only. You see, I know deep down in my soul that there is that special someone for me. There is something that draws me to Aaron's face, but that's as far as it goes."

Virginia sat on the other side of the bench. "So, you have a physical attraction towards him?

Her face wrinkled like a raison. "Huh?"

"You think he is handsome and like the way he looks."

"Well, sure. Who wouldn't? But I know in my soul he is not the one. It's so complicated."

Sympathetic eyes stared at her. "It will all work out one day. You'll see. Keep the faith. I pray every day for you."

"What about you, Ms. Virginia? It seems you and Tyrus have an attraction. What are you waiting for?"

All flustered she replied, "Oh nonsense, child. We're just friends."

"Un-huh. Sure."

Virginia gently slapped her knee.

"What's going on over there?" Tyrus asked inquisitively.

"Not a thing, nosy," Virginia replied shyly. "Hey, Garrett, you ready to go?" He was staying at her house until they could figure out what was going on. He hopped up off the floor and ran to put his dish in the sink.

"Ready now." He opened the door. "Whoa!"

A huge shadow flew over at that moment and stopped over the stable. It freaked him out and played with his mind. "Uh, guys, what is that?"

They all ran to the door and looked out. Nobody spoke. Tyrus took a picture while Harry snored lying back in the recliner. A lightning bolt shot directly at the stable. The eyes in the sky formed what appeared to be laughing eyes. Smoke started climbing.

"Fire. Everyone, grab a hose quickly," Tyrus urged frantically. "Tania, can you get the horses out of the stable?"

They were snorting and raving, running around the stalls. Grabbing the hose, Tyrus looked up just in time to see Ember float over the stable gate. The fire was spreading at the exit to the pasture, so she opened the gate to let them run out front. "Watch out!" she yelled as they stampeded to safety.

"Tyrus?" Virginia yelled.

He was in some kind of stupor.

"Tyrus!" Virginia yelled again. He looked over and she motioned to the fire. A quick shake of the head and he was on it. Jacob came up the other side, and within minutes it was out. They soaked the ground so that no embers could ignite again.

Just as they walked out front of the stables, the huge shadow drifted off. None of them would mention it, but they stood in shock as an unholy laugh echoed throughout the sky.

After about five minutes, they all came to their senses. "What was that in the sky?" Garrett asked still dumbfounded.

"Nobody knows, son."

Virginia pulled Tyrus aside. The rest of the gang was rounding the horses up. "Why did you just stand there as though you saw a ghost?"

"It happened again. Tania floated above the stable fence. My mind won't comprehend it, and I feel like I'm going mad. How is it she doesn't know it happens? How can that be?"

"Let's get the horses rounded up and ask her. They'll be safe in the stable."

"Face it. We're sleeping in the stable tonight. Tania will refuse to leave the horses."

"I figured," Virginia answered.

Now that the horses were secure, they called Ember over. "Little one, are you aware that you floated over the fence to open the gate?"

Eyes of fear popped up. "I have no idea I did that. Are you sure you didn't see me climbing over it? Why wouldn't I notice something like that?"

"It's true there was a lot of smoke, so maybe it covered the boards as you climbed. Other than that, with these strange occurrences, nothing makes sense. Maybe someone has the power somewhere to block your thoughts, along with your memory. That's total Sci-Fi malarkey, but nothing else seems to make sense."

"Oddly enough, I agree," Virginia said stunned.

"Hey, Ms. Virginia. Maybe we should get to your place and check it out," Garrett suggested. His light blonde, red hair blew out around his face in the wind. The cold weather gave him rosy cheeks, covering up his tiny freckles. He had a cute, loveable face.

"Good idea. Come on, son."

"Send me a text as soon as you check everything out, please," Tyrus threw out on their way to her truck.

"Okay. Night all."

"Sweet dreams," he followed up.

"Tyrus, I have to sleep in the stable?"

"I figured as much. Let's go in and wake that slouch up so he can get some sleep, and we'll grab some sleeping bags."

"Oh, Tyrus. I heard the poor man say he hasn't slept in days."

"I'm just joshing. I completely understand. We'll keep all of this secret until the morning."

Inside he shook Harry's shoulder. "Har-Har, get to bed." Ember giggled at his nickname. She whispered, "Hardy-har-har," and laughed again. Then she switched it around in whispers. "Harry-har-har." Louder laughs emerged.

Blinking his eyes, walking wobbly up the stairs, Harry asked, "What's so funny?" His nose lifted and he made a loud "Mhhm, Mhhm" sound with it. "Do you smell smoke?"

"Nothing, Har-Har. Just get some sleep and take those mudmuckers off before climbing in that bed. Seriously!"

"Yeah, yeah." The door clicked close.

"Jacob, you can sleep in my room. Just leave the door open so you can hear yelling, or anything of concern."

"Sure, boss." His eyes lighted up.

They grabbed their things. Ember put on a warm onesie and carried extra blankets plus her pillow. Tyrus carried the sleeping bags, his pillow and a shotgun. "Lock the door, Jake."

"Yes, sir." He watched them round the corner, then swiftly ran back to the kitchen, poured a glass of milk and scooped out another piece of pie. He plunged into Tyrus' favorite recliner and watched the rest of the game.

Tyrus laid outside of the stable in a cubby out of the wind. Ember lay on thick hay as the horses circled around her. A pony lay down next to her. Tyrus shook his head at the phenomenon in front of his eyes. He knew darn well no other person could ever get away with that. They would be trampled on. Somehow, some way, they all slept like puppies.

Chapter Twenty-Four

Virginia drove in quietly. She had a key, so she and sleepy Garrett went inside to start breakfast. Homemade muffins baked, scrambled eggs sizzled, and creamy, chocolate Malt-O Meal gurgled on the stove. A pot of hot chocolate kept warm on the burner.

Thumpity-thump-thump played a tune down the stairs. The kitchen door rattled back and forth as wide-eyed Harry stood in anticipation.

Sleepy-eyed Garrett's whole body took up the couch, head resting against a crocheted pillow and watching Bugs Bunny say, "Eh, what's up doc?" He chuckled.

"Oh Harry, fix yourself a cup of coffee."

"Thanks, Virginia. I will."

"Sleep well, I hope?"

"Ah, yes ma'am."

She pushed the kitchen door open and yelled, "Garrett, please wake up Jacob and go out to the stables to get Tyrus and Tania."

"Sure." He stuck his head in Tyrus' room, wondering where Jacob slept. The chest of a body rose up and down under the blankets. "Tyrus? Tyrus, is that you?"

"No, idiot. It's me."

"Jacob! What are you doing in Tyrus' bed?"

"Sleeping. Duh."

"Get up!"

"Get out!"

"Ms. Virginia, Jacob won't get up." They were cousins but acted more like brothers.

"I'll take care of it. Now, get out there and find Tyrus and Tania."

"Yes, ma'am," he answered frustrated.

Tyrus and Ember had already cleaned the stalls and were feeding the animals. The dogs jumped around them on the walk back to the house just waiting for their breakfast. Their paws scratched against the linoleum as they skidded through the kitchen door where a bowl of fresh water and bowls of feed awaited them. They slurped and guzzled down their food.

"All right, Cain and Able, out with you."

"Ms. Virginia, can't they stay inside for a little bit?"

"Of course, dear. Of course."

"Mornin' all," Tyrus said as he stumbled into the kitchen. "Har, sleep good?"

"The best. I feel like a quarter bucks."

"Huh?" Garrett questioned him.

"Have you not noticed our inflation? I can't afford to sleep like a million bucks." He used his usual grumpy disposition tone. It brought welcomed laughs.

"Sit down all," Virginia demanded. "Garrett, please grab the pitcher of orange juice out of the frig."

"Yes, ma'am," he said scowling at Jacob. "Jacob, you idiot."

"What's your malfunction, Garrett?"

Garrett looked around at everyone's faces. Then he pointed to Jacob. "Pig, there, ate all the pie but a sliver."

"How do you two ever get anything done?" Ember asked quizzically.

They sneered at her.

After cleanup, the boys attended to their chores. Even on Saturday they had chores to complete before they could go into town or anything. Tyrus cleaned up the glob on the porch swing and the mess it made on the deck underneath before he and

Harry sat down. He wore gloves because of the disgust. "Hey Harry, have you ever seen anything like this before?"

He bent down and made his lips wide as his head tilted back. "Never. What is that repulsive smell?"

"I have an idea. Why don't you take a sample and find out."

"Yeah, I guess I should." He ran out to his cruiser and grabbed some evidence bottles and scraped some into it holding his breath. "Weird."

"That should do it." Tyrus ran into the house to wash his hands, even though he wore gloves, to get the potent smell off of them.

Harry swung back and forth. Tyrus took a seat on the rocker. He pulled up a picture and handed it to Harry. "This is what you missed last night."

He used his fingers to enlarge the picture and studied it before speaking. "What in the world is that?"

"Tell me what you think it is."

"It's lunacy. That's what it is. But honestly, it looks like a huge pair of wicked eyes in the sky. Your turn."

"That's the same thing we all came up with. This...thing shot a bolt of lightning at the stable and it caught on fire. We put it out quickly, then it disappeared. Do you believe in that old tale about the Thunder Bird?"

"No, but I'm rethinking it after all the cuckoo things lately."

"Well, wonder if it could be that."

"Who knows at this point? I remember now smelling smoke last night. Why didn't you tell me then?"

"Because there's nothing you could have done, and you needed sleep."

"I guess you're right. Well, I received a text from Emma. She wants me home. I'll drop this specimen off first."

"Hey, Harry. Something weird happened again last night."

"You mean weirder than that picture?" said smugly.

"Believe it or not, yes."

"Let's hear it."

"Tania floated above the fence in the stables last night. She was terrified for the horses and hurried to their safety. Nobody else witnessed it. She swears she has no idea she did that. And get this: It looked like pixie dust or something bazaar like that sparkled all over her."

He rubbed his jaw. "How could she not know it? Maybe the smoke interfered with your vision."

"First off, I believe her. The way she answers is genuine. Secondly, I thought about the smoke, too, but I know what I saw. And, thirdly, there's a crazy thought about somebody blocking her mind to keep her memory from coming back, as psycho as it sounds."

"Heck, Ty, nothing makes sense, so why not? I gotta go. I'll let you know what I find out." His feet shuffled to the cruiser.

Tyrus dropped his heavy head in his hand propped up by an elbow resting on the arm of the rocker. The guys and Ember ran up excitedly.

"You okay? You look worried," Ember asked.

He shook it off, his thoughts rather mawkish. "I'm fine. Really. More mentally tired than anything." With sad eyes she forced a commiserating smile. She kept the guilt to herself.

"Boss, could Tania come with us to town?" Jacob asked. She was wiggling back and forth.

"Sure, why not."

"We know. Keep her in sight at all times."

"Right. Here's some cash for lunch and an ice cream soda. I'm sure you'll all want some."

"Thanks, man," Jacob replied. Ember studied him humorously. There was still a barrier between their expressions and her lack of knowing how to express thoughts.

Chapter Twenty-Five

The three of them ran around town. They laughed, went into stores, spoke to the locals, tormented Ember with hair pulling and had a great time. They ate in the diner for lunch, and now that they walked enough to bring on hunger, in the nick of time the soda shop came into view. They looked back and forth at each other and dodged for the shop.

Garrett yelled, "Last one there is a"—

—"rotten egg," Ember finished the saying for Garrett after hearing it a million times.

Ember sipped a delectable chocolate soda fountain treat. The guys were too interested in stuffing their faces with the goodness in front of them to notice her far-off gaze. She studied the horse pictures carefully, beyond interested and beyond her capability of wondering why it had such an effect on her. Especially, the white stallion. She kept studying and studying it.

"Hhhh!" Garrett sighed.

"What? What's wrong with you, man?"

Garrett pointed to Ember. She was lost in thought. Jacob, with a scorned face, looked over. At first he didn't notice it and huffed out loud. Then his eyes caught sight of something really strange. The birthmark above her left cheekbone was swirling with bright, glittery colors. His hypnotic eyes glanced back at Garrett. He shrugged his shoulders.

"Tania. Tania, can I ask you a question?" Jacob asked.

She gazed at him with a faraway look. "Sure."

"Can you feel that birthmark swirling? Does it vibrate or something?" He and Garrett were twenty-one and twenty-two years of age, constantly full of questions. His light-brown hair shined in the fluorescent light and his fair facial skin turned an unhealthy pallor.

"Mhhm?" she asked, still lost in thought.

He pointed to it. She felt her skin. Her mouth dropped. She ran to the restroom and looked in the mirror. This is something she had never witnessed before. Why not? She walked back to the booth in a daze and sat down without speaking, staring straight ahead.

Ari gave Skyfire special attention since Ember's abduction. Using a unique style of a brush, he combed his coarse hair and made it soft and shiny. Something flashed under his mane. Something Ari never noticed before. He folded back Skyfire's mane and studied it. It wasn't something that could be detached. It was a permanent fixture. At least it appeared to be permanent. A little, rectangle knob stuck up in the shape of a lioness. It swirled and various colors glittered. Standing in awe, Ember's face came right to his mind. A message was sent to the families to meet him in the stables, NOW.

They all arrived in a flash. Skyfire felt uncomfortable and neighed, moving around. "It's okay, boy. It's okay," Ari whispered gently, rubbing his humongous neck. They could see the flashing light from where they stood. He lifted strands of his mane so they could see it clearly.

"Ah, yes. I forgot all about that. Now, that's a good sign. Skyfire and Ember were born with the same mark. Skyfire was created specifically for her. When this occurs," Berthold said pointing to the fascinating replica of her birthmark, "it means hers is too. This is good and clarifies that she is alive and well. It wouldn't do any of this if she were dead. Or heaven forbid, transformed to evil."

They all breathed a sigh of relief. "How come her mother and I have not been told about this same birthmark on Skyfire?" Arwood asked perplexed.

"The truth is that it would reveal itself at the appropriate time. It's always been invisible, which is why I guess I forgot all about it, so it appears now is the right time for revealing it. It has brought us much needed relief, wouldn't you say?"

Heads shook in agreement.

"I need some sleep. I haven't slept in days. Then I will make Addley think I've fallen in love with her. I'll make her believe it. You just watch and see," Ari said convincingly.

"There's more trivia if any of you are interested," Berthold said suspiciously.

"Sleep can wait. Let's hear it," Ari said.

"We all know Ember has gold streaks in her hair and gold specks in her eyes. Do you know why?"

"Let me tell them, Bert," Valeska insisted.

"All right my dear."

"Because she is rich with love, kindness and loyalty. Gold is a mineral that people associate with being rich." She looked upward and smiled. "It's true. That girl is rich with more love and goodness than any monetary thing could offer. If I had to make a choice of being rich with love and kindness or of a monetary value, I'd choose just what Ember spreads with her richness."

"But you have both, monetary, love and kindness. Why would you have to choose either?" Ari asked confused.

"I am aware of that and with much gratitude, but I was using the words in a way we could relate to for clarification. Ember has such a special place in the Lord's heart that I can't even figure it out. Of course, I know she is special and the sweetest, forgiving and kindest person I have ever known. Maybe that is the reason. It's a darn good one."

"But of course my dear. Of course," Berthold commented.

Chapter Twenty-Six

There was a break in the disturbances. Nothing bad had happened in days. Ember tried coaxing Aaron to ride horses, but he said his stomach didn't feel too good. Every time he came over, the visits would be shorter and shorter.

But on the next day he came over all bundled up and wearing thick gloves. He attempted to hold her hand. She groaned but let him.

"There, see? I guess I'll have to wear gloves forever if I'm to date you."

"Date me?"

"Yeah, why?"

"I told you, Aaron. We're friends. Nothing more. We will never be anything more than that."

He huffed and puffed. "That's not fair. Look how hard I'm trying. Look at the extent I'm taking to be with you. It's pretty offensive to feel like the girl I love gets sick by my touch."

"Love? I don't love you, Aaron."

"Yes, you do! You're just scared. A big scaredy cat. Well, a little scaredy cat. You have to at least give us a try."

"No, I don't. The person I'm meant to be with is out there somewhere. I feel it in here," she said with a hand over the heart. "I don't feel it with you."

He started pulling her behind him towards the woods. His eyes turned dark, and an evil expression began to materialize.

Having difficulty because of her trembling fingers, she finally pulled away. "Let me go!" she said with an angry face.

"No, I won't. You don't get to decide if we date or not. I'll decide."

Staring at him with wide eyes, fingers still trembling, she asked. "What is wrong with you? Why can't you let it be?"

Something in the sky caught his eye. His face more pallor than usual. At first his skin tone wasn't noticeable, but as weeks went by, it became more and more pale. "I'm really sorry. I don't know what came over me. Of course we'll just be friends. If you decide later that you have feelings for me, we'll discuss it. Will you forgive me for acting like such a brute? Please?"

"Yes, but we're going back by Tyrus," who was standing up on the porch moving their way.

"Sure, I deserve that. After I acted like such a jerk, of course you want to go back. Come on. You're right. Tyrus looks like he wants to battle me."

How was he going to fix this? She wouldn't trust being alone with him ever again. He had to come up with a plan and quickly. He pondered how she had always disgusted him with her goodie-two-shoes perfectness. But now, is possible to fall in love with her? No, it just can't be true. Impossible. He never felt anything for her in the past, plus he didn't like sweet, goodie-two-shoes girls and she was definitely one of them. Since the transformation wouldn't be complete for a couple more weeks, maybe his conscience was allowing him to think and feel good things. It felt good to him but confusing at the same time. The queen made him take on Ari's appearance to see how Ember responded and if she would remember him. To her pompous satisfaction, Ember couldn't pull the memory of the real Ari up. The queen could relax and savor the day Ember is tricked into becoming one of them.

"You guys okay?" Tyrus asked.

Ember was quiet and replied unconvincingly, "Yes, we're fine."

"Okay," he said still staring at them.

"I'll catch up with you in a couple of days, all right Em—I mean Tania. Sheesh, I'm tongue tied."

Tyrus couldn't quit staring at him. He walked fast to his truck. "Ugh! There is that smell again."

She pinched her nose together. "P.U."

He walked around to see if that goop was sitting on the ground somewhere but didn't find a thing.

"Virginia is bringing over some mac and cheese."

"Oh, yummy."

"Let's feed the animals before she gets here."

"Sounds like a plan."

Virginia pulled in, waved and carried pots and bags inside. While she was in there, Jacob came zooming over to the stables. Garrett lay listless against his back in the bed of the truck.

"We got to get him to the hospital. A lightning bolt came out of nowhere and struck him."

Tyrus looked at the sky. It was clear and bright.

He and Ember dropped their buckets and ran to him. They carried him to Virginia's truck and laid him on the truck bed. "Get Virginia, Tania, please."

She ran inside and was out with Virginia like a flash.

"Tania, fix him," Jacob cried.

"How? I can't—"

"Try, please," Tyrus urged.

A film of tears spread over her eyes. "I'll try."

She did exactly what she had done with the animals but so far, nothing happened. Ember prayed in a language they never heard, except for the few times she used it. A slight glow shadowed her and Garrett. Her pleading got stronger. Begging God. True, contrite pleading.

Garrett stirred. She felt him move and then he jerked up. His eyes blinked open. She sighed loudly.

"That's remarkable," Virginia commented.

"It wasn't me. I pleaded with God. He heard my prayers. Thank Him, not me."

They all looked up to heaven and did exactly that.

Inside the house, they made Garrett comfortable. "We should take him to the hospital," Jacob insisted.

"Yeah, we really should," Tyrus agreed.

"I'm fine," Garrett scolded them. "If I start convulsing, getting some kind of superpower like Tania," she gasped at his remark, "then you can take me. I feel just fine. Really. Hey, is dinner ready?" Oh, yeah, he was totally himself.

Jacob sat in the living room with Garrett while the rest of them set the table and placed the food on it.

"You sure you're okay?"

"Jake, I haven't felt this good in a while. I think that bolt gave me super energy."

"What did it feel like to be hit by lightning?"

His index finger rubbed between his mouth and nose. "From what I can remember, because it happened so fast, it sort of felt like daggers and needles poked through my skin and out the other side of my body. It was far worse than the jolt I had when I got shocked by that outlet."

"Ouch!"

"Hey guys, come on. Dinner is served," Ember blurted.

They all kept watching Garrett as if he would fall over dead any second. His eyes lifted, feeling the stares. "Guys, I'm fine. You're creeping me out by watching me like that."

Mumbles of sorry slurred as they returned to eating.

"Son," how Tyrus referred to the guys, "did you see anything weird before that happened?"

"No—Wait! I remember the sky got dark all of a sudden." They all observed each other's faces.

"Did you see what it was?" Virginia asked.

"No. The bolt hit so fast, I didn't have time to look up."

"What about you, Jacob?" Tyrus asked.

"My mind was focused on fixing the fence and this disgusting goop on a board. It smelled like death."

Very carefully, so as to not scare them, Tyrus quickly glanced Virginia's way.

"But wait," Garrett said remembering. "Just before I became conscious, I smelled this beautiful fragrance. Not that I know what cashmere smells like, but if I had to describe this scent, I would say warm cashmere woven with sunbeams and marshmallow. Maybe I got shocked more than I thought." That description would have never come out of his mouth before.

Tyrus lit up at his description, since he, himself described that fragrance as he walked up to Ember the first time, and never would he have come up with something so bizarre.

Virginia was still concerned and spoke up. "Tyrus will help me clean up and I have hot fudge sundaes for dessert."

Ember and the guys stormed to the living room in anticipation.

"Ty, something has to be done. We can't go on like this. Maybe we should speak to the sheriff about bringing in military power. This thing is way out of our league, and we are not equipped to stand up against whatever that thing is. Whose turn is next? Will one of us die?"

His hands automatically ran through his hair. "You're right, but what do we say? I am at a loss to think this through."

"Including the doctor, sheriff and us four, we have witnessed these things with our own eyes."

"What about Tania? They will take her from us and perform extensive research on her. It's not fair to her either," he said almost in a scold.

"That's true. I can't bear to think what they would do to that sweet girl, all in the name of science."

"Tomorrow morning I'll visit Harry. We'll come up with a plan. You're right. Who's next and will it be fatal?" Tyrus said rubbing his jaw as he stared at the floor.

Tyrus poked his head out the door. "Come and get it," he said happily to keep them from seeing his worry. Then he stepped out of the way quickly. The kitchen door swung back and forth making the sound of an Old West saloon door. Smiles were big, eyes wide and pure joy flooded the room. All the whipped cream mustache faces brought laughter.

"Jacob, I think it's best if you stay with me tonight. This will give Garrett a chance to recuperate," Virginia said with concern.

"But he's fine." Garrett's lips formed downward at Jacob's lack of concern.

"Jake, she's right. Now get your stuff together and get going. Go on!" Tyrus demanded.

Jacob used the back of his hand to wipe his mouth and then wiped his hand on his jeans. "Yes, sir.

"You big baby," he whispered in Garrett's direction. Garrett busted up laughing.

"Hey, Ms. Virginia lets me watch whatever I want, eat what I want and go to bed when I want. She's really cool."

"Virginia, go on home. We'll clean up. Thanks for all you do. I just had an idea. So that we can all stay together safe and sound, how about we bring your critters and their food here tomorrow? We can make it work, and you and the guys will be comfortable enough. What do you say?"

Her lips scrunched together tightly. "I don't know..."

"Please, Ms. Virginia." Ember's expression was begging.

"If you mean it. Well, all right."

Tyrus' face lit up like a star. "Good, then. We'll make it work."

Chapter Twenty-Seven

Ms. Prissy ran around Tyrus' property eating every flower and plant. "Oh no. How do we stop her?" Ember asked.

"I'm afraid we can't, unless you lock her up."

Baaa, baaa kept ringing through the air. They found a place for all the critters. Cain and Able were ecstatic about her and the animals moving into the house and barns. They usually slept in their soft, plush beds. Tyrus had planned on getting chickens again for his coop, but now Virginia's chickens filled it just fine. They had a huge running area and double fenced with tiny holes and cement poured around the length of the fence and coop to prevent anything from digging its way in or out. Many times, he would hear her yell names talking to the rooster and chickens. She got such a kick out of them. Henrietta, one of the chickens that had to stay in a cage by itself because the other chickens picked on her, followed Virginia around. Henrietta loved it when anyone would spend time talking to her.

Everything was working out perfectly. They sat around watching television, playing board games and eating popcorn. Much laughter in the house. Tyrus enjoyed it more than he ever thought possible. Ember felt like she had a real family. Her head turned slowly observing each and every one of them. Her smile was warm, but something stirred inside of her. She just knew there were more loved ones out there. She plopped a hand over her heavy heart and couldn't help but feel melancholy. A thought hit her of loved ones scattered in the wind, just like the leaves and debris blowing around in the wind outside the window. She pressed harder on her heart. A very mean thought hit her hard. *I'll never know. I just know it. Love to me feels just like those leaves scattering in the wind. Soon they will fade away, and love, as though they never existed. Just like my life.*

"Hey guys, Jacob is going out on a date tomorrow evening," Garrett said teasing him.

Nobody had noticed the shift in Ember's mood. That was how she wanted it. She didn't want to hurt any of them.

"Shut up, Garrett."

"Come over and make me." He started to stand up.

When Jacob took off for him, Tyrus yelled. "Sit back down. Both of you."

Quietly Virginia asked him, "So, who's the girl."

"Her name is Melissa. She's in the young adult group. We're going out after church tomorrow night."

"She's a cute girl."

"She's not a girl, Ms. Virginia. She's a young lady and I'm a young man."

"I see your point, but if you look at it from my age, you're kids. I'll be sure to watch how I address you from now on."

"Where are you taking her?" Ember couldn't resist asking.

"Folks are seeing the Aurora Borealis. We're going to drive out and look for it, after getting some fries and a milkshake."

"Big spender, Jake."

"Shut your mouth, Garrett."

"I'm only kidding. I think she's pretty."

"You two do know you're not brothers; right?" Tyrus asked.

Their noses wrinkled.

He let out a snicker. "Just checking."

Ember walked to the picture window and stared out. In her heart she felt someone was waiting for her. She looked down at her finger as if a ring should be around it, twisting the finger with the other hand. The feeling inside was so strong. Those enchanting eyes wandered out to the beauty before her. Alaska was magnificently beautiful. Her attention was drawn to the area where Virginia's house was sitting. She couldn't see it because it was too far away.

The sky was dark, wind howling and snow flurries swishing by. Thunder echoed and shook the ground; it was so loud. Lightning lit up the sky. She pushed her face up against the window.

"Whatcha see out there, little one?" Tyrus inquired.

"I'm not sure, but it almost looks like smoke over there."

He jumped up and rushed over. "Over where?"

She pointed. He squinted. His eyes popped open. "Boys, get to the truck."

"Tyrus, it's not safe out there. Garrett has been struck with lightning already."

"You're right. Garrett, stay here and Jacob, follow me. Dress warm. It's icy cold out there."

"Where we going?"

Virginia looked out the picture window and she gasped. "Is it?"

He shrugged his shoulders. "I hope not. We're going to check it out."

When they arrived at Virginia's place, lightning was striking the house and barn over and over, like it was putting on a light show.

"Would you look at that. I'm not going anywhere close to that. It's a death sentence," Jacob said with a stutter in his voice.

"I have never seen anything like that in my life," Tyrus said staring. "The bolts are directed at her house and barn, as though intentional. I don't get it. I don't understand any of this."

Her house and barn were burning to the ground. They couldn't get near it, even if they tried.

"How am I going to tell her? How?"

Jacob dropped his hand on Tyrus' shoulder and looked at him seriously. "Looks like you'll need to marry Ms. Virginia."

"What foolishness are you yapping about?"

"Come on Tyrus, we all know you two like each other. What are you waiting for?"

He rubbed his neck area. "I spose it would be nice to have her around all the time."

"Yeah, and now she has nowhere to go."

"True. Believe it or not, I've actually wondered about it."

"There you go."

"Regardless, she's going to be devastated," he added as he looked over at Jacob.

"Oh, yeah. That's really sad to lose all your stuff in a flash."

"Who's next? Us? Will our place be burned to the ground, too? We have to do something, but what? What do we do?"

"Let's deal with Ms. Virginia first," Jacob noted.

The truck turned around and putted down the road. Tyrus was really dreading this conversation.

"Jake, get Garrett and Ember to go in the kitchen when we get there so I can speak alone to Virginia."

"Yes, sir."

"Hey guys, let's go to the kitchen to get a snack," Jacob said as he rushed through the front door.

"Oh, not you Ms. Virginia. Tyrus wants to talk to you." Garrett and Ember kept looking back at Virginia wondering what was going on.

Virginia turned as Tyrus stomped the snow from his boots. He came in and closed the door, eyes not leaving hers.

"It's bad; isn't it?"

"I'm afraid so."

"My house has been burned to the ground; right?"

"Yes," he said not able to look at her.

"The barn?"

"It's gone."

She dropped onto a chair and bawled. He crouched down and laid a hand on her knee. "I'm so sorry, Virginia. You have a place to stay."

"My things. My memories. What if my animals were still there? Oh-my-gosh!" She broke down again.

"We'll make new memories together." She looked up to his eyes, tears still streaming down her cheeks.

"Not sure if I'm evaluating this right, but maybe it was the

Lord directing me to get you and your animals to move over here for a reason. You wouldn't believe what I saw if I told you."

"Oh really? I doubt that."

"Lightning bolts were directly hitting your house and barn over and over. It was uncanny."

"Is your house next? When's it going to stop?"

"I'm wondering that myself. Maybe I should take Tania on a trip to get away from here for a while. Maybe that will stop this madness for a while."

"Or make it worse."

"I don't know what to do Virginia."

"I do." She laid a hand on top of his. "Let's pray." He nodded.

Chapter Twenty-Eight

Tyrus drove Virginia to her house. Ashes were smoldering and you could hear hissing as snow mixed with soot dropped on the ground. It was nothing but ashes. His hand rested on her shoulder. "We'll get through this."

Their feet crunched in the snow. Coals of wood had glowing spots in areas. Everything was gone. "I do have my insurance agent's number. You know James Sanders. He's my agent. When we get—"

She couldn't finish the sentence using the word "home".

"Virginia, there is something I want to ask you, but I'm not sure if this is the right time or right place."

Her brows drew together as she studied his face. "What on earth is it?"

Perspiration beaded up on his forehead in the ice-cold temperature. "I don't know how to ask this but let me try. My feelings for you are strong. I guess what I mean to say is I think I love you. I was just too scared to admit it to myself. The kids have brought it to my attention that just you and I won't admit it, but they see it. Is it possible you feel the same way?"

She gulped and her freezing, rosy cheeks grew even redder. "I um...never knew you felt that way. The kids have said the same thing to me. You don't have to treat me as a charity case."

"I'm not."

"Nor should you feel guilty."

"I'm not."

He grabbed her hand and turned her to face him. "You brighten my day. It's been six years since I lost Mary. It always made me feel like I was cheating on her when I thought about you and me together. But she would want us both to be happy. You make me happy, Virginia. If you don't feel the same way, please be honest and we will continue as friends like we are now."

"I've been in love with you for years, but I felt like I was betraying Mary also."

He licked his lips a few times. "What do we do now? I'm rusty on the dating stuff."

"We just let it happen the way the good Lord intended and see where it goes, except there will be no hanky panky without a ring."

"Oh, absolutely not! I understand that." A mischievous smile formed. "But there's no reason I can't do this." He pulled her close, she trembled, and he placed a long smack on her lips. "Was that okay?"

"Very okay."

"Good, because we've wasted enough time fiddling around. I mean to propose right after Tania, and I come back from our trip."

Her forehead wrinkled. "What trip?"

"I did some prayin' last night and I believe the good Lord is telling me to take Tania away for a couple weeks. Maybe three. It's for all our protection. The boys will be on lookout, and I bought you all phones that can't be traced. Hide it just in case someone from who knows where comes looking for us. I will not tell you where I am going. A note will be left on the coffee table in the morning telling you that we went away.

"If there are eyes in the sky, then they'll be able to tell we're gone. Only pull that phone out of hiding when you're certain they can't hear. Nobody knows where we are going. Nobody. If you feel threatened in any way, call me and I'll turn around and come home. I'm hoping this will buy us all time and give us an opportunity to try and help her regain her memory."

"I'm a little nervous, but I understand. Um, so you're going to propose?"

"You bet." He pulled her up close again, held his hands on her waist and kissed her softly, with much more passion. Her knees felt like buckling under.

"Something just came to my thoughts. Jacob's father will be hanging around until I get back. And his wife. That should provide more protection. The guys will take turns sleeping in the stable each night.

"Two out there at night. This way they can release the animals quickly if something like this happens again. Everyone sleeps downstairs and have coats, boots, and keys ready to run out that door."

Fear grew in her eyes. "I'm terrified, Tyrus."

"Don't be. You were the one who inspired me to talk with the Lord. I believe He moved you and the animals here on purpose. It wasn't a coincidence. I trust Him. You should as well.

"It may not be the best, but I bought some homemade pizzas in town this morning. Let's celebrate tonight before the morning. I will ask Tania to pack the little she has.

"Are you okay with this decision?" he asked.

"Yes, I am. It's the right move. We can't allow whatever is out there to destroy her. She's special. I mean, supernaturally special. One day we'll know it all."

He squeezed her hand. "Let's go home."

She jerked her head at him in shock. Then she relaxed. "Yes, let's go home."

Upstairs, Ember packed. Her shoe fell beneath the bed and she bent down to pick it up. A book laid under the bed. She grabbed the shoe and then the book. She plopped on the bed and looked at it. It was a child's book named *Ember Pines*. She studied it, turning the pages and realized something looked familiar. But what? What? What? What?

The girl in the story looked just like her, but at a younger age. A horse's picture was on the next page. Its name was Skyfire.

How beautiful and mighty he looked. Something swirled under his mane, but she couldn't tell what it was. She pulled the book close to her face and saw that the birthmark on the girl was the very same birthmark as hers.

"Hhhh!"

Chapter Twenty-Nine

After hugs and kisses inside the house, Tyrus grabbed Ember's hand and ran to the truck. It was still dark out. Virginia's eyes blurred as they drove off. "Guys, put these phones in a safe hiding place here in the house where they can't be found by anyone but you. Check on them from time to time to be sure they are charged. This is a secret between us and nobody else. Use them to text me if an emergency comes up. Keep them in the stable with you at night but hidden well."

"Yes, ma'am."

"This note stays on the coffee table until they return, and I don't know when that will be."

~

"How far do we have to travel?" Ember asked Tyrus.

"You'll see. I can't tell you where we're going for your own safety."

"I'm so sorry I brought this trouble to you. It's all my fault. All your troubles are because of me. Virginia lost her house because of me." She couldn't control the flood if she tried. Water flowed from her eyes like a river.

"Hold on there, little one. You are what brought joy to my

life once again. And it's because of you Virginia and I are getting married."

Wet blotches covered her shirt. She wiped her eyes. Sniffling, she replied, "Really?"

"Really. You mean a lot to all of us. We all love you and would do anything to protect you.

Anything!"

"Thank you for being so kind. I don't know what I would have done without you. Without all of you."

They drove all night. When she awoke, palm fronds blew in the breeze, the sun was bright and warm and the sky cheerful blue. The sparkling ocean was on both sides of the road. Dolphins leaping up and down showing off their skills. Sea gulls squawked endlessly.

"This is so beautiful."

"We're almost there. We're staying on the beach."

"Beach? What's beach?"

"We are staying in a house that is on the beach. The beach is made up of white sands, sea shells, and ocean water comes right up to the sand. That's the beach."

Her mouth opened wide with a smile. "This is so exciting."

"You know what, let's go in that supermarket and get some groceries to take to the house."

"Mmmm, I'm starving."

"How about baked potatoes, salad and a whole bunch of desserts?" He had a wide smile as he said it.

"A whole bunch."

They were still dressed in Alaska attire. People sized them up and down. He heard someone say, "Look. It's Grizzly Adams." He rubbed his scraggly beard. "I'll have to fix that," he said to himself.

"Hey kiddo. Tomorrow, we get new clothes."

"But Tyrus, can you afford it?"

He smiled. She was so considerate. "Yes, I can. We're getting swimsuits, too. See those people." he pointed. "They're wearing swimsuits so they can get a tan and go in the water. I'll explain it all at the house."

She clapped her hands. A few guys with great tans walked by. "Hey there. Hi." Of course, her head tipped down and pink rose on her cheeks. Tyrus glared at them hard, so much so that they walked away fast.

Carrying groceries in the house, they both admired the wrap-around porch. An inviting porch swing and rocking chairs were calling their names. It was perfect. She smiled every time the sun caressed her skin, squeezing herself.

"I'm starved. Let's have donuts and cereal. It's almost lunch but who cares; right?"

"Right," she agreed.

Ember walked out of her room the next morning with a yawn that took up her whole face. She froze in place. "Where's Tyrus?"

"Sitting right here reading this newspaper," he said with amusement in his tone.

"You don't look anything like Tyrus." She took a step back.

"Tania, it's me. I shaved my beard and mustache at the barber shop two buildings down from us early this morning. I left you a note on the table."

She scurried to the table and lifted the note, looking back a few times at him as she read it. Walking up to him to get a closer view, she examined his face. "Wow! Must feel better with that fuzzy shrubbery off your face. That had to itch."

His head fell back with laughter. "A souvenir shop was next to the barber, so I went in and bought us some swimsuits and warm-weather clothes. Take a look in the bag."

Her lips and eyes lifted in unison. She pulled them out and inspected each piece of clothing.

"If you don't like, we can return them and find something else for you."

Her arms squeezed the bag to her chest. "I love them."

"I wasn't sure if you wanted a bikini or one piece, so I got you a cute one piece."

Thinking about what he said, she cocked her head.

"A bikini is a swimsuit in two parts. It shows your stomach and back."

A hand slapped the gasp coming out of her mouth. "Oh, no. I'm not wearing that."

He studied her face. If you looked at her from the back, you'd swear she was a child, but when she turned around, it was clear she was a beautiful, young lady. Her charm and sweet, helpful disposition were precious to him. He'd seen how most children and young adults act. Probably no fault of their own, but they could be pretty self-centered.

"Pancake mix is ready to drop in a hot pan. You hungry?"

She licked her lips. "I could eat that table, I'm so hungry."

"Looks like a hunger emergency. Let's get to it." His hand-made circles around the top of his head and annoyingly he shrieked out a siren alert.

"Stop! Stop!" she pleaded with hands covering her ears.

They both laughed. The mild sizzle was proof they were cooking. Pure maple syrup was warmed in the microwave and plates pulled out of a cabinet. After napkins and silverware were added to the place settings, she sat down and twiddled her fingers anxiously. With a plate of pancakes on the table, she stuck a fork into a couple just that fast.

Butter oozed onto the plate and Tyrus poured syrup from a small pitcher. She devoured a huge bite of pancakes and moaned with delight. Now able to focus, she looked hard at Tyrus. "You know, you're quite handsome without all that scruff. I've never seen your hair that short. It looks nice. You look younger and so very handsome."

Not good with compliments, his smile quivered and his head dropped to look at the pancakes.

"Ms. Virginia will be crazy about the new look."

"Do you really think so?"

"Un-huh. And that snazzy shirt is playful. So not like you."

"Hey. I'm on vacation and it's a good time to lighten up."

His shirt looked like something Tom Selleck would wear on *Magnum P.I.*

"What do you say we take a walk on the beach after dishes are done?"

"I say, yes," she said excitedly.

After cleanup, she yelled back as she skipped to her room, "I may be a few minutes. I want to try on these clothes."

"That's fine. I'll be out on the back porch."

Ember tried on clothes, twirling in front of the mirror. He had bought her five summer outfits. The one-piece swimsuit was white with a few flower designs in spots. It was a little tight but gave that tiny body some curves. Folding the outfits, a small corner of the book she brought along stuck out under the pillow. Eventually she would show Tyrus, but not yet. It was too unsettling. She turned a few pages and saw a man and woman. Her eyes teared up, but she didn't know why.

The boy was beautiful and looked so familiar. Actually, he looked like a boy version of Aaron. And, that tiny girl could be her as a child. The resemblance is striking. She tugged it back under the pillow and went out to the porch.

Treelin was forced to take on the appearance of Ari, but the queen didn't want him to use Ari's name just in case Ember was able to identify him using that name. She didn't know but wasn't going to take the chance. With Treelin disguised as Ari, it was to make sure her memory didn't come back. If her memory did come back, he would be able to report to the queen immediately to take further precautions.

Tyrus looked up almost in shock. Not in a million years did he expect her to have such attractive curves. Why can't he quit thinking of her as a child? It was driving him nuts.

"You look beautiful."

Her lips puckered and shyly she thanked him.

"How about that walk?"

She rubbed her hands together. There were spots of sand that the sun shot scorching rays on it. "Oops. We need to go back."

"Why?" Her voice was sweetly distraught.

"We both need sunscreen and flip flops. This sand is burning a hole through my foot."

She didn't know what a lot of things were, but like always, in a short time she would figure it out.

White lotion smeared her face while she kept rubbing the

lotion on her arms and legs. Tyrus rubbed some on her back and she did the same for him. Being a little self-conscious of seeing him with a shirt off, she still managed to rub it on.

"This reminds me. Stay right there and I'll be back in a second."

She stared at the gorgeous ocean. Two teen boys walked by with golden tans. They waved to her. She ignored them, not thinking they were looking at her. Children giggled as the waves chased them farther up the shoreline. Tyrus walked out wearing a pair of sunglasses and handed her a pair. She put them on and wrinkled her nose at the feel. Glancing around, she was in awe at the different colors the glasses produced.

"Now, off we go."

At the shoreline edge, they walked half in the teasing waves and half on the wet sand. Her hands felt the water, lifted seashells and she splashed her feet in the water. Now she acted the part of a child. Two teen girls walked by wearing string bikinis with thong bottoms. Her mouth dropped. They noticed and stuck their noses up in the air at her.

"What kind of parents would let their daughters wear something like that?" Tyrus said disgusted.

"I sure don't know," she mumbled with a shake of her head.

They sat on the sand and wiggled their feet in the water. He looked over and his brows immediately furrowed. She caught him staring at her feet. "Is something wrong?"

"Oh, no. Just watching the water rush up and down."

"It feels so wonderful."

"Beats that frigid cold, right?" he said with a sigh.

"Right."

He tried to examine her feet without her noticing. *I swear it looks like patches of fur on the tops of her toes. How is it I never noticed before? Because we're covered head to toes in Alaska.*

In her hands she held a Fargo worm snail and a Lightning whelk shell. Tyrus bent over and observed them. She threw them back in the water and started patting the wet sand into shapes. Once again, he was mesmerized by what he saw. Blotches of fur, it looked like to him, rested on the tops of her fingers. Evidently it was only seen when she got her hands wet.

He dropped his head back and tried to question himself at what he was seeing and wondering if perhaps it was some type of medical issue or some type of physical imbalance.

A handful of warm water hit him in the face. He shot his head up. She chuckled and moved backwards. He jumped up and chased her in the water. It was up to her chest now.

"Tania stop. That's far enough. You probably don't swim, so you should move up closer." She obeyed and a wave crashed over her head. It knocked her backwards. Tyrus grasped her arm so fast, it hurt somewhat."

"Ow!" she gurgled out. Her face formed a weird expression. "It tastes like salt and like yuck."

"That's because it's salt water."

Fish started swimming around her, dolphins circled her and even a small shark. People on the shore started to panic and called out to them. Tyrus pulled her to the shore and the fish and other ocean creatures followed as closely as possible, jumping up and back down. Sea gulls and pelicans landed in the water next to her. While everyone else was freaking out, she was laughing.

A crowd of people gathered around her. "Are you okay? Do you need a doctor? Did any of them bite you?" On and on the questions came.

Tyrus stood in front of her with his arms extended back. "Back up please. You're scaring her. She's fine."

People were still snapping pictures at all the movement at the shoreline. A shark's fin dipped back down under water to be seen no more.

He and Ember went to the porch and sat on rockers. The creaking sound washed out the sound of waves breaking on the shoreline.

Tyrus was perplexed by a lot of things, and Ember kept thinking about the sea life. Finally, they both got up and took showers. Then they would decide where to go for dinner. And then plans included a sunset walk on the beach. He crossed his fingers that nothing weird would happen with the sea life. Just getting her to safety was on his mind. How would he keep attention off of her when these strange things kept happening? Locking her in the room sounded promising, but of course he wouldn't ruin her fun because he was overly cautious. Like normal, he'll deal with it when it happens. "Make no mistake, it will happen," he mumbled under his breath.

Chapter Thirty

A knock at Tyrus' door in Alaska. Virginia answered it. "Hello Aaron."

"Hi Ms. Virginia. Is Tania around?"

"No, she's not."

"Oh, when do you expect her back?"

"Not for a while."

He tossed his head back and squinted one eye.

"Here, read it yourself." She handed him the note.

"I'm too upset to read. Would you mind reading it, please?" The truth was that he couldn't read, but nobody knew anything personal about him.

She read it and the look on her face grew concerned. "Son, you look like you've seen a ghost."

"This is bad. Really bad."

"No, it's not. They're coming back. Tyrus felt worried for her and wanted to take her away from all the weird stuff happening. Have you noticed anything strange?"

"No! I have to find her. You must know where they are."

"I have no idea. I read you the note. He doesn't want anyone to know where they are, including me. Did you know my house was burned to embers?"

"Ember," he mumbled. He ran off shouting to himself. A gray sweat started falling down his face. Virginia watched completely confused. His truck squealed out of the driveway. Sludge spit out from the tires. His reaction looked suspiciously petrified, as if it was a life-or-death situation.

❧

Tyrus couldn't believe he was actually sitting in a rocking chair rocking back and forth on the porch listening to the waves. In fun he pinched himself. Every corner, every change in the sky caused concern, though, but now the ocean sounds were soothing him right into a nap. Tania walked out and informed him dinner was ready. She made grilled cheese sandwiches, accompanied by chips and fruit. She gently clutched her fingers between his shoulder blades and whispered, "Dinner is ready." His head shook and he looked around licking his lips. Dry mouth.

"Hey there, little one."

"Didn't you hear me?"

"No. Did you say something?"

"Yes. Dinner is ready."

His head pushed back and his mouth folded inwards. "You made dinner?" he asked almost frightfully.

A big smile, she replied, "Grilled cheese sandwiches."

"For real?"

She nodded her head not understanding his misgivings. He didn't want to offend her and hopped up. After a thorough examination, he smiled. It had a few burnt spots, but definitely edible. They chuckled through dinner.

"What do you say to a sunset walk?"

"I say, what are we waiting for?"

She wore a cute pair of shorts and cotton sleeveless shirt. Flip flops clacked annoyingly against the linoleum floor.

"Come on little one. We need to get around that corner of beach to see the sun go down." They jogged slowly but effectively. A small crowd gathered to see the brilliant colors appear and disappear just that fast. It was always worth the time.

They sat on the rocking chairs and squeaked back and forth.

Tyrus worked up the courage to ask her questions. "Little one, do you have any suspicions about where you came from?"

"Actually, I have a lot of them, but right now they're all 'cuckoo for Cocoa Puffs'." She picked that phrase up from Garrett. "Give me a little more time and I may have some things to share, but I need to be more certain about my thoughts. What about you? Do you have any new information that will enlighten us?"

"Like you, I need more info to substantiate my findings. Honestly, I don't think you're from this world. There's something otherworldly about you. Seriously, I am wondering if you fell from heaven, and the bump on your head from the fall is why you lost your memory."

"Get out of town."

He broke out in a rambunctious laugh. "Your English has certainly improved. You would have never used slang like that at first."

"That's true. Well, you can't hang around Garrett and Jacob very long and not pick things up fast. I miss them, you know. You may disagree, but it started feeling like a family. You and Virginia, Garrett, Jacob and me." She became very quiet. He picked up on her thoughts.

"You're wondering about your own parents, aren't you, little one?"

"Yeah, I am. Wondering if I even have parents or if they miss me. I don't know."

"From spending time with you, I would say, yes, you have parents, and they have to be very loving and really special."

Her head slanted one way, and her cute nose wrinkled slightly.

"You wonder how I know, don't you?" he asked her.

She shrugged her shoulders expecting him to elaborate.

"It's simple. You're too charming and sweet NOT to have a great family. You're special, and I mean that sincerely."

"I think the same thing about you. And Virginia. And Garrett and Jacob. Well, they can be annoying at times." She laughed it off.

"Oh no. We have discussed this together and we're in full agreement that you're just different and special. We all have irritating things about ourselves. Except you, you don't have any of those things. It's very inconceivable. I always thought Mary walked on water, but being around you, even I could point out her flaws. That's how special you are."

"That is so sweet. Thank you."

"Well, I'm going inside for a snack. You coming?"

"In a minute. I have some things to think about."

"Just be on the lookout, little one. Oh, by the way, that good-looking young man keeps walking back and forth and always looking this way. I think he likes you."

"Hhhh," she sighed frustrated. "How many times do I have to tell you that someone is out there for me? And probably looking for me. I don't want to date—whatever that means—or get to know some guy. It upsets Aaron that I won't be his girl-friend. I think that's what he called it."

"What makes you think that? I mean, you have no memory, so what are you basing it on?"

"Something in here," she said pushing down on her heart, "tells me. I can't explain it."

"I see. Well, it won't hurt to make friends. You can tell that boy right from the start that you aren't interested in dating. If he still wants to hang out with you, then it will be much easier to strike up a friendship, or he'll just leave you alone. Play it by ear.

"Do you have any idea how beautiful you are? You have this enchanting mystique about you. I think it makes those young men crazy."

It looked as though the sun set on her face. "That's just embarrassing."

"Now see, most young ladies who are beautiful know they are. You have no idea and that makes you extra-special."

"I am not comfortable with this talk."

"Okay, little one. Just be aware of your surroundings, for my sake."

Her smile boomed with fondness for him.

"If that young lad gets the courage to walk over, let me know. I want to make sure no harm comes to you."

"Sure."

The breeze blew her hair out and back down. Moonbeams glistened on her gold streaks. She was a sight to behold. She rocked slowly in thought. That book was more than a coincidence. The girl looked like her, gold streaks and all, when she was a child, not that she could remember herself that young. The charming boy looked like he could be Aaron, as well, when he was a child.

Pictures of the little girl's parents had a sweetness about them, so loving and they, too, felt familiar to her. Could they be her family? Silly girl. It's a book. "I'm grasping at straws. That's what Jacob would say. Whatever it means."

She couldn't get the book out of her mind. Images of the evil queen flashed back to her memory. Why did a child's storybook freak her out? It wasn't making sense. Well, her life didn't make sense.

"Hello."

Her thoughts jerked back to reality. Head turning to find where the voice came from. The moonlight reflected off of his eyes and she cringed. "Who are you?"

"My name is Todd. I noticed you hanging around with your dad on the beach and thought I'd stop over and meet you. I hope that's okay."

He was as cute as a young man could be. "He's not my dad. More like a guardian, but I love him like a dad." Tyrus was listening at the door and his macho image melted like ice cream on a blazing hot day.

"I need to let him know you're here. Do you mind?"

"No, not at all."

Tyrus scooted to his chair and almost fell back in it from the quick movement. The door opened slowly.

"Hey, Tyrus. That young man you pointed out to me earlier has stopped over to meet me. Is that okay?"

"Of course, but I will move to a chair where I can observe things. Gotta keep you safe, little one."

"Yes, and you do that very well." All her teeth showed, and she went back outside.

"Would you like to sit down?" she asked Todd.

"Thanks. I think I will."

"Oh, do you want a soda or water?"

"No thanks. I'm good. So, what is your name?"

She thought for a moment, because it was a made-up name. He noticed but wasn't certain how to interpret her avoiding the answer. "Tania."

"I never heard that one before. It's very pretty...like you."

Instantly, soft pink rose in her cheeks. The breeze caused the trees to sway and moonbeams were blocked each time, so the light didn't expose her cheeks.

~

Back in her homeland, Ari sat in thought analyzing everything that took place just before and after Ember's disappearance. In a flash, his temper rose and his face became red as a beet. He stomped around, kicked a few things that were in his way and mumbled with an angry voice.

"Son," his mother said, "What has stirred you up so?"

He stood up tall, opened his mouth and shut it just that fast. Her head pushed back a little and her nose wrinkled. "What is going on with you?"

"Mother, I have no idea what just made me so furious. If I had to guess, I'd say I feel jealous."

"Jealous? Of who?"

"That's just it. It's the kind of jealousy I felt when Ember and Aldric used to laugh together. I wanted to deck him and make him get away from her, but that was before we found out we were meant to be together."

"So, you're jealous of someone you can't see or even know. No logical reasoning. It just came upon you?"

"When you put it that way, then yes. How weird is that?"

Her fingers fiddled with her lips. "Very weird."

~

This question was eating away at Todd: "Let me ask the basic question: Do you have a boyfriend?"

"I'm not interested in dating right now."

"Why not?"

"I have too much going on and it's just not a good time."

"Are you on vacation?"

"Mmm hmm. What about you?"

"I live down a little ways in a condo. It's super nice."

"It is beautiful here. I live in the cold. Right now, there is two feet of snow on the ground."

"Yikes! Don't you get tired of the cold?"

"No, not really." Soon he would be asking questions she couldn't answer. Tyrus had told her to keep it under the radar. Of course she didn't know what he meant, but when he explained the definition, she understood. It was time to go inside, before things got uncomfortable. She changed positions a few times already.

"You seem nervous. Am I making you nervous?"

Her cheeks puffed out and then deflated. "Truthfully, I don't like questions. I understand they are necessary in getting to know each other, but they make me nervous."

His forehead wrinkled. "Okay then. Well, maybe we can play Frisbee or something tomorrow. I'll introduce you to some of the local hangouts. We always have a few laughs. It will be fun."

"I'll see. I would need to check with Tyrus."

Why would a grown lady need to check with a guardian? Weird. Really weird. "Catch ya tomorrow then."

"Yeah, catch ya tomorrow." That was a new one for her. Catch ya? Is it a game? Sheesh.

Chapter Thirty-One

A light pounding on the door alerted Addley. She walked over and opened it. Her smile was wide and her eyes bright. "I never expected to find you at my door. I figured you would be out looking for Ember."

"I needed a break. It was bringing me down. You always know how to cheer me up, so I thought why not visit my good friend." Ari cringed inside after saying it.

She flinched at his choice of "friend" word. "We always make each other feel better. You are right about that. Come on in."

Realizing she has to be responsible for Ember missing, he didn't feel safe going into a den of lions.

"Let's go to our favorite spot." He wanted to punch that pleased smile right off her face. His eyes pierced her face, but she wasn't paying attention. *How can she be so happy while Ember was missing? A friend would be just like Sharley. Hey, I haven't seen Sharley around.*

"Have you seen Sharley around?"

She pulled at a piece of thread avoiding eye contact. "Nope."

"That's odd, now that I think about it. I should pay her a visit as well."

"Not now. You're all mine." She wrapped an arm around his and pushed up next to him. She leaned her head up with a satisfying smile. He played along and smiled back, squeezing her arm in his. The way she had been acting practically spelled the words out that she was guilty.

"Where do you go when you leave for days?"

Her eyes crossed. "How do you know if I go anywhere?"

"Let's see, oh, yeah, Sharley told me she has seen you leave several times."

Her mouth puckered. "Well, Sharley should mind her own business."

"So, where do you go?"

"To visit my aunt or grandmother."

"I see."

"You know, your muscles are so strong. Did you get bigger and stronger? Your arm muscles feel like weights."

"I may have been working out a lot more. It helps with my frustration levels."

"Of course. Ember."

"How come you're not out looking for her? You are close friends," he asked in a casual tone.

"My mum won't let me. She's afraid something sinister is going on."

"Do you sense it as well?"

"Me? Nah. Everyone is grasping at straws. Did it ever occur to you that Ember wanted to be alone? Or maybe she likes another guy and is unhappy with the arrangement. There are just no signs that she has been abducted."

His fingers formed fists, but he released them quickly because she must have felt him tense up and looked up to his eyes.

"Ember has never been irresponsible and it's not in her character. She made it abundantly clear that she loved me."

"Or wanted you to think that."

"How long have you been so skeptical?"

"I guess I picked up on the vibe hanging around her," Addley answered smugly.

He rolled his eyes.

"Here we are. This place is so serene. It causes me to look up and praise God."

"No need to get all religious or anything." Her voice had a noticeable incandescent timbre.

He grabbed her hand. Her heart did flip flops. He pulled her over to the boulders they normally sat on together.

"I miss our time together. We always had fun." He turned his head around and formed a disgusted expression.

"We still can. I'll always be here for you." She laid her head against his arm.

"You always understood me. I think you understand me more than anyone else."

"Even more than Ember?"

He formed an ashamed expression. "Yes, I'm afraid so."

She pushed her head up and kissed his cheek for an extended amount of time. "I always felt that way, too. We're good together. This may sound insensitive, but I always thought you and I were better together than you and Ember."

"You don't say?" He was hating everything about what he was doing, but there wasn't a choice. She would cave under the influence of love if she really felt that passionate towards him. He had to make it look real. He cupped her chin and touched his lips with hers. She felt faint. Then he deepened the kiss, making it more passionate. Her body twitched with pleasure.

He pulled away and looked tenderly in her eyes. "I always wondered why you and I weren't meant to be together."

She gulped, and at first, speechless and breathless. "Me too," she replied with dreamy eyes and in a floating-on-clouds articulation.

How long has she waited for this moment? She finally got it but it's not enough. Too much time had been lost because of Ember, and she wanted to make up for lost time. She stood to her feet, placed hands around his face and kissed him, then longer, and longer. She took a breath and repeated it, melded her body against his, pleading him to accept hers. Arms wrapped around his neck, she pulled herself up on his lap. Moans of pleasure escaped her throat, and her heart raced with urgency.

"Help! Help me!"

Ari pushed her off and stood up straight. He adjusted himself to the yells coming his way.

"Prince Ari. Help me. Please."

Everything had gotten so casual that everyone always referred to him as just plain ole Ari. Actually, that is the way he wanted it. The urgency in her tone caused him to go into "prince" mode.

"What is wrong?"

"Oh, Prince Ari. It's bad. Sharley has been missing for days. She's gone. No sign of her anywhere. I have searched and searched all known locations where she may be, but nothing, and no one has seen her."

Addley's face turned bright red. *Who cares,* kept playing in her mind.

Ari looked at her. "I need to deal with this. Are you okay to go back on your own?"

"Sure," she said infuriated.

"I'm sorry. This needs immediate attention."

"So do I." She huffed off.

Sharley's mom looked mad and confused. "Your Highness, I'm confused with your relationship to that...that girl." She was being decent and respectful to the prince, even though she felt repulsed.

Once he felt positive that Addley had disappeared from them, Prince Ari remarked, "Please excuse me. I have to do this right now." He spit on the ground a few times and turned back to her. "Ewe, do you smell that?"

"That is disgusting. What is it?"

"I have suspicions. Hhhh!"

"What is it, Prince Ari?"

He grabbed her arms, his face serious. "You can't tell a soul. Promise me."

"I promise."

"You may not understand this right now, but believe me, it's not what you think," he whispered in her ear.

"It's for your safety, as well as everyone else's." He held a hand to her ear and whispered. "I am pretending to be in love with

Addley because we know she is behind the missing of Ember. I'm trying to get her to think I love her, so she'll feel comfortable and confide in me where Ember is, and possibly, now, where Sharley is.

"But, for right now, here's my concern. She just kissed me, and I let her. It's only to earn her trust. I had to spit the filth out of my mouth, is what you saw. If she has converted to become an Eryndonite, will her kiss turn me also? I never thought it through?"

"Dear Prince, the only way you can turn is if you accept the mark of that beast, King Eryn. The sooty liquid that drips from an Eryndonite is toxic to our touch but won't turn you. It will kill us though. You didn't accept his mark, did you?"

With quickness, he answered, "No! Never would I do that."

"It's sort of the same thing as in the scripture, when in the end days, if they accept the mark of the beast, there's no turning back. That is why we take such huge precautions in keeping the Eryndomnites out. They are so deceptive. Somehow, they got to Addley. I've seen the trance in her dark eyes after she comes back from being gone for a few days.

"Prince Ari, we have to figure out who's been infected and fast. They may have Sharley."

"I haven't been called 'prince' in a while. It kind of took me by surprise."

"No disrespect, but I always felt it was wrong to address you and the kings and queens as anything less than royal. We look up to you all. It is important to us to address you with the respect we feel towards our royal leaders."

"And all this time we felt such formal address made the people of our kingdom feel unimportant. I had no idea we had that all wrong. I will certainly bring this to the attention of the king and queen immediately. We will become the kingdom we once were.

"Now, I was just asking Addley if she had seen Sharley. I was planning on visiting your home today and find out where she's been."

"Prince Ari, I have a very bad feeling. A feeling that she is badly injured. Maybe even dead. There has been a stench that makes my stomach nauseous. I think we all know what is causing it?"

"We are investigating all of it. That saddens me about Sharley. She was Ember's closest friend. I fear I have made a mistake and misjudged her harshly. I will get right on it. Why don't you get your family and come to the king and queen's home —I mean castle. It's time we refer to royalty as it is and not water it down. The Lord appointed us, so we need to uphold His respect, or gain it back, rather. I will send guards your way and I promise to give it my utmost attention."

She thanked him and bowed in respect. It renewed his appreciation for their roles. He bowed back to her.

Chapter Thirty-Two

Ember finally had some time to herself and could sit in the bedroom alone without being worried for her safety. Her hand slowly pulled out the book under the pillow. For some reason, she felt stupid bringing it to Tyrus' attention. Hasn't her presence put him through enough? She certainly didn't want to cause him more anguish. She felt a love for him, a fatherly love.

"How stupid is this? Who would even jump to a conclusion that this book had anything to do with me?"

She turned the pages and saw a picture of a very hairy man with pointed fangs and a disgusting liquid dripping from them. The book described his walk as a quick tap, tap, tap, and then he would stop, repeat it again and stop, and do it over and over again. How strange. His name was Tarant. But what freaked her out is that this little girl had gold streaks in her hair just like hers, and a noticeable birthmark located on the same spot of her face just like hers.

This was just uncanny. There is absolutely no way she could tell Tyrus right now. He is finally relaxing.

"I'll wait until we go home. Yes, that's a better idea. Why cause him more grief?"

Ember appreciated how Tyrus left her alone in her thoughts. She expected him to ask her lots of questions about Todd. It was coming, that much she knew, but at least she was allowed privacy in her thoughts until she could express these concerns. She walked out to grab a snack.

"How's the game going?"

"Lousy," he replied with a detectable anger.

"How about a bowl of ice cream with marshmallow and hot fudge?"

"Yesssss!"

"I'll make it. You just watch the game."

She handed him a bowl of heavenly delight and a bottle of water. She grabbed hers and sat down on the couch next to him.

"Did you enjoy your time with Todd?" And here it is.

"Sure. He's nice."

"You guys going to hang out?"

"I guess. He wants me to meet some of his friends. Do you think it's a good idea since I have no memory?"

"It all depends on what he wants to do. I will not be okay with you going anywhere except out there on the beach. It's too risky and you cannot tell them anything about why we're here. Nothing."

"Duh."

That remark took him by surprise, and he fell down laughing. That caused her to laugh. Trying to catch his breath, he said, "You're"—and he busted up again. It just struck him funny to hear this always sweet and loving young lady mock him and so brilliantly. "You need to quit hanging out with Jacob and Garrett. I can see they have an influence on you. But I love it."

"They have taught me so many words and sentences. They said it's not natural how quickly I have picked up English terminology."

"Mmm. I never gave it much thought, but yes, you have picked it up incredibly fast. I think it shows your intelligence."

"What do you mean?"

"That you are smart, very smart."

Talk about a self-esteem booster, she smiled ear to ear.

"Have you heard from anyone?" she asked.

"No, and I haven't contacted anyone. It's too risky. If something goes wrong, they know to use the secret phones and call me.

"You, Virginia and the guys feel just like my own family. Tyrus, what if my family is so horrible that I ran away? If we find them and they are, what does that mean for me? Think about it. If my family was so bad that I had to escape, I would never want to find them and I would never want to leave you all.

"I mean, I get it. I've done nothing but cause grief and trouble for you all. I wouldn't blame any of you if you kicked me out."

"Tania, I want to make something perfectly clear. You are just like my own daughter. Virginia and the guys feel like all of us are family, too. Neither one of us would be happy if you left us, and we certainly couldn't live with ourselves if you were killed or abducted. Never wonder how much we love you. All you need to think about every day of your life is that we are your family and love you very much, until you've had enough of us."

Drops the size of a dime dripped from her eyes. She jumped up and embraced him. "That makes me so happy. So very, very happy."

He patted her back almost in a motion of burping a baby. "Me, too."

Chapter Thirty-Three

Todd came over around 11:00 a.m., hoping in the back of his mind that Tania would change her mind about him. His fingers were crossed. It's not that he was a conceited, spoiled rich brat, because at times he played that card well. With good upbringing from parents and grandparents who did not try to impress the world with their small fortune, they chose a more humble approach to life and in raising him.

Did they give in and provide Todd almost anything he wanted and needed? Pretty much. The best schools? Pretty much. A Jeep Rubicon? Yup. But they also provided discipline and attended church regularly. He didn't get away with acting like a rich kid. Mostly, he was spoiled with love. Adored.

Not just his family, every girl in the area and school adored him. His very blonde hair streaked by the sun's glistening rays, a healthy tan, and a toned body with the help of the best exercise equipment made, he was always checking his attitude. One time he tried using the rich, spoiled brat method of getting out of trouble by saying he couldn't help it he was born to privilege. His parents provided him with the good ole privilege of restriction and isolation. It really backfired.

Because of his humble upbringing, he noticed something different in Ember, Tania to him. She was enchantingly beautiful, and innocent with an adorable, sweet spirit. Because of his looks, his confidence and wealth, most girls were impressed by those qualities rather than who he was as a person, but not Ember. She would be a challenge, and he was willing to find out.

A knock on the door brought Tyrus out of the kitchen. Just as he opened the door, Todd started to bang again, just missing his face. "Gee, I'm sorry, sir."

"That's quite all right son. Won't you come in?"

He stepped inside feeling confident. "My name is Todd, sir. I live in the Grandview of Bay Beach condominiums."

"Nice to meet you. My name is Tyrus, and I have walked the beach in that area. That's a tropical paradise."

"Yes, sir. I'm very grateful to live there."

"Here comes little one."

"Hello," squeaked out.

When she smiled, he could only conclude that the sun had fallen into the room. She wore a sunny racerback tank top and basic white cotton shorts. She walked in front of a sunray, and her gold streaks shined, almost blinding his eyes. He squinted a few times, then stared in awe.

"Hey, you want to come on the beach and meet some of my friends?"

She looked to Tyrus, eyes widening, mostly from shyness. He winked.

"Todd, if you keep her out in front on the beach that will be fine. There are reasons I don't want her to get out of my sight." Todd raised an eyebrow. "But it's nothing to worry about in the least. After all, she may be a tiny thing, but she is very much a young lady and is of age to do what she wants. It's for her protection she isn't to wander away." The other eyebrow raised.

"Sure. I understand. We'll keep her out front on the beach. You're welcome to join a noisy bunch of college kids if you want, sir."

"Thanks, but no thanks. I think I'll sit on a rocker and drink some quenching lemonade."

"Don't you drink all of it," she said sternly shaking her index finger.

"Not on your life, I wouldn't."

Her smile brought the sunshine in once again. Todd held the door open. "Nice to meet you, again, sir."

"You too. Have fun kiddo."

Todd kept his word and didn't try any unwelcome moves. Surprisingly, he was easy to talk to. She jumped as a gaggle behind them grew louder with each squishy step in the sand. "Here they are. Right on time."

After greeting Todd, he introduced Ember to the group of excited young adults. The guys gawked and most of the young ladies were very welcoming, with one or two already changing colors from normal to green. Like any group of college-aged boys and girls, they occupied themselves for hours. Todd pulled a cart with water and sodas. Ice cold. Ember grabbed an orange soda. She took a taste and stared out at the ocean licking her lips.

"A penny for your thoughts."

"Mmm?"

"Whatcha thinking about?" Todd was dying to know. She fascinated him.

"This soda is delicious. I have never tasted anything like it."

"You've never tasted orange soda? Come on. You have to be from Mars or something. Every kid in the world has probably tasted orange soda," Tiffany, one of the girls, remarked full of hostile jealousy.

Todd pulled Ember away. "Don't pay attention to her. I'm sure you've seen the movie, *Mean Girls*. Well, meet the leader." Tiffany heard him and stuck her snobby nose up his way.

"I've never seen that movie."

"It's not important."

The other guys started throwing the bikini babes in the ocean. Ember's face grew to panic hearing them scream and laugh. They headed her way. "Todd, I can't swim. I mean, I don't think I can."

Before he had a chance to react, the other guys grabbed her arms and pulled her into the water. As they threw her, a big wave toppled over her. Todd looked for her with eyes like saucers. "She can't swim. Find her. Now!"

Everyone's faces turned from laughter to serious. They

walked out, water up to their chest, and no signs of her. Tyrus ran towards the beach with a life preserver.

~

After foraging the area for Sharley, the teams returned to Ember's castle. On the walk there, Ari's heart skipped a beat. Then another one. His hand grasped his heart, and he stopped with his foot in midair.

"Son, what is it?" King Dillon asked.

"I don't know, Father. Intense emotions of fear, or sometimes jealousy takes hold of my whole being. Right now, it's a fear deep down in the gut of my soul."

"Your soul has a direct link to Ember's. You were probably unaware or never told that."

"Unaware, yes! Who should have explained that to me?'

Letting out a frustrated sigh, he replied, "Me or your mother. I'm sorry son."

"That's okay. When Ember arrived here, everything was nothing but chaos. Then when it settled down, we were immediately thrown into our roles as prince and princess; no time in between."

The fear subsided and he felt immediate relief. He exhaled a long and relieved sigh. "She's okay," he said in a low, thankful voice.

"Did you say something?"

"Yes. I said she's okay. The fear is gone."

King Dillon hugged him while looking up to heaven.

~

Tyrus and Todd were in panic mode. Tyrus stopped searching, and with a look like he saw a ghost mumbled, "She's okay. Look."

She was laughing up a storm riding on the back of a dolphin. It brought her up as close to the shoreline as possible. Everyone searching stood back and became speechless. Tyrus ran over and grabbed her hand to help her off. As he held onto her so she could catch her balance, a big wave washed over them, almost knocking Tyrus and her off balance, but at the same time, pushed the dolphin up on the beach, unable to get back to the water.

Screams were heard. Sounds of distress came from the dolphin. It was writhing in fear.

Tyrus looked at her and said, "You can save him. Go to him."

She looked into his confident eyes questioning him. Then she pushed her way through the crowd up to the dolphin. Tyrus ordered everyone to get back. She bent down and laid her body, heart touching on the dolphin. A glow encapsulated their bodies together. Shrieks and sighs of not believing what they were seeing echoed through the air. The glow covered the water and them. Her eyes were clasped shut, focus as high as it has ever been. The water came up and over them, pulling them out to the ocean. Once in the water, little splashes that looked like tiny fish popped up and down and underneath them. But, it wasn't fish. Nobody could tell what it was. Excitement in the nearby conversations grew louder.

Deep enough now, the dolphin leaped up in the air and down into the water several times.

Whatever was popping up and down in the water somehow and someway carried Ember back to safety. There was so much activity in the water, it sounded like a mild sound of Jiffy popcorn on the stove.

She jumped up and stepped onto the beach and the popping stopped. Everyone stood as though they were hypnotized. Even Tyrus, who should be used to such crazy things.

"How did you do that? What was that?"

And then, "She's a witch," Tiffany yelled out.

That was enough to grab Tyrus' attention. "If anything, she's an angel." His glare caused Tiffany to turn and walk away. "Come on, little one. It's time to go home."

"Home, like by Virginia?"

"No, not quite, but soon. Very soon."

Todd ran up to them. "Hey, don't worry about Tiffany.

Nobody likes her. We can't seem to get rid of her. I think what you did is so cool. How did you do that?"

She stopped walking and looked him straight in the eyes. "I didn't do anything. I have no idea if or how I did anything." She turned away from him. "Tyrus, I am sleepy."

"Then sleep you shall get." He gently tugged at her arm.

"Could I see you tomorrow, Tania?"

She stopped, turned her head, frowned and shrugged her shoulders. They walked away faster. Todd just stared as they walked away, thoughts spinning in his mind like he was on a roller coaster. "She's magnificent. I'll bet she is an angel."

"What's that you said?" his friend Shawn asked.

"That young, beautiful lady has to be an angel. Did you see her glow?"

"Who could have missed it? It's a little freaky but really exciting."

"Yeah, she is exciting. I really don't think she is aware of the glowing or that she had anything to do with the rescue of that dolphin. But how and why would an untamed dolphin just happen to stop by and offer her a lift home? That's just weird."

Shawn patted his shoulder. "Strange things happen every day. Do a search on the internet and see for yourself. It will blow your mind."

"You're probably right. Now, more than ever, I want to get to know her better. The only thing that would make me wonder if she were really a witch is this spell I feel about her. I am under the influence of a magical love potion or something. She takes my breath away.

"And what's so strange about that, you're probably asking yourself? Look at all the gorgeous girls I have contact with on a daily basis. None of them make me feel like she does, and I don't know anything about her. Well, except that she's mysterious and enchanting."

Ember could sense they were watching her. She turned back for a second before going into the house. Todd waved. She nodded her head and walked inside.

"You know what else is striking about her?" Shawn asked.

"I'm more than certain you're going to tell me."

"Those gold streaks in her hair. I was watching the sunlight hit them and—you're going to think I'm nuts—they sparkle like real gold jewelry."

"No, I've wondered the same thing. Not only that, but that birthmark above her cheek. It has a shape like a female lion. Your turn to think I'm nuts, but I swear, I swear I saw it sparkle and swirl. How? Why? What?"

"I think it is fair to say none of us have ever met anyone like her."

"Oh! And one more thing. Did you hear the language she used in speaking to the dolphin?" Todd asked.

"No, I didn't."

"I've been around the world traveling with my parents. There is not another language I have heard remotely close to the words and the melody in her tone. Anywhere."

Shawn walked directly in front of him and stopped. They kept staring in each other's eyes. "Todd, maybe she is an angel. It's possible."

"And makes the most sense. I can tell she feels uncomfortable about what happened. She won't come out with us anymore. I will get to know her. I have to. I just have to."

"Don't give up. Keep going over there and talk to her. You should probably go by yourself without a raucous bunch like us."

"Yeah, that's a good idea."

Excited about seeing her tomorrow, Todd jogged home on the beach.

Chapter Thirty-Four

All throughout the Kingdom of Ma Oz, droplets of a sooty goo were found in various places. It was physical proof that evil had regained entry into their province. Teams were assigned to track down the goop, and covered in protective gear, they cleaned it up so that the people in the kingdom didn't come in contact with it since it was toxic. It wasn't a virus, but it was evil converted to a form of muck and mire. The stench smelled of death and decay. It was literally evil poison.

The unholy kingdom where the toxin originated was found in Brimstone Mountain. A hellish, evil and terrifying place. The fallen people from the Kingdom of Ma Oz became creatures that transformed into ungodly, deformed bodies. Their skin actually took on a sooty ash texture and it would progress to the point it constantly dripped the goopy toxin. Once their transformation was complete, you could not recognize the person they used to be.

The wicked king and queen could use their powers to disguise themselves as normal everyday people for the sole purpose of converting the people from the Kingdom of Ma Oz over to their evil empire. That and to destroy their arch enemies, the good and Godly King Berthold and Queen Valeska. King Eryn and Queen Malvoil had almost conquered the Kingdom of Ma Oz twice before, but the folks sought God's intervention. The Eryndomnites were defeated and once again thrown into the bone-chilling Brimstone Mountain.

When the people of Ma Oz let their guards down, that somehow, not knowingly, invited the Eryndomnites in but through disguise. Now the main goal is to conquer and destroy Ma Oz. That is how Addley was led astray. She wanted to be in a relationship with Prince Ari so badly that she compromised and fell into their trap. Daily, she has begun to transition into one of them. But the transformation wasn't at a critical place where her touch would severely burn Ari. Although, that moment was getting closer and closer.

That's why anyone who was in disguise or in transformation couldn't be around the people of Ma Oz for any lengthy amount of time. Their disguises would begin to drip the toxin and deformity would progress.

Addley was called to Queen Malvoil's court. Creatures of stench and disgust watched her with evil eyes as she entered. They moaned and hissed. Fear grabbed at her insides of what was left of them.

"So, you wanted an audience with me?" Queen Malvoil said eyeing her cautiously.

"Yes, your Empress."

No longer was she to be addressed as queen, but empress is what she demanded of her underlings.

"I have exceptional news. Prince Ari has shown affection to me. Real, true affection. It won't be long before I bring him to our side. With Princess Ember out of the picture, this will bring us victory."

"Yes, I have seen with my own eyes. Job well done. Now, your time is running out and there is no way for me to halt your complete transition. You must move faster."

"But I won't look like one of them," she said turning to see what she could possibly become.

"It matters not. Obeying my commandments are all you need to be concerned about. If you fail, you will wish for instant death." How ironic. Death is just what people who accept the mark transition to. They look and smell like death.

"Be gone and be quick."

Addley ran out and through the portal that was closed for two thousand years, but her selfishness was just the act that opened its door. Selfishly, Treelin was in love with her and followed her pathway to evil just to be near her. Except, he accepted the mark much earlier than she had and his transition was at critical stages.

If only they could foresee the future. Would they have taken this route and placed their family and friends in evil's path? The battle will take on countless casualties.

~

King Berthold sat in a darkened room by himself, staring at the walls. His thoughts were great and in shame. Queen Valeska walked in and with a fling of her fingers, lights brightened the room. "There you are, dear husband. I understand the level of torment you feel. I feel it as well. Is there more? Anything I could discuss with you? I am in this with you."

"My dear. The road ahead is long and tiresome. Scary and shameful. I fear we have failed the Lord yet again. We allowed a falling away to happen right underneath our noses. Not wanting our people to think us arrogant and pompous, we even lowered our own ruling status. What have we done to our kingdom? My heart is full of shame and distress. We can't even blame the Eryn-domnites. By being accepting to new ways of thinking, we have failed this people."

She lowered her head in shame. "Yes, it is true and heavy on my heart. No matter how exhausting, how terrifying it will be for the kingdom, repentance is needed first and foremost. We were warned that if we turn our backs on truth and righteousness, the battle would be more severe than before. The Eryndomnites power would increase. There isn't time. You must call all peoples to the courtyard and deliver the truth. Something tells my soul that we need more help than what our kingdom can provide."

"Yes, it must be done at once." He ordered his assistant to summon the people. In the highlands, in the valleys and in the river and streams, the bells rang out. Every breed, realm and individual heard the bells. They stopped what they were doing and made their way to the courtyard. It was a sight all fairy-tale lovers would pay to see. Like the grains of sand, the courtyard and beyond were filled to capacity. All kings and queens, princes and princesses, and all subjects joined the king and queen on the platform. There were too many to count.

King Berthold walked up and looked out amongst his people. Tears dropped down his face. Then with courage and boldness he asked them to bow their heads. They did. His prayer of repentance and protection was heartfelt, deep sobs accompanying it. The rest of the kingdom joined in with the prayers and broke down at the emotional distress they were all under, waiting and seeking a day of retribution and restoration.

All in agreement with the prayer, they split up and went back to their realms and prepared for battle. Just before they left, lights flashed throughout the sky and a devilish laugh echoed through the clouds. Trembling and fear took its toll on the people. King Berthold apologized for allowing the kingdom to get to this place. "We should have learned from the past battle, but no, eat, drink and be merry was foremost in the mind of our inhabitants on a daily basis, royalty included."

The king and queen made a solemn promise to their people that they would return to God and follow His written Word. The crowd roared with support and agreement.

Chapter Thirty-Five

P rince Ari made his way through the crowd, shaking hands, embraces, and in search of Sharley's family. On the way, he saw Addley and Treelin standing by themselves away from the crowd. They wore forced smiles, and their eyes were so dark, and even stranger, they looked like empty vessels. His body quivered at the realization that they stood out so differently amongst the people of Ma Oz.

Addley came out of her trance as the echo in the sky diminished and connected her gaze to Ari. She smiled and waved. He waved back but then turned around to find Sharley's family. Finally, he realized if he was determined to find them in this crowd of people, a different approach was needed. He rose above them. He glowed with royalty and waved. Using his extra-sensory hearing and eyesight, they were spotted. He was at their side within seconds.

The people of Ma Oz all had an extraordinary presence, and for royalty to stand out amongst them, their appearance was grand and full of the highest level of enchanting imagination.

"Dear Adelina, I couldn't leave this gathering without speaking to you. I want you to know we are making progress and have some extremely good leads. Once we determine the clues are pointing us in the right direction and not a snare of the Eryndomnites, we will be in touch."

"Prince Ari, I have prayed for this day, this gathering and this determination to repent and return to the good Lord's ways. This is most precious to me. I still believe Sharley is in grave danger of dying, but I also have utmost faith that we will be victorious once again.

"Do not worry, I know you are doing everything in your power to find her."

He kissed her cheek. "God bless you and all who worship Him."

With gratitude, she bowed, and he flapped his way above the crowd. But what he saw as he looked around the kingdom was disconcerting. The areas where the toxic goo was cleaned up had turned the vegetation, rocks, stones, and rivers to decay. The destruction took his breath away. He went immediately to report what he saw to the King and Queen.

~

With haste, the evil queen entered the King's quarters. "Eryn, I am overwhelmed with concern."

"Why is that, my dear queen?" His words were derisive, and he ordered all the women and men out of his quarters.

"First of all, please address me as Empress. We have very few of our people on earth. The princess is missing, nowhere to be found. She is key to our victory. The plan was to bring her forth in the Kingdom of Ma Oz and use her for leverage to get the prince, king and queen to submit to our authority. She is so beloved by all, even by their God, so it is our best choice of weaponry."

"Well in that case, FIND HER. Never forget, I rule over you as well. You may have powers, but mine are more powerful. Don't test my abilities, Queen," he mocked her.

Showing her spunk and vile temper, traits he adored in her, she retaliated. "Do not try and intimidate me. I am not subject to your orders as the peons serving us."

His head fell back with laughter. The disturbing laugh echoed through the walls and trails of Brimstone Mountain, causing his people to cower in fear.

Queen Malvoil loved being intimate with him and this was how she got his admiration. "I'll see you later, Emperor."

He formed his fists into a ball and held them up to his mouth. His eyes grew bright, and a wicked smile molded. "Ooh. You have redeemed yourself. I like it. I'll see you later, Empress."

"Just being near you stirs my blood and gives me inspiration. I will find both girls and enjoy a good way to terrorize the people of Earth." She laughed loudly, in diabolical and demented tones. Oh, how it stirred his insides.

Chapter Thirty-Six

"Your majesties," Prince Ari said as he entered their castle. "We are close to having some answers to the whereabouts of Princess Ember and Sharley. While you addressed the realms, our guards did a search of Addley and Treelin's room. We found a journal with analytical symbols and equations. One of the entries had Ember's name next to it. Our specialists will apply the formulas and demonstrate what they mean. They are certain something vindictive is involved."

Queen Valeska clapped her hands together. "That is marvelous news. I always knew in my heart that you would be the man the Lord chose for Ember. I'm so glad she has you."

"I am the blessed one, my queen." He bowed in respect. "But now I have to do something I dread even more than battle."

Her eyes furrowed. "What could be worse than that?"

"I have to pretend to be in love with Addley."

"Uh. That does make sense."

"She is believing the lie. That part, as horrific as it is, could be our best method of finding them. If she keeps believing I am in love with her and confides her dark secrets, we'll have Ember and Sharley back in no time."

"I will pray for God to shield you with His protection. You have seen firsthand how tricky and conniving they are, and sadly, they get results."

"Yes, please keep me in prayer. And Queen, if I might add something, it appears Sharley's mother would make a great advisor to the royal team. I am very impressed with her wisdom and courage."

"Thank you for informing me. They are staying in the larboard chambers that abide seagirt. I will formally bring her in as spiritual counsel. I don't know what has taken me so long to get around to it, because I meant to do it before. Her wisdom is most valuable indeed."

"Yes, your majesty. Well, I must be off and carry on my duties to find my beloved."

On the way to Addley's, he drug his feet and shuffled through the path. Addley sat outside on a natural vine-made swing. She swung back and forth in the breeze, observing the soot that was beginning to drip off various areas of her body. Some dripped down over her eye, and she quickly wiped it away. She stared at it on her hand, realizing her whole body would take on this disgusting form.

She was so obsessed with Ari that she ignored her mother's guidance about taking the mark of King Eryn. She reminded her of past battles, except Addley was a lot younger and a lot of it disappeared from her memory. Looking back, her mom explained how she witnessed the transformation during the battle and how gross and spooky it was to watch.

When Addley called out to Queen Malvoil for help while entering unsafe territory, the queen was disguised in beauty and kindness. She pretended to have compassion for Addley and won her over to the dark side. Her foot burned even now with the fiery brand of a demented looking worm, King Eryn's iconic symbol. She sucked in air at the pain and squinted her whole face.

The story of how Malvoil became the queen came back to memory. Her mother had told her that Malvoil was madly in love with King Berthold. So much so that she would do anything for him if he would choose her over Valeska. But, he was tuned in to the Lord's instructions and followed His ways. When he rejected Malvoil, she ran out to the creepy, crawly landside of the Eryndomnites. Their king thought she was the most beautiful woman he had ever seen. Knowing she was out for blood and revenge, his kind of woman, she accepted his proposal and mark without hesitation.

Of course, King Berthold's ego was flying high at the attention, but good won out over evil. He could see a vindictive side to her, but that beauty caused him to be almost possessed at times. Not only did Valeska have incredible beauty, but it was her inner beauty that won him over, and wanting to please his Creator and Lord was even a stronger reason. Now, Malvoil wants nothing more than to destroy him and his beautiful, powerful kingdom.

After their wedding, the good Lord decided to appoint mates to each and every inhabitant in the kingdom and not take the chance for evil to influence or take hold of the kingdom. Their kingdom was secretly created to help guard and care for the Lord's creation on Earth. They were a pure and loyal group of subjects. Much was given to his people. Realms into every area of the Earth, but secretly, and humans were none the wiser about their existence.

And now that Malvoil had arranged to slowly infiltrate the earth with her poison, the failure of King Berthold would cause extreme sadness and shame. She applauded her wickedness and pictured him bowing to her in the end. She mocked the Lord and used His words before she left Ma Oz.

"In the end of days, yes, 'every knee shall bow'," but she added to the Word of God, "to me and King Eryn." It was one of the most disturbing exits the king had ever witnessed.

Chapter Thirty-Seven

T he Kingdom of Ma Oz was a most enchanting and beautiful place. Everything in it was pure and clean, fertile and blooming. If it didn't sparkle and glisten, it would shine and glow, every inch of it. It truly was as special as the Garden of Eden.

Queen Valeska rose up to great heights in the sky. Her appearance was the most magical depiction of God's harmony in creation that there ever was to be. She had dainty qualities but also the strength and boldness of the fiercest warrior.

She looked out over the kingdom. A hand covered her mouth as tears flooded her face. She could see evil destruction creep in and it was devastating. Physically disabling.

∼

Ari walked up startling Addley. With a hand to her heart she exclaimed, "Don't do that. You gave me quite a fright."

"I'm sorry. We never got to finish what we started." His smile was mischievous and a lie. He had to make it appear sincere. She pointed to the vine swing sitting next to her. He sat down, holding the vines with both hands and watched her. "What did you think of the gathering today?"

She waved a hand down. "Too mushy. Overrated. The usual."

His face scrunched together. "I felt empowered and rejuvenated."

"Oh brother. You buy into everything they say. I guess you have to, since you're a prince and all."

"Maybe there's truth to that."

"So, I guess you came to tell me that you have to remain loyal to Ember, who isn't here by the way, and who doesn't understand you either. I'm here and I understand you. We're good together and you can't deny that."

He reached for her hand. To him her touch made him feel nauseous, but he suppressed his revolt. She smiled and brought his hand to her lips. She kissed it affectionately.

With warm, but secretly vulgar eyes, he jumped up and pulled her off the swing. "Let's take a walk. Someplace we can be alone where no one will walk up on us. I know just the place."

Her body tingled inside, and heat flushed her cheeks. "I am under your command. Lead me to your secret places." She squeezed her body up to him and welded her arm tightly to his body. They walked to a mountainous entrance. As she walked through it, her eyes lit up. A waterfall dropped harmonically into a serene pond, the area lavished with different colored flowers and trees that moved to the beat of the breeze. The natural fragrance was scintillating.

"How is it possible I have never known of this place?"

"This was Ember's and my secret garden. The king and queen had it created solely for our eyes only. No one else would be able to see it. Since you're with me, you get to experience the magic of this place."

"The fact that you are bringing me to a secret spot set up for you and Ember touches my heart in ways I can't describe." She lifted his hand to her heart and smiled up at him. Stars in her eyes.

He dropped her hand and turned around, head slumped down. "You must think I am a most horrible prince. Here my betrothed is missing and all I can think about is how much I like spending time with you." Feeling an urge to stick a finger down his throat, he coughed instead.

She pushed her way in front of him and made him face her. "Ari, I could never think such things. We can't help how we feel about each other. I think you and Ember jumped to conclusions since you are prince of the animal kingdom, and she was labeled princess of the animal kingdom. But obviously, they got it wrong. That's why this isn't working out between you and Ember. I was supposed to reign as princess of the animal kingdom."

"But that can't be. You don't have a bond with the animals of the world like Ember has. But, maybe, she was meant to be with someone other than me and me someone other than her. Maybe that's how we got it mixed up. Everyone just assumed because we are both connected specifically to the animal kingdom, God placed us together."

He grabbed Addley's hands that cast off an undeniable evilness, and said, "Do you think it's possible that you and I are meant to be together? Is that even possible?"

She held his face in her hands and looked tenderly in his eyes. For her, this wasn't a fake performance. In her mind, she was unequivocally in love with him. "Yes, yes, it's possible. Look how well we get along and how good we are together. I have loved you since we were in napkins. Oh, Prince Ari, it's me you love, not Ember. It's me."

She kissed him and moaned with excitement. Ember was always a pain in her side and if she were to die, so be it. Good riddance.

Feeling like he was about to regurgitate all over her, he pushed her back. "This is happening too fast. We need to slow things down and make certain before jumping into this relationship. I owe Ember at least that much. You understand, don't you?"

"No, I don't understand it. We have waited a long time to be together. We don't have time to wait!" She started sweating, her eyes were turning dark, and a sooty substance began to drip.

"What is that smell?" Ari's nose pushed upwards.

"I forgot. Mum has something I need to help her with. I'll see you tomorrow." She was gone so fast, a streak flashed through the air.

The prince sent a message for the cleanup crew to make haste. They showed up in suits that would protect them from contamination. Ari saw firsthand the truth. Addley was infected with the evil. He saw the soot drip and the fear in her eyes about him finding out. What he didn't know is how hard it has been for her to accept the fact that she will look as hideous as fellow Eryndomnites who were infected and the end result of the transformation. It was a ghastly sight and one she never gave thought to, until it was too late.

Prince Ari demanded time alone. Yes, he despised her with every ounce of his being, but there was a time she was one of his best friends. He never felt romantic feelings for her, and he was unaware that she had always felt that way towards him. How did he miss that? Suddenly emotions of regret, anger and sorrow filled his soul. No one could ease the pain he felt, and now, she would turn into pure evil, soon to lose her own soul and memory of who she was in the kingdom. Maybe losing her memory was a blessing in disguise.

Addley had long auburn hair with natural bluish highlights. She was beautiful and once upon a time charming and delightful to be around. If she would have confided in him, he could have prevented the whole thing. But he never knew about it. Guilt was eating him up. Once somebody accepted the mark of King Eryn, there was no turning back. Everyone in the kingdom was aware of that fact and everyone at some time in their life caught a glimpse of one of the kingdom's people who transformed into one of the Eryndomnites. It was a grotesque and grim sight to behold.

As much as he loves Ember, there was no encouragement or sympathy that could ease his pain. He just needed time alone.

Chapter Thirty-Eight

A pounding on the door alerted Tyrus and Ember. She peeked through the blind. A sigh escaped.

"Who is it?" Tyrus asked.

"It's Todd. I really don't feel like answering questions about how weird I am."

"Weird? You are the most interesting and enchanting person I know. There is nothing weird about you. Todd obviously recognizes that. Go on, greet him. Make a friend."

"Okay, but if he makes me feel insecure about my 'special gifts,'" she said making air quotes, "I'm coming back inside." A light knock hit the door again. The door creaked open slowly as she stuck her head out. Her voice was low. "Hi Todd."

"Hey there. I told you I would come by."

"Why?"

"Because I happen to like you, and just as a friend. Calm down there. I see that face of worry. Are you bothered by my visit?"

She shrugged her shoulders and wouldn't look up at him. For Ember, she had to look up to everyone because she was so tiny.

"What? Is it about yesterday?"

A shrug again.

"Please come out and sit with me." His face was so sweet and honest. She hesitantly walked out, and it looked almost like the bench was too hot to sit on the way she fidgeted.

"I'm not bothered at all about yesterday. Why should you be?" Todd exclaimed.

"Because you're not the one they're making fun of. I am. To be called a witch is the most insulting thing anyone could say about me."

They both looked out towards the beach just as Tiffany walked past, staring at them both with evil eyes.

"If anyone's a witch, it's her," he said pointing.

Ember chuckled. "Don't you think she is beautiful?"

"Sure, but her heart is ugly. She is a spoiled brat and digs her fingers into guys with money. It's never about love or companionship. It's always about social importance, money, fame and power. It's a real turnoff for me. My friends aren't like that either. We all met in our youth group and have the same interests."

"Oh, really. That's nice. Maybe it's because you're so nice to look at that she can't help herself."

His head pushed back, and he sculpted a pleased and confused expression. "You think I'm nice looking?"

"Is there something wrong with that?"

"No. I like hearing it. It's nice to hear sometimes. Like you, you probably have no idea how beautiful you are; do you?"

Pink appeared on her face instantly.

"I don't mean to embarrass you. Would you like to walk on the beach? Just you and me? Tyrus is welcome to walk with us."

Her eyes squinted as her face leaned sideways against her shoulder. "I don't want to be made fun of."

"That's not going to happen. My friends adore you. Even the girls who like me can't help but adore you. They think what happened is super cool. So do I. And you have no idea what happened?"

"Absolutely none."

"Let's forget about all of that. Why don't you ask Tyrus if he would like to take a walk and feel the breeze." He held his arms out. "The weather's too beautiful to ignore." Her hair was flying in the breeze, sparkling like gold, and an unidentifiable earthy and beautiful scent flowed from her. As she rose, he closed his eyes and sniffed. *Warm cashmere woven with sunbeams and marshmallow.* His eyes popped open. Under his breath, he said, "Where did that come from?"

The rocking chair creaked back and forth as she exited it. She ran into the house and was back out in a few minutes carrying flip flops in her hand. Hair pulled back in a ponytail. Tyrus stepped out and locked the door. "Thanks for inviting me. I was looking forward to taking a walk, but this one," he said pointing at her head, "was too embarrassed and wouldn't walk with me. You have a gift of making her feel comfortable."

That's not the first time he heard that. His smile widened. His parents worked hard to keep him from being a rich, spoiled brat. *Guess it is working.*

They walked, Ember stopping to admire a shell or two, feet splashing as the waves rolled in and the sun beating down, its warmth welcoming. It was a glorious day. Until Tiffany walked back and passed them mumbling the word, "witch".

"If you will excuse me for a moment, I have to take care of something." Todd walked up to Tiffany.

They watched.

"I don't know what your problem is, but I think you owe Tania an apology."

"Pbbbbbt," she spat out.

"I'm not kidding. Why do you treat her so hostile like?"

"She's weird, and she doesn't fit in with us."

"See, that's where you're confused. She fits in perfectly with us. You don't fit in with any of us. Do us a HUGE favor and go somewhere else. You are not welcome with us anymore."

Her eyes grew big and her mouth dropped wide. "Because of her?"

"No. Because of you. Now, leave us alone. We don't share the same interests or agree with your arrogant and snobby treatment of people. We aren't like that." He turned and walked off.

She huffed loudly. "Your loss."

"Happy loss."

She huffed again.

"Well done," Tyrus said shaking his hand.

"Thanks, but I don't like hurting people's feelings, and she seems to get a thrill out of it. It had to be done. So, are you going to be staying for a while?"

"Can't be certain. We will return home as soon as it is safe for Tania."

"This is killing me. Why can't you tell me what's going on? I won't breathe a word of it."

"It's too dangerous for you, as well as for us. We can't tell you anything. And if you run into anyone who asks about Tania, you have never seen her. Please make sure your friends don't release her whereabouts to anyone. Please."

"Yes, sir. I would never do anything that would cause her harm. Never. My lips are zipped."

He looked with empathy at her. What horror was she escaping? If she would let him, he'd pull her into an embrace and make her feel protected, but common sense told him that would make it worse.

They were at a stretch of the beach that was void of people. That popping sound they heard yesterday started creating a huge sound and it was following them. Todd couldn't figure out what was popping up and down so fast and why it was so tiny. He knew fish, and this just wasn't fish. Then, out a little farther, dolphins clicked as they leaped in the air, performing and following them.

"Wow! This is amazing. I have lived here all my life and have never seen anything like this. What's happening? This is so cool."

Tyrus knew it had to do with Tania, but he didn't know why or how.

"Todd! Todd! Wait up!"

He turned. Shawn was running towards him waving his hands.

"Hey man, what's up?"

Panting from running so far, he caught his breath. "Some guy is asking for Tania. I remember you said to keep her presence quiet. That's what you told me in secret at your house the other day. I just wanted you to know."

"Did you tell him she is here?"

"No. I just acted like I didn't know of her."

"What was his name?" Tyrus asked in a panic.

Talking to himself first, he said quizzically, "Ari or Arnold, something with an 'a' sound."

"Could it have been Aaron?"

"Yeah, I think that's it."

"Where is he now?"

"He walked the other way down the beach. I turned and walked to the condo and ran behind it on the beach. I checked for you at Tania's house before this guy came up to me. Your mom said you would be there."

"Tyrus, I told you Aaron has been acting weird. How did he find us?" Ember asked with widening eyes.

"I don't know but we need to sneak into the house, get our things and get out of here."

Todd looked sad. "As much as I hate to see you leave, I can help. Follow me and I'll get you there the back way. I'll keep watch and if I see him, I'll walk past your window and knock loudly.

"What does he look like, Shawn?" Todd asked.

"If you were a girl, you would be swooning over him. Big, muscular, golden hair, gorgeous to women. Women were snickering and whispering as he walked by, but he ignored every one of them. Thankfully, I was the lucky one he chose to talk to, because someone else may have given her up. You'll know it's him when you see him."

"I'm scared, Tyrus."

"Come on. Follow me. Shawn, keep a watch out for this guy. Text me the second you see him."

"You got it."

All the popping and performance in the ocean stopped abruptly. The three of them ran through paths, sea grass and even sandspurs. "Ooooch! Ouch! Yowie!" was spouted. Finally at the front door, not in view of the ocean or beach, they ran inside and grabbed their things. Tyrus placed a call and left the key in the aforementioned hiding spot. He shook Todd's hand.

Todd walked up to Ember. "I know this will make you uncomfortable, but all I ask is that you allow me to hug you goodbye."

A wide smile covered her face. "I will miss you, Todd."

"Not as much as I will miss you. I guess I'll never see you again?"

"I'm afraid not, but here," Tyrus said handing him a torn piece of paper with his number on it. "Keep in touch and alert us to any potential threats."

Precisely at that moment, sunrays beamed over Ember's hair and face. Todd stood breathless as the gold in her hair gleamed like twenty-four carat gold. It literally glistened. And that face was flawless ivory skin with a mixture of sparkly glitter and silk. He almost reached out to feel her face but was too stunned by the enchantment he would never lay eyes on again.

"Todd, you okay," she asked in a sweet voice. Waving her hand around, she finally got his attention.

"Sorry. Being around you takes me to a fantasyland. Yes, we must hurry, I know." He embraced Ember for seconds. Kissed her cheek and said, "Farewell Princess, for there is no other word I could call you that would suffice." She smiled warmly and slammed the door shut. The car squealed out of the driveway never to be seen again.

Tyrus pressed numbers to connect to Virginia. In a minute she answered almost out of breath.

"Are you okay?" he asked concerned.

"Yes. I had to run upstairs to get my phone. Is anything wrong?"

"Yes. Aaron is here asking for Tania."

"What? How did he find out?"

"I have no idea. I was hoping you would know."

"I'll check with the guys later. All I can tell you is that Aaron stormed out of here when he found out she was gone. He was all out of sorts, sweating, dripping small blobs of sweat even."

"Something strange is going on and he's part of it," Tyrus admitted.

"What will you do now?"

"I have to think, I'll contact you later this evening. I love you," he whispered into the phone.

On the other end her face flushed, and she whispered it back.

"Where to, Tyrus?"

"Drive. We just need to keep driving until we find a safe place to rest."

"Is there such a place?"

"Probably not. Pray, dear. Pray."

Chapter Thirty-Nine

Ari walked into his own family's castle. Instantly he became enraged and spewed anger. Thuds and smashing sounds rang out.

"Hey, hey, hey, cool down there. What is it?" Queen Melisande asked.

He shook his head. "I don't know. This rage comes on me out of nowhere. Like I said before, I'm instantly jealous. You don't think she found another guy where she's at; do you?"

"Son, of course she wouldn't be with anyone else. I don't know. I have no idea what's happened to her or if she's of sound mind. There's just no way to know."

"Mum, I have evidential proof that Addley has accepted King Eryn's mark."

She slapped a hand over her mouth.

"I saw her eyes darken, a grayish sweat bead up on her skin and that squalid goop started dripping from her. It was so upsetting. She was one of my best friends. She will never be able to take back that act. It's over for her. Completely over. I'm so saddened, even though I know she is behind Ember's disappearance. How could this happen? How could she think she is in love with me?"

"If only I knew that answer. All I can come up with is that

she refused to adhere to the decrees, and that, dear son, is for her to answer. It is the only place you will hear the truth."

His jealous fit subsided and now he had to make further plans to get Addley to confide in him. He was mentally and emotionally exhausted. Queen Melisande was heartbroken watching guilt and sorrow consume him.

~

Sitting in a park somewhere in Kansas, Tyrus pulled out his phone and called Virginia. Ember was sound asleep in the back seat.

"Hello there," she answered cheerfully."

"Hi. Can't talk long, just in case someone is able to monitor our conversation, and you know as well as I do that things have been too weird to let our guard down."

"Yes, you're quite right. So, to answer your question, no, the boys haven't seen Aaron since he sped out of here that day. I explained to the sheriff and let him read your note. Harry didn't like it, but he understood why you did it. No one knows where you are."

"How could Aaron find us?"

"Can't believe I'm cuckoo enough to say this, but maybe those huge eyes in the sky have been following you."

"There's nothing cuckoo about that statement. It was so relaxing not to see all the weird stuff, but that didn't last too long. There were times I thought clouds passed in front of the sun, but now I'm wondering about that. When will this end?"

"Oh, Tyrus, we're all living in fear. I hate it, but I could never do anything to compromise that sweet girl's life."

"Nor could I. I still need to figure out what would be the best plan of action. If anything happens, contact me right away. I love you, VA," his new nickname for her. She laughed. Didn't know how she felt about being referred to as the state of Virginia though. What happened to terms of endearment using the words honey or dear?

Tyrus fell asleep, nerves on edge, but yet, way too exhausted to keep his eyes open.

Chapter Forty

"King Berthold, it's not as though I get enjoyment out of deceiving Addley; nor do I enjoy pretending to be in love with her. My heart feels like burning embers. It hurts deeply to know Addley chose evil over good. It kills me. And watching her body slowly begin transmutation, breaks my heart greatly. We were best of friends. I had no idea how she felt about me.

"Please don't worry. My heart belongs to Ember. I physically ache about her disappearance. I will be careful with Addley. Right now, she is the only one who can help us. I have to continue onward," Prince Ari confessed.

"Its obvious Queen Malvoil is using Addley to trap you. This scheme has her written all over it. If she can, she will set it up where you watch your fiancé and I watch my granddaughter die. She would love to see our pain.

"If they can trap you, then it will be much easier for them to get you to buy into their lies. This isn't the first time we have witnessed their skullduggery behavior. You were too young to remember the details from the last time they deceived our peoples. Be extra cautious and vanish from their sight at any moment you feel an ambush or fear for your life."

"You are correct. I don't remember all the despicable details of the previous battle and what led up to it but, King, I will take precautions, along with fasting and prayer before my next visit to Addley. This has to work. It just has to. King, is there any chance, even minuscule, that she can repent and be saved from such destruction?"

"You have no idea how much I wish that were true. Compare this to Revelation, chapter fourteen. People who accept the mark of the beast have no opportunity to repent. But God makes sure everyone hears the truth before they have to make a choice. Unfortunately, this is the same scenario. I'm really sorry, Prince Ari."

Tears spilled down his face. He walked away with his head down, drops splashing on the floor. It was time to visit Skyfire. He did this daily to comfort him and check the symbol underneath his mane.

When he arrived at the stable, he didn't expect to see such a disturbing scene. Skyfire laid on the ground. He never does that. Ari ran up and shook his massive shoulder. Skyfire neighed weakly. "Get up, boy. Please get up."

But he didn't move. Ari took off in a flash to get help. His mom and dad came and performed their normal magic. He rose, but still it seemed he was depressed. Do animals grieve? But he wasn't just some animal. He had supernatural powers and was Ember's protector. He loved her.

A checkup continued and a thought clicked inside Ari's mind. He pushed his mane up and stared at the symbol. It glowed and swirled but the colors had faded. What does that mean?

"What do we do to help him? We have to do something."

"Son," King Dillon said resting his hand on Ari's shoulder, "the only thing we can do is bring Princess Ember back home. You must visit Addley and bring this to a close. Now."

"Yes, father. I'll go there now." To see Addley so vulnerable by his presence and to the evilness waiting to transform her completely, this was torture; but she brought this on herself. Ember is too important to the wellbeing of the animal kingdom to lose his courage now, not to mention to him.

He walked up to her door. He reached out to knock on the

door but pulled his arm back fast. Taking a few deep breaths, he resumed his task and knocked softly. The door opened slowly and Addley peeked around it. When he smiled, a soft smile spread across her face, but those eyes looked odd. Almost like she was there physically, but mentally and spiritually absent from the body.

"Addley, are you okay?"

The voice that came out of her was like an echo that traveled outward. Very strange. "I am fine, Prince Ari. Are you fine?"

He blinked his eyes a few times before able to answer. "I am fine, thanks."

"Do you need something?" still echoing.

"I just stopped to see you and ask if you want to go for a walk."

As if whatever had ahold of her mind let go, her eyes blinked forcefully until she could regain her own thoughts. "Oh, hi there. When did you get here?"

Ari just stared at her for a moment with a dangling, open mouth. "Just got here. Wanna go for a walk?"

"Yes. I would love to. Can we just go down to the river? I'd rather not walk so far away from home this time."

"Sure, whatever you want." He grabbed her hand and looked down at her face. Guilt eating away at his insides. Even he couldn't deny how she looked at him. Absolute devotion and love her face showed.

Addley stared at him with dreamy thoughts. Maybe what she had to do to get him to love her paid off after all.

He mentally gave his mind a good headshaking. Skyfire was losing hope, and he can't live another day without Ember. Time to put on a good show.

Squeezing her hand, he smiled down at her more. "I don't know why, but I can't seem to get you out of my mind."

"Then don't," she replied sincerely. The truth is that he couldn't get her out of his mind because of guilt, sorrow and even hatred for what she did to Ember.

"So, how long have you known that you were in love with me? There has never been anyone else you were in love with?"

Thinking, she kicked a pebble that was in the path. "Always. I can't remember a time when I wasn't in love with you. There has never been even the slightest crush on anyone else. Never."

"You know, I never knew you felt this way. Ever."

"Yes, I know. When that stupid girl came, you didn't want to spend as much time with me. That made me angry."

"I bet it did. Do you still feel that strongly for me?"

She looked mischievously into his eyes with a slanted smile. "Oh, yeah. Maybe even stronger, now that you feel the same for me."

She saw his expression change. "Hey, you do feel that way for me; right?"

"Of course. I'm here with you instead of looking for Ember. You do the math."

Addley cuddled up to him.

"I bet you hated Ember when she came here," he said sneaking a glance at her face.

"More than you know. Everybody loves Ember. She's always sweet and caring, kind and funny. Talk about boring."

"Well, you have to admit she is also brave. Remember how she stood up to the Eryndomnites?"

"Yeah, so what."

"You were her friend. Did you ever like her?"

With disgust she answered, "No. It was all a ruse." She released an exasperated breath.

"Yeah, all that goodie-two-shoes stuff could get boring."

"What about you? How did you manage to pretend to be in love with her all this time?"

"It wasn't easy," he pretended to smirk. "But I always had you to turn to. We always got away from the suffocating, endless training and all the tiresome stuff that goes with being a prince. Thanks for always lightening my load." That part he meant. Addley always found something crazy for them to do. But so did Ember. He just never shared that with Addley. Why, he and Ember could laugh for hours, explore and find the most unique things. She even got into some thrill-seeking sports. That little lady had no fear and knew how to have fun. She also knew when to be serious, caring, a confidant and affectionate.

Just thinking about her caused a train of tingling to run through his veins. Yes, he truly loved Ember. But he also loved Addley as a friend. Choosing her friendship over the true love of his life wasn't negotiable.

They strolled hand in hand by the riverbank. They talked about her disapproval of the king and queen's rulings and choice of offering comfort to the inhabitants of the kingdom. If she heard anymore praise to the God of heaven and earth, she would throw up right there and then. It was repulsive to her ears. Next time she would refrain from courtyard gatherings.

"This might be a sore subject, but what do we do if Ember comes back?" he asked hoping she didn't see through his eagerness to find out the truth.

"Don't fret. She won't be back."

"You say that like you know what's happened to her. If you know for certain that she is dead or will never come back to Ma Oz, please let me know so I can make arrangements to wed you, my love."

"Hhhh!" Her hands patted her heart. A film of tears covered her eyes. "Oh Ari, that is what I've been waiting to hear my whole life. Now that I am of age to wed, and Ember out of the picture, I'm breathless at the possibilities. If only I would have gotten rid of her sooner." Oops, her face revealed.

"No, please, go on. We have to make arrangements, but we will need to keep them quiet. The king and queen won't take kindly to our plans." He kissed her cheek. "You know, I'm sick and tired of following every demand, having to agree with their ways of thinking and having no life or privacy. Maybe I should denounce my royal lineage to the throne of the animal kingdom. I want freedom to go where I want, think what I want and not have to worry about the consequences of being proper all of the time. It's exhausting. You have no idea." It was hard to say these things.

"Oh, but I do. I have seen you mentally and emotionally, and even physically depleted of energy. More so now with all this stupid Ember stuff going on. You don't have to hide anything with me. There is nothing you could ever do to change how I feel for you. Even denouncing your birthright to the throne. I say, do it. Be accountable to only yourself. Those pesky animals will be fine without you. Your parents can handle them."

"Now see, that's information you have not been privy to. If anything happens to my parents and even to me or Ember, just losing one of us could cause the utmost destruction to the animal kingdom. Ember and I took an oath to uphold our roles and protect this kingdom. If any of us fails, it is the animals who will suffer. That makes it so much more difficult for me to ignore my role in the animal kingdom."

"Oh, pish posh! Nobody lives forever. You need to think about yourself for a change. Look how miserable you are. Come on, Ari. We could live a life of pure seduction, pleasure and adventure. Don't compromise your needs any longer. It's your turn to be happy. I'll bet Ember already has another boyfriend."

His thoughts seethed with anger. Was he hiding the raging red heat that consumed his whole body? He had to keep up the pretense.

"You have a point. Will you come with me to the castle tomorrow while I do it?"

Her mouth dropped. "Yes, oh yes, I will. Just think, you and me forever," she responded folding her hands on her heart.

Yeah, just think, smelling like decay and looking like a blob of vomit. Thanks, but no thanks.

Her body started twitching and sweat beaded up, turning to sooty ash, and slowly it began to drip. She looked down and gasped. "I need to go. Mum is waiting for me. Come to my place tomorrow so we can walk together."

"But wait, you didn't finish telling me if Ember is alive or what."

It was too late. Just as before, she was gone with a flash of light diminishing with each passing second. His anger rose to great heights and a boulder sitting feet away exploded to tiny pieces. *Time to make arrangements for tomorrow. Surprise, surprise.*

Chapter Forty-One

Virginia, Jacob and Garrett spread out on the couch and recliner to watch movies. She was in a tizzy worrying about Tyrus and Tania. Were they still being watched? All three of them sat up in a flash and stared out the window. A big shadow glided by causing the window to vibrate. Garrett rushed to the window, but it had already passed.

"It's back. Whatever it is, it's back!" he roared looking at Jacob and then Virginia.

"Don't panic. Let's see what happens. We don't want whatever it is to hear us. Act natural."

"Ms. Virginia, shouldn't we let Tyrus know about this? What if it throws lightning at us like it did your house?" Jacob commented. Fear was in their eyes.

Whispering, "Let's hide all our phones under that broken piece of wood flooring by the door. I was able to pull it up enough for our phones to be stored there. Then, we'll take turns sleeping on Tyrus' bed, the couch and recliner. We need to stick together. Keep your weapons with you at all times." Jacob's parents had been staying out in the barn.

The ground was hard as ice, so they didn't see any dust scatter as a truck drove in. Someone knocked at the door. They looked helplessly at each other. Virginia motioned with her head for Garrett to peek through the curtain. His finger gently created an opening enough for him to squint an eye through. He stood up.

"It's Aaron."

Pounding was louder.

"I'll get it. Be calm.

"Aaron, what a nice surprise. Won't you come in?"

Aaron's body language looked like a drug addict in need of a fix. He walked in and looked around the stairs and adjoining room. "Is she here? Is she back?"

"Still no word from them. I am so worried about them," Virginia replied.

Jacob jumped in to make her statement sound legit. "Miss Virginia. Don't think that way. They'll come back. They wouldn't leave us and never return."

"I suppose you're right." They put on a great performance.

"Call me the second they return!" It wasn't a request.

"Of course we will call you. You must be worried yourself."

The door slammed and Garrett peeked through the curtain as he sped out of the driveway. "Hhhh!"

"What is it, Garrett?" Jacob demanded to know.

"That shadow passing over. It looks like a dark cloud, but it's not. Very spooky."

"Has it passed out of sight yet?" Virginia inquired.

"Yes."

"Grab your phones and anything else you may need and hide them. I'll give Tyrus a quick call," she whispered.

"Ms. Virginia, do you know what they want with Tania now?" Garrett asked with big eyes.

"Sorry, no."

He dropped his head. "This may sound goofy, but I feel like we are all a family now. I miss us all hanging out together."

"And seeing all the cool and strange things that happen with Tania," Jacob added.

"You young men are special. Everything will work out. The Lord will protect. Now, get your things and I'll make a quick call."

Tyrus' phone rang. Ember looked over with scared eyes. He answered quickly. "Virginia?"

"Yes, it's me. Aaron was just here looking for Tania and the huge shadow flew over again. You must find a place to hide out for another week, at least. Don't come home without calling first."

"Thank you." Then he whispered, "I love you." She whispered it back.

~

"What, Tyrus?"

"Aaron is back in Alaska and so is that huge shadow in the sky."

Her hands covered her mouth to keep from screaming. Mumbling through her hand, "When will it stop?"

"I'm afraid it won't stop until we get your memory back. That's the only way we can figure out what's going on."

"I just wish I knew how to do that."

"Me, too. Me, too, little one."

The phone woke her up. Tyrus looked at the display to see that it was a spam call. "Where are we?"

"Nebraska. We're not in Kansas anymore, Dorothy."

"Huh?"

"No! You've never seen that movie?"

She shook her head no.

"I'll have to fix that. Everyone should see it at least once. It's the best movie ever created."

"Can we rent it?"

"Not yet. I'm thinking we will hang out in a national park. That way the animals may be aware of your presence. They all seem to have a special bond with you, as if it's natural to you and them. What a better source of protection. For you, anyways."

"Don't think like that. Anyone who has ever been with me is safe, if I make it so. They'll listen to me."

"That's true enough."

"Hey Tyrus, tell me the truth. What do you think is going on? Where do you think I'm from?"

He scratched his head, thinking: *Didn't we already have this discussion?* "I have no proof of anything. According to your lab results, your anatomy is slightly different than ours. What I mean is that you have human organs but also parts of your body favor an animal, mostly part of a lion."

Her mouth dropped.

"That's not all. Even your blood type is different from any person on earth. I'll tell you what I think. I think you're somebody very special, maybe even royalty from a different planet or something. For some reason, somebody doesn't want you around. You pose a threat to them. Jealousy, power or money is usually the main culprit."

He could tell she didn't understand. "Look, I am letting my imagination get the best of me. We'll figure it out."

"Does that make me strange?"

"That makes you special."

She drew in a huge amount of air and tried letting it out but broke out in a cough. He patted her back.

They pulled into Nebraska National Forest at a campground area and parked. They both froze as a dark shadow hovered over the park. She slouched down in the seat.

"Hey, don't worry. Around here it could be an eagle or probably a pterodactyl."

One side of her top lip lifted.

"Kidding. I'm just kidding." But was he kidding? He surveyed the sky before allowing himself the opportunity to relax and sleep. It was too chilly to open a window. They both cuddled up with heavy blankets and laid their heads on soft, squishy pillows.

A raucous raccoon family digging in trash cans woke Ember up. Snoring loudly, Tyrus never heard her get out of the car. She walked up and crossed her arms.

"That isn't very nice of you to make such a mess." They ran up and climbed on her legs. She picked up one at a time, kissed their furry heads, tickled their tummies, and then put them back down. Tyrus awoke and rubbed his eyes. When he sat up and looked forward, he saw her playing with the raccoon family. It was simply adorable to see the interaction. She tiptoed back to the car and quietly opened the car door. A rush of cold wind blew in, causing Tyrus to pull the blanket up to his head. After she got situated, he spoke.

"How are the raccoons doing?"

"Huh! I didn't know you were awake. They are so adorable. I don't think there is one animal I'm not in love with."

He turned to look at her. "That doesn't surprise me in the least. Now, get some sleep. We'll have to find a restaurant in the morning."

"Mmm, I'll dream of waffles."

"I'll join you; now, sleep time."

Something patting the window woke them both up. Tyrus' mouth dropped to his feet. At least it felt that way. His eyes could work as golf balls. "Yikes! Don't m . . . o . . . v . . . e."

A big ole bear scratched at the window. Ember sat up and rolled her window down.

"Tania, what are you doing?"

"Shhh, don't scare him."

"Tania, please roll that window up."

Her hand went out the window and she scratched its bent head. It made the cutest humming sound. Then she spoke. Tyrus leaned his head back to hear. It was, again, an indescribable language. It was beautiful. The bear was focused on her words. She kissed its head and put the window up.

"How are you not terrified of a ferocious bear?" he asked while keeping his eye on the bear walking away.

"Don't ask me how, because I don't know, but I sensed that the bear wasn't worried. If something bad was around, I think—and I'm not sure why or how I know—I would have sensed fear in the bear."

She noticed his shocked face. He opened his mouth, but no words came out.

"Like I said, I don't know what I said or if the bear could understand me. I'm guessing. It's weird, because something inside of me makes me believe we connected somehow."

"Girl—young lady, woman or whatever you prefer to be called —there is nothing you say that surprises me anymore. Not a thing."

She grinned but looked puzzled at the same time.

"I have an idea. Let's go home. I'll check with Harry and ask him to let me park my truck in his garage. I hid it at a friend's house down the road, but I have to return this rental when we get close to home. If it is safe, I'll have Jacob pick us up and Virginia can pick us up at Harry's. Thinking about it, if whoever is after you finds my truck, I don't want to put them in any danger. Harry can handle them. Besides, his garage doesn't have windows. I'm running out of ideas."

"I guess we should do whatever it takes to keep people safe. We should try. Besides, I miss everyone, including all my animal friends," she admitted.

"Did I tell you that Mr. Horns has been grouchier than ever?"

"No, you didn't. How do you know that?"

"While we were at the beach, Virginia told me when I phoned her."

"He's all show. I'll get him to accept you. That should help."

"No, he only accepts you, like all the animals. You know very well that's the way it is, little one."

"Have you tried rubbing his neck?"

"Nope, because a very sharp horn is right next to it."

She giggled. "It's kind of funny, but I miss Todd. He ended up being okay and a lot of fun."

"That is a fine young man, yes. You ready to go home?"

She nodded yes and climbed in the backseat to sleep a little more. The car engine roared, and they headed home.

Chapter Forty-Two

While he drove, Ember pulled out her book and studied the pictures. Her fingers rubbed over Flora and Arwood's picture. Something drew her to them. She turned and studied Prince Ari's face. It was so odd to her how much he looked like Aaron, only younger. If she stared too much longer, she would need glasses.

She turned the page to Skyfire and the girl, who had all her features but younger. Her mind took in every color and anything that kept nudging thoughts at her. Weird. Something was sparkling under Skyfire's mane. At the same time, she felt a vibration on her birthmark. She placed a hand over it and felt a mild tremble. What in the world.

Back in Ma Oz, Ari brushed Skyfire. He started shaking his head and neighing. Ari stood back and saw sparkling colors flash under his mane. He quickly pushed strands of hair out of the way and saw it clear as day. It was so vivid that it looked like fireworks exploding. His hand felt it to see if it was hot. But instead, a vibration tickled his hand. He removed his hand and just watched it. Skyfire had a renewed strength about him.

"You know something, don't you Sky?"

His muscular head bobbed up and down.

"You can feel her. This is good. Really good. She's alive. We'll find her boy. Today is the day we find out where she has been taken."

Skyfire took off running around the pasture, leaping and galloping at a much faster speed than a regular horse. Ari could barely see him as fast as he was running, and a hint of smoke trailed.

~

Jacob pulled Tyrus' truck into Harry's driveway. The rumble and clanging of the garage door ended, then he pulled right into the garage. It rumbled and clanged all the way down to a loud thump as it hit the cement floor. Tyrus had called Harry the last time he stopped for gas, so he was aware of the plan. Jacob thanked the sheriff and ran out the side door. Virginia waited for him to climb in the truck. They took off and would meet Tyrus at the rental return in Seward. It was a bit of a drive, but full of anticipation. Garrett fooled around with the radio station, driving Virginia and Jacob up a wall. It was close to dinnertime and Virginia brought with her some biscuits and jelly to hold them over until they got home. Spaghetti was sitting in a crockpot. Meatless, of course.

A happy reunion it was. After quick hugs, they all drove in her truck with endless chatter, except when their mouths were full of biscuits and jelly. Tyrus and Ember hid. Trying to act as natural as possible, the guys and Virginia checked the house and property to be sure it was safe. Barks and snorts were continual. The dogs and Mr. Horns must have sensed Ember and got excited. Hooves pounding the ground, the horses ran back and forth around the pasture. Virginia purposely didn't turn on the outside light so they could make it into the house without being seen. The guys brought in the luggage through the back door because it was darker there.

"You look good with a tan," Garrett told Ember.

"Speaking of a tan, you do as well. But something is missing,"

Virginia remarked rubbing her chin. Then she looked back at Tyrus. "Hhhh! It's your beard and mustache. They're gone."

"Wow! That knocked five years off of you, boss," Garrett spoke.

"What a handsome face. Don't you ever grow that bristly beard and mustache back. It hid way too much of the good, strong stuff," Virginia insisted.

"All right, enough of that. I smell something really good," Tyrus said changing the subject.

"I just have to bake the garlic bread and dinner will be served. Please be sure the drapes are closed tightly. Looks like you and I will be bunking together, Tania."

Ember just smiled at Virginia.

After dinner they discussed everything that happened. Before long, Tyrus' head fell back, and snoring took over. The guys escorted him to bed, and they used the living room to sleep. Ember and Virginia were so exhausted, when their heads hit the pillow, they were out fast.

After breakfast the next morning, slush splattered on the driveway. Tyrus and Ember hid, while the rest of them made certain there was nothing that would create suspicion of their return.

Jacob answered the door as Aaron pushed his way inside. Looking around fretfully, he asked, "Have they returned yet?"

"Nope. Check for yourself." His brows arched. "You okay Aaron? You look deathly sick." Aaron glared at him with hatred.

"We have looked everywhere for them. They didn't just vanish into thin air, did they?"

"Your guess is as good as ours," Garrett spouted annoyed.

"Wait! Before you leave, you said 'we' looked everywhere for them. Who is we?" Virginia asked. The guys stared him down. His face was looking worse by the minute. "I meant me."

"Why are you looking for them?" Jacob asked accusingly.

"I miss her. That's all."

"Looks like you miss her too much." Garrett closed the door and stood in front of it. Aaron slowly began to sweat.

"I've gotta go. Move out of my way."

"Or what?" Garrett countered.

The sweat started to turn to globs of soot. He began to panic. He shoved Garrett aside and ran out the door. Jacob bent down to examine the glob that was more than sweat. He pinched his nose together. "What is this disgusting stuff? It dripped off of Aaron."

Virginia and Garrett bent down and quickly stood back. "I don't know, but by the smell of it, it smells like decay. Death."

They both locked eyes. "This is not normal. Could he be an alien?" Garrett said with a horror-filled face.

"Who knows. Please use gloves and disposable wipes to clean this up. Throw it in the trash can outside. Check for more on the porch or driveway. We can't leave that stuff around. I have this feeling that it's toxic."

The guys crinkled their faces and did as they were told. Scrubbing the skin off of their hands, it felt, because they did not want to chance the result of coming into contact with that contamination.

Jacob's parents left so they wouldn't be in the way. Even though they sensed something was wrong, nobody spoke about it. Besides, they and Jacob had a standoffish relationship, so it was more than the right time to leave. Jacob and Garrett asked if they could work in the pasture. Tyrus agreed as long as they stuck together and carried a shotgun. He and Ember would have to remain in hiding.

He tinkered with repairs while Ember helped clean up in the house. She dreaded it and hated housework, but she didn't complain. Virginia had kept the place nice and clean, so there wasn't much to it. The guys had been taking care of the stalls and feeding all the animals. Miss Prissy was begging to come inside. She wouldn't be quiet.

"Please, Tyrus," Ember pleaded.

"Just for a little while, but you stay with her. Virginia will need to open the door and we will need to get out of the way."

Excited clicks ran through the kitchen door. Ember played with her for an hour or more. Then Virginia escorted Miss Prissy out to the stable, against Ember's contesting.

Four wheelers skidded on the driveway. Frantic voices outside grew louder. At first Tyrus grabbed Ember and hid her in a closet that was set up so nobody would recognize it as a hiding spot. The door flung open and slammed against the wall. The guys were trying to catch their breath.

"Boys, you're scaring me," Virginia responded.

"We...We found a young lady, tiny like Tania, lying in the pasture. We can't tell if she's alive or dead." Jacob rushed the words out of his mouth.

"Oh my. Oh my. I need to ask Tyrus what to do. Sit tight."

She poked her head in the closet. "The guys found this tiny lady in the pasture, but they don't know if she's alive or dead." She heard Ember gasp.

"Have them drive your truck and bring her in the house. Maybe Garrett can use his truck to bring the doctor out. That is, unless he's added more dents to it and not able to drive it," his questionable face said.

"Okay. Don't come out until we feel it's safe." She instructed the boys what to do. They took off.

The young lady was bleeding from the head. At first, they were scared to touch her and kept withdrawing their hands. Finally, Jacob insisted they just pick her up. Before long she was lying on a blanket in the bed of the truck and Garrett was riding in the back with her.

Virginia held the door open as the guys lifted her carefully out of the truck bed. They brought her inside and laid her on Tyrus' bed, then Garrett sped his tires in the gravel and drove to find the doctor.

Tyrus and Ember came out of hiding and examined the little lady. He felt for a pulse, but it was really weak. They wrapped her in blankets and kept a clean rag on her wound.

Tyrus stood back and looked at Ember. "Tania, does she look familiar to you?"

She stared and stared, wanting a memory to come out, but as usual, she couldn't bring it up. Frustrated, she paced the floor. "I just can't figure anything out. When can I be of help? When?"

Virginia's warmth comforted her. "Don't get upset. It's not

your fault. But take a close look. She is about your size and age. I am getting a strange feeling about her like we do about you."

"Yes, except I have no feelings or memory. None. But I have something to show you both."

"She's a magnificent little lady, just like you," Tyrus mentioned. "Correct me if I'm wrong, but do either of you see her hair or face glittering?"

Ember and Virginia both nodded yes.

"I'll be right back," Ember said.

Virginia and Tyrus looked confused at each other. Within seconds Ember's feet tapped quietly down the stairs. She held a child's book out. Virginia grabbed it.

"I don't understand."

"Just look through it and see if anything looks familiar in any way," Ember pleaded to Virginia.

She and Tyrus sat on the couch together and looked closely at the title. They turned to the first page, but nothing stuck out. They turned to the next page and the one after that until they saw a closer view of the little girl. She turned to look at Tyrus, then to Ember.

"I'm not quite sure if this is what you intend for us to see, but the little girl does have a resemblance to you," Virginia noted.

"Look at her hair and eyes. Look above her left cheekbone," Tyrus added.

Virginia pulled the book up closer, grabbed a pair of reading glasses and viewed it more clearly. Her eyes looked forward like she had seen a ghost. Tyrus followed suit. Ember crossed her legs, and the top one wiggled up and down constantly.

"This little girl has the same glittery hair and skin, and specks of gold in the eyes, a lot like yours," Virginia said pointing to the picture.

"And the girl who looks like you has the exact same birthmark in the exact same place on the face as you do. And I may be a little delusional but is that birthmark on the girl's face swirling with glitter?" he asked dumbfounded.

"Oh my word. How can that be?" Virginia asked mystified. She felt the birthmark on that page and jumped back with a gasp. "It vibrated. I don't understand any of this. Where did you get this book?" Virginia asked stunned.

"I found it under the bed upstairs."

The palm of Tyrus' hand smacked his forehead. "The young lady who used to live here must have left it. She was a child's author. What's the author's name, Virginia?"

"Just Galaxas. No last name."

"That's her. She wrote it. I have met her, and she too had strange things about her. Not like horrible, strange or weird strange, but like she didn't fit in with Earth strange. I can't explain it. But wait! Galaxas and her mother had a light green or gray skin color. Sometimes Aaron has a grayish tint to his skin tone. Maybe this has something to do with them, not Tania?"

"Except that Aaron is looking for Tania, not Galaxas. Now I remember that girl. There was something really special about her, too. People called her a freak because of her skin and eye conditions. I found her most pleasant and impressive, like you, Tania. There wasn't a bad bone in her body. She was sweet, intelligent, creative and a kind young lady. Such a pity people made fun of her condition. I wonder where they went," Virginia said looking up in thought.

"This could really be of help to us if we could find her. Maybe she has some information that would be beneficial," Tyrus wondered out loud. "Unfortunately, we have no way of finding them."

"Don't give up, any of you," Virginia said in a scolding voice. "There's this feeling in the pit of my stomach that when all is revealed, we're not going to be able to comprehend any of it. We are going to find out things about Tania that will bless our soul. You wait and watch."

Two vehicles pulled in the driveway. Doctor Wilson walked into the house with Garrett. Bag in hand. He led him directly to Tyrus' bedroom.

"Her pulse is low. We need to get her to my office so I can better treat her. Since you know nothing about her, we will have to test her blood and see what type it is. Let's not waste time. Put her in the back of my car and you two boys follow me. I will need help in removing her from my car. Have you contacted the sheriff yet?"

Jacob searched Virginia's face. "I was just about to do that. He'll probably show up at your office."

"Good. That's good. No time to waste, help me move her boys."

Ember sat with her fingers crossed. It would be nice to have someone else around like her. Maybe all the attention wouldn't always be on her and even better, maybe they are sisters or good friends. Her shoulders rose as she inhaled her hopeful thoughts. Pipsqueak, shorty, and fairy girl the guys were always calling her. Alone in her room, she remembered walking in the room to see the tiny lady lying there, lifeless and so young. Something sentimental had stirred her heart, but two and two wouldn't come together. It never comes together. She bowed her head and wept.

Chapter Forty-Three

The phone rang, shattering the nerves of everyone in the room. Ember ran down the stairs. All waiting to hear news of the injured lady's progress.

Virginia listened to the person speaking on the other side of the line. "Uh-huh. Oh my. Really!? We'll get back to you."

They crowded around her. She pushed her head back, needing space. Tyrus noticed and used his hands to move everybody back. "Go ahead, Virginia."

"You probably already guessed. I don't know why it shocks me anymore. So, she has the same blood type as, guess who?"

Everyone turned to face Ember. "Me?" she asked confused pointing to herself.

"And that's not all. The girl—I'm sorry for calling her a girl. It's just that you both are tiny like a child."

"Virginia, we all know that. Go on, please," Tyrus impatiently insisted.

"The little lady elevated slightly from the bed a few times. It freaked the doctor out."

Once again, all eyes landed on Ember.

"Will she survive?" Garrett asked concerned. "She is a real beauty."

"She needs blood, and Tania is the only one with her type. We need to get her over there now."

It sounded like a stampede, as fast as they ran for the door. "Wait! We have to be sure it's safe to leave," Tyrus reminded them.

"I'll drive quickly to the bunkhouse and grab something and return. That way if someone is watching, it won't look like anything strange to them. As I leave, hide behind the house. When I return, I will run into the house carrying something and you and Tania climb in the truck, dark side of it. Then I'll come out and drive off again."

"That's better than nothing. Go ahead," Tyrus instructed.

Garrett walked out, yelling back towards the house. "I'll be right back. I need to grab some stuff at the bunkhouse, Jacob."

To make it look sincere, Jacob shouted back before closing the door. "Okay, but hurry. The game is going to start."

Out along the field fence, a few eyes watched the whole production. Jacob had driven like a teenager down the drive. When he returned the clothes, a box in his hand, he entered the house, leaving the truck parked where one side of it would be in the dark. Thankfully the ceiling light didn't work so Tyrus and Ember could crawl in the backseat without being noticed.

The door to the house swung open. "Why do I have to go? I'll miss the kickoff. You're a jerk, Jacob."

"Just go, or I'll knock your block off," Jacob said frustrated, playing his part.

"Okay Rock'em Sock'em Robots. That was corny; huh?"

"Garrett!!!"

"Hey, you want to play with them when I get back?" Garrett asked in sincerity.

"No! I'm watching the game." This time Jacob's frustrated tone wasn't an act.

"Just popcorn? Because I'm not going back out," Garrett informed Jacob.

"Yes. Just go!"

He jumped in the truck and sped out. Their plan worked. They arrived at the doctor's office and quickly ran inside. Garrett went to the store to get popcorn before they closed and left his truck parked there. It was just blocks from the doctor's office.

Inside the office, the nurse hurried Ember to the room and began to draw her blood. She would have to remain there all night. Tyrus planned to stay as well. The IV dripped into the young lady's veins. Her color was brighter, but the only thing that proved she was alive was a very low pulse. The doctor listened to Ember's pulse to compare with the patient lying on the table. Embers was still weird compared to a human beings, but faster than the unconscious patient's.

The doctor placed a hand around Tyrus' shoulder and pulled him aside. "I'm concerned about this one. If she doesn't pull through tonight, I suggest taking her back to your house and keep her comfortable. Maybe she'll be the memory boost Tania needs."

"Thank you, Doc, for all you've done and for keeping this hush-hush. Harry should be stopping by shortly. Go home. Tania and I will be fine on our own. If anything happens, I'll call you right away."

"If you mean it, I may just do that. Thanks."

"Thank you. Now, get out of here."

"Garrett, you need to head home to keep up appearances," Tyrus said in an authoritative voice.

"Okay, Boss. Take care and call me if you need help with anything." He took one last look at the unconscious lady, laid a hand on her arm and left.

When Garrett opened the door, Jacob yelled, "What took you so blasted long?" He wasn't kidding, though. Garrett's wrinkled face, a little defensive too, showed his confusion.

"You going to just stand there or make popcorn?"

Garrett threw the box at him. "Go ahead."

"You two calm down. I'll make it." As Virginia entered the kitchen she heard snorts, and under-the-radar words she would never use, along with a few threats of a boxing match. "Boys!"

"We're not boys!" Jacob reminded her.

"Men, please come in here."

Not wanting to miss any of the game, they both huffed into

the kitchen, eyes of missiles waiting to be ejected. "Please calm yourselves down." She lowered her voice. "I just want to ask how the patient is doing."

Garrett lowered his eyes. "It's not looking good."

"Oh my. That dear, sweet young lady. It's just terrible."

"Tyrus and Tania are staying the night."

"I figured as much. Go on now. I don't want you to miss that important game." The television exploded with cheers from the living room. Jacob and Garrett looked into each other's eyes. Their hands formed a fist as they exited. She heard more grumbling and those darn under-the-radar words that she would address if it happened again.

"You like her, don't you Garrett?"

"What foolishness are you speaking of?"

Jacob formed a knowing smile. "You know that little injured beauty."

Garrett pushed his body around to face him as he relaxed in the recliner. "Why do you always get the recliner?"

"Simple, I'm the oldest."

With a puckered mouth, Garrett began to rise.

"So, are you in love with her?"

Words spitting from his mouth. "You act like a child. How could I be in love with someone I have never spoken to? Idiot."

"You're right. But you're attracted to her."

A fist formed, and carefully formed words emerged. "Have some respect for her; would you? How insensitive can you be?"

Jacob pushed his hands out a few times. "You're right. I'm sorry. I don't know why I'm acting like such a jerk. I'm sorry, Gar."

Garrett's fist relaxed and he stepped backwards.

Jacob jumped off the recliner. "Here, you sit on it. I have been hogging it."

Eyes wide and wondering if it was a trap, Garrett cautiously walked over and jumped down fast before Jacob could change his mind. Jacob gave a quick nod of his approval and relaxed on the couch, legs reaching to the other side, head resting on a pillow.

Drat! Why didn't I think to do that? Garrett thought with puckered lips.

The kitchen door swung open and rattled back and forth a few times before it stopped. The guys sat up eager to dispose of the delectable tastes awaiting. Inside their mouths it felt like pop rocks were exploding, it was so tasty. Virginia set the tray on the table and each one of them grabbed a bowl and soda. Moans of joy followed.

"Hey, Gar, is this a different kind of popcorn?"

"Yeah. I thought we could give it a try."

"Good choice. Hey, I'll play that robot boxing game with you after the game if you want."

"Sure. That would be great."

Virginia giggled to herself. They could grumble and berate each other with a fierceness and turn around and be best friends that quickly. To be young. Carefree. A long life ahead.

~

After breakfast and chores, Jacob made up an excuse to go into town. He was picking Tyrus and Tania up, and unfortunately, an unconscious young lady who showed no signs of improvement. Virginia worked to replace clean sheets, comfy pillows and to air out Tyrus' bedroom for her.

Jacob drove Virginia's truck to the back door. As fast as possible, they carried the young lady into the house, IVs of all sorts inserted in her body, and an oxygen concentrator was necessary, nasal prongs attached to her nose. She was tiny enough that Tyrus could carry her while the others supported the other devices.

The mood in the house was filled with reticence.

Ember walked sluggishly to the window. She lowered to sit on the window seat and held her chin in her hands, elbows resting on the glass. She jumped sky high. When she turned to face everyone, her eyes showed fear. Stuttering at first, she pointed. "Some people are standing outside in the driveway."

Nobody had paid attention to her sitting in the window,

because they were too gloomy to notice. "You're not supposed to sit in the window. What if they saw you?" Garrett scolded her.

"Do you know who it is?" Tyrus asked.

Her head nodded no.

"How many of them are out there?"

"Four."

Tyrus jumped up and peeked around the curtain. Garrett had closed them. "It can't be!"

Chapter Forty-Four

Standing like a popsicle, Tania confessed, "I'm scared."

"No, Tania. I'm sorry for scaring you. I know these people. I just don't understand why they didn't drive up in a vehicle and why they are walking."

"Who are they, Tyrus?" Virginia huffed, throwing one of her hands up, trying to peek out the window.

"The people who owned this house previously. Let me go out and speak with them."

"I know Galaxas, Nebulane and her husband, Mitchell. Can I come?"

"Wait! I can't go out there. Virginia, if you feel it's safe, bring them inside."

A knocking on the door stirred all of them. Tyrus motioned to Ember to hide. They hid behind the kitchen door, ears up against it.

Virginia opened the door, and a big smile spread across her face. "Nebulane. Galaxas. Mitchell. What a surprise," she rattled off staring at Troid.

"We expected Tyrus to open the door." After saying that a hand flew to Nebulane's mouth. "I noticed your place has been burned down. I'm really sorry."

"Please come on in and take a seat. Guys?"

"Oh, sorry." They jumped up and studied them with suspicion and inquisitive eyes.

She pointed to each of them, "Jacob, Garrett, please meet Galaxas, Nebulane, Mitchell, and ..."

"Troid," Galaxas added. "My husband." Virginia gave an approving nod.

"They owned this home previously." The guys nodded suspiciously, still not speaking.

"Jacob and Garrett work for Tyrus and live in the bunkhouse."

"Where is Tyrus?" Nebulane asked.

"Why, I don't rightfully know," Virginia stuttered.

Nebulane's brows rose.

"What brings you by?"

"We received telecommunication that something was wrong here, plus we wanted to see the place again. It looks nothing like it did when Galaxas lived here, except for that rattily screen door." She chuckled.

"Yes. Tyrus wanted to turn it into a ranch."

"Well, it looks great," Mitchell said joining the conversation.

"Telecommunication?" Garrett said out loud like it was a word that belonged in a Sci-Fi movie.

"Long story," Galaxas inserted.

The guys were intimidated by Troid's so very tall, muscular build. They couldn't take their eyes off of him or Nebulane and Galaxas, because of their skin and hair tones and unnaturally thick eyeglasses.

"Virginia, is something going on around here?"

"What do you mean?"

"I sense fear, and to be honest, I can see Tyrus and some tiny lady through the kitchen door. Confide in us. We may be able to help," Nebulane remarked with sincerity.

The kitchen door squeaked slowly open. Tyrus and Ember walked out.

Slapping both hands to her mouth to cover the gasp, a loud "Hhhh!" escaped. Troid grabbed Galaxas' arm and made her face him.

"Are you in danger?"

Head in a constant shaking, she managed to say, "No-no-no. It's not that."

"What is it then?"

She got up and walked to Ember. Ember's face showed terror. Galaxas picked up one of her hands, looked shocked and pleasantly surprised, and then whispered, "Ember?"

Virginia stumbled backwards as Tyrus grasped the wall.

"What did you just call her?" Tyrus asked.

Galaxas turned to him and recited her name. "Ember."

"Pines?" Virginia asked with unbelief.

"Yes, that's right."

Tyrus and Virginia were speechless and lightheaded. Mitchell and Nebulane grabbed ahold of their arms and helped them to sit on the couch.

"It can't be," Virginia commented staring at the coffee table.

"Can't be what?" Garrett shouted loud enough to have all eyes on him.

"Who is Ember Pines?" Jacob threw out.

"I wish I had my book," Galaxas said looking to the floor in thought.

"Just a minute. I'll be right back." Ember ran up the stairs, almost in flight.

Troid pulled Galaxas into his arms. "You said she was real. Amazing."

Ember walked up to Galaxas and held the book out to her. She took it and tears blurred inside her customized glasses. It was the first time Troid wore them, and he was always fussing with them. He hated wearing them.

"I don't understand. How can this be real?" Galaxas mumbled to herself.

"So, she is the girl in that story?" Tyrus hesitantly asked.

"Yes. I know it's her. I feel it inside my soul, and she is identical right down to the birthmark. But I don't understand. Why are you here? You're not allowed to be seen by humans."

"Neither were we," Nebulane interjected caressing Galaxas' shoulder.

"What? I am so confused," Tyrus said, dropping his head in his hands.

"So, Tania, or Ember, is a real fairy?" Virginia said embarrassed, not looking at anyone's faces.

"Yes, she is a fairy," Galaxas replied with warmth. "That's evidently not how they refer to themselves where they're from, but that is how we identify them. I'm thinking they are called Ma Ozions."

Tyrus needed an explanation before an asylum was to be notified to pick him up. "I found Ember on the ground around the side of my house. She was unconscious but woke up the second I touched her. She has no memory of who she is and how she got here.

"That explains the glowing, elevating, powers to heal animals and the bond," he spoke like he was carrying on a conversation with another person in his head. Then he looked up. "Something weird is going on around here. This huge thing in the sky that looks like a pair of wicked eyes keeps tormenting us, and a young man named Aaron keeps looking for her. He's a weird one, too. This disgusting goop falls off of him lately and he runs off when it starts happening."

"Oh no! The Eryndomnites have regained access into the kingdom. They'll destroy it and Ember."

Ember was quiet all this time. With a soft voice, she asked, "My name is Ember, and I am a fairy?"

Galaxas looked at her with sympathetic eyes. "Yes, and a very special one. You are a princess for the animal kingdom. You have powers to heal and take care of them." She choked up realizing the story she wrote was true and seeing how special Ember is.

"Do I have a husband or boyfriend?"

"Yes. When you grow up, or grew up, you were to marry Prince Ari."

"Aaron reminds me of someone, but I'm not sure why."

Tyrus handed Galaxas a picture of Aaron from his cellphone.

"Wow! That looks exactly like Prince Ari grown up. You say he acts weird, and this sooty stuff falls off of him?"

"Yes, that's right."

"First off, in my story it is part of a transformation from good to evil. It appears he was disguised to look like Ari to keep tabs on you, Ember. They can't be around for too long of a period before their disguise wears off. Your life is detrimental to the animal kingdom and even mankind. Our people are assigned as watchmen throughout the solar system. We noticed the commotion and decided to come back here to see if help was needed."

"So, you're aliens?" Garrett's surprised voice asked.

"You can say that, but we call ourselves watchmen, God's soldiers in the air, sort of a form of like angels. We're the good guys. He even created us with Jesus' eyes as described in Revelation. His eyes were 'like a flame of fire', and so are ours. Troid, would you mind showing them."

He lifted the glasses away from his eyes and rays of light shot out. His eyes looked and shined like miniature suns.

Tyrus had to wave a magazine near Virginia's face. This was all too much.

"We're sorry, Tyrus. I know this is a lot to hear and accept. I was sent here to escape an evil army taking over our planet. Galaxas didn't know about our world until Troid came searching for her. You see, our mates are determined at birth. Everything is good now on our planet and King Troid and Queen Galaxas are a mighty team; good, honest, blessed of God. We believe the Lord sent us back here to help," Nebulane explained.

"I fear we are running out of time. Please explain all that is happening," Galaxas urged.

"At the moment, we have an injured girl in my bedroom that is probably one of Ember's," stopping for a moment to digest her name and royalty, "people. The guys found her unconscious with a wound to the head," Tyrus mentioned. "Diagnosis looks bad for her," Tyrus said, face showing questions of his sanity.

"Mom, you have to try," Galaxas said with force.

"Not sure if it will work, but I will try."

"Try what?" Garrett asked worried.

"God gave me a blessed gift of healing. I will try my best. I'm not sure if it will work on the inhabitants of Ma Oz because of their God-given powers. Please direct me to the room."

Garrett walked over and opened the door. Nebulane went in and looked with sorrow at the innocent victim. Please allow me to close the door and pray before I begin."

Nobody spoke, but many heads dropped and praying hands formed. In minutes, a glow came from underneath the door. It kept growing in strength. The suspense in the air was climbing and intense.

Ember gripped Tyrus' arm. The glow faded and the door slowly opened.

Drained, Nebulane walked out taking big breaths. Faces in the living room looked glum.

Then a sight like a ray of sunshine walked out. She was healed. The enchanting young lady ran up to Ember and hugged her, tears splashing on their arms. Ember was stiff, so Sharley stood back and looked in Ember's eyes.

Noticing the confusion in Ember's face, she acknowledged, "Ember, it's me, Sharley."

Groans of happiness filled the air. Tyrus almost looked sad, as though his thoughts betrayed his innermost fear of losing Ember, Tania to him always.

Galaxas walked up and placed a warm hand on Sharley. "She has no memory. None."

"That doesn't surprise me. Addley tried to kill me, her and that witch, Malvoil."

"They almost succeeded, I dread to say. My mom, Nebulane, is the one who was given the powers to heal you."

Sharley walked up and embraced her. "Thank you so much. You not only rescued me, but probably Ember, as well. Hhhh!"

"What is it dear?"

"Addley is trying to trick Prince Ari into marrying her. I'm almost positive she has accepted the mark of King Eryn. They are going to destroy our kingdom once again. We have to stop them."

A truck skidded on the icy driveway to a halt. Jacob peeked through the curtains. "It's Aaron!"

"Everyone hide," Tyrus demanded. "But wait! Sharley, would you peek out and see if he looks like this Ari fellow?"

She peeked out and almost fell over. "It is him."

"No, it's not," Galaxas interrupted. "He has to be an Eryndomnite disguised as Ari."

"Everyone, hide now."

Jacob, Garrett and Virginia sat down trying to calm themselves down before answering. Fat chance of that. A fist pounded heavily on the door.

"Stay cool," Virginia reminded Jacob.

He opened the door. "Aaron, we meet again and so soon."

Aaron barged inside. "I know she's here. Where is she?!"

"You're referring to Tania, I presume."

Dark, evil eyes peered through his. "You know I am. I want to know where she's at."

"How many times do we have to tell you she's not here?"

"I don't believe you anymore."

"Search the house then. Go on."

Aaron ran down the hall, peeked his head in Tyrus' bedroom. "What's all that stuff?"

"Virginia came down with a terrible virus. The doctor put her on IVs," Jacob shot forth.

She pretended to have a coughing attack. "I'm much better. I may need some oxygen, Jacob, if you don't mind."

"I'll get that now."

Aaron rushed around, ran upstairs and back down. His clothes showed a dampness. The book *Ember Pines* rested on the coffee table. He gave it a skeptical once over, and since he couldn't read the English language, returned his attention to the room. "You'll be sorry if I find out you're hiding her."

"We allowed you the opportunity to look around. We don't know where she is at. And by the way, who do you think you are coming in our house and speaking to us like that?" Jacob snarled.

Stench filled the air, and a sooty blob fell off of Aaron as he slammed the door behind him. His vehicle clanged and screeched on the drive out.

Everyone rushed out to the living room.

Sharley squeezed her nose.

"Gross, more of his goop dripped on the floor. I know. I know, clean it up," Jacob said disgusted.

Sharley examined it. She backed away fast. "This soot is toxic. It will kill us."

"Will it kill us?" Jacob asked as he gulped.

"That I don't know."

As Jacob reached for the door handle to check that they were alone, some of the soot was on the handle and his hand wrapped around it. He stopped suddenly, turned around and fell to the floor.

Chapter Forty-Five

"Hot water and soap now. Please. Antibacterial wipes and bleach, also," Nebulane insisted.

Virginia had boiled water for tea and poured it in a kettle with dish soap. It sloshed all over the floor, making a trail from the kitchen to the living room where they laid Jacob on the couch. Gloves and a garbage bag were handed to her, and she moved quickly to clean it off Jacob. Garrett wore gloves to remove the garbage bag and gloves from Nebulane.

"Please give me some room." She tilted her head to heaven and prayed in the tongues of angels. Her body leaned over his and a glow encompassed both of them, almost identical to Ember when healing animals. Jacob's body wiggled and shifted. He let out a moan. Soon his eyes tried to open. It took a few times and then he stared around the room. Nebulane stood to her feet.

"I feel just horrible. My head and body aches, and my throat burns. I feel dizzy. What happened?"

"You touched that toxic gooey stuff," Tyrus answered leaning over him.

"It's poisonous?"

"Lethal," Sharley interjected.

They scoured the room and porch area, taking no chances.

Nebulane urged them to gather together and make plans for the upcoming attack.

"Sharley, do you know how to get back to Ma Oz?" Galaxas asked.

"I don't. I just know there has to be a portal somewhere."

"Troid, get in touch with Raiden and Annalee and tell them to transport here immediately and the reason why, please."

"I was just getting ready to do that."

"Sharley, I happen to know you have powers to help us, if needed. As soon as it gets dark, I'll use my eyes to look around for that portal. Maybe the guys who found you can show us that location. It has to be around here somewhere," Galaxas advised taking lead as the queen.

"Galaxas, are you suggesting to enter their realm?" Nebulane asked with a definite tremor in her elocution.

"Yes. It is not safe to bring the Eryndomnites to Earth. People on Earth will have no chance against them. They already have too much to deal with. We need to fight them in their territory."

"I hope our powers will work there."

"Have faith, Mother."

"Is he your husband?" Sharley asked Galaxas looking at Troid.

She smiled with much affection. "Yes, he is."

Sharley gulped. "He is the most gorgeous thing I've ever see, green skin and all."

Galaxas stared at her in disbelief.

"Did I just say that out loud?"

Galaxas nodded her head.

"I'm so sorry. I guess I'm eager to meet my predestined mate. That hasn't happened yet. It's not as though your skin tones are loud. They have a tint of green, is what I meant to say. Please forgive my directness."

"That's okay. I'm just glad everyone else was preoccupied and didn't hear it. I do love that man."

Sharley touched her hand. "I can tell. Maybe I'll take the time to tell Ember about home."

Galaxas looked pleased. "That's a good idea."

Troid walked over to Galaxas. "I heard that conversation."

"That's because you have elephant ears."

"I do not." He touched his ears. She laughed. "I told Raiden to bring a lot of cheese pizza. I'm so excited about that."

She rubbed her stomach. "Gosh, it's been so long. We have to get a recipe."

Just as their stomachs growled, there was a knock on the door. Troid could smell the pizza from where he stood. "Stand back!" He wanted first dibs on the pizza making it sound like an urgent matter. "I'll get the door. Stand back everyone." Galaxas broke out in laughter.

Sharley was once again enamored by the presence of another gorgeous guy, Raiden. Galaxas strolled over to her and nudged her elbow. "You're doing it again."

"I don't mean to be a flirt. I'm really not that way. The only justification I have is when Ember got engaged, it caused a desire in my heart. What's taking so long?"

"Did Ari turn out to be quite handsome?"

"Are you kidding? Between these two guys and him, they could rule worlds."

"That good, huh?"

"Oh yeah."

"Hey, it will happen for you. I think once all of this chaos ends, you will be struck by lightning love."

"Maybe you're right. Those two earthlings aren't so bad either."

She pulled Sharley with her. "You got it bad, sister. Don't you go near my man or Annalee's until that is taken care of for you. Got it?"

With a sheepish grin, she answered, "Got it."

"Wow! Looks like you were on the money about the trouble," Annalee mentioned looking apprehensive at Sharley and not knowing why.

"How was the visit with your mom?"

Annalee grabbed both of her arms, a couple of tears dropped, and a sentimental smile developed. "Great. She got help and quit drinking and she attends church. She has a lot of health issues due to alcohol consumption, but she is so different. Mom was kind and welcoming and treated Raiden like a piece of treasure. My heart still has a pitter patter beat going."

Galaxas, extremely happy for her, drew her into a tight embrace. "My heart is leaping inside."

"How are you doing about finding out Ember is real? I'm saying, mind blowing."

Thinking before speaking, Galaxas answered, "Maybe God put her story in my mind for just this occasion, so we can help her."

"I was thinking the same thing. Look at my arm." She held it up. "Look!"

The hair on her arms stuck straight up. "Annalee, I could never survive one day without you. I thank God for you." She couldn't help but think how Annalee never knew about her own secret power. The power to bring laughter to intense situations.

"Back at ya. Now, let's kick some butt. By the way, now that I'm pregnant, does my butt still look toned? I can't tell." She was twisting her head to a very uncomfortable position to check.

"You're still the biggest goof. Since you're with "chili," you get this instead of a shove."

Galaxas puckered up and kissed her cheek so hard that Annalee groaned in pain."

"How do I deliver a bowl of chili?" Annalee cracked up after saying that.

"What foolishness are you speaking about?" Galaxas said with a raised brow and scrunched up nose.

"You said since I'm with chili."

Galaxas puckered her lips. "You know very well I meant child."

Annalee rubbed her face where Galaxas kissed her. "That mouth been working out or something?"

"Or something," Troid interjected with a mischievous smile on his face as he walked up. "Did Galaxas tell you the news?"

"What? What news? I will knock your socks off young lady unless you tell me now." Annalee rolled a fist around. Nebulane and Mitchell joined them to listen to the news again. Their smiles were pretty revealing.

Galaxas grabbed Troid's hand and spilled the beans. "I'm going to have a little Troid."

"Or a little Galaxas," he added with a proud smile.

She and Annalee jumped around and screamed like girls.

"Hey, you are not going to battle in your condition. I won't let you," Annalee said forcefully.

Placing a hand on her shoulder, Galaxas replied. "That's why we're here. I feel it in my heart that God wants us to fight with them and that's why He had me write this story. I have to go. I'll be careful."

With a removal of her hand, Galaxas summoned Jacob, Sharley and Troid to follow her to search for the portal.

Sharley noticed a spot that had a very tiny amount of sparkle. "This has to be it."

"Mark the spot, please," Galaxas demanded in queen formation.

Throwing hands up to their faces to cover the scent of rotting decay, Galaxas and Troid gave each other a knowing look. Brimstone Mountain.

Chapter Forty-Six

Ari walked over to Addley's, stomach in knots, and feeling like he couldn't catch his breath. He swallowed hard before knocking on the door. When it opened, Addley was dressed in a soft, lilac fabric dress. It had the look of ragged, romantic cut fabric that blew every which way in a breeze. A flower crown rested on her head.

"You look beautiful."

She folded in her lips and fluttered her lashes. "Thank you, my prince."

"When we get back here, I need to know if Ember is alive or not. Otherwise, our wedding will be null and void because of our laws. We have to do this right."

"Are you asking me to marry you?"

With a fake tenderness in his eyes, he admitted, "Yes, I guess I am."

"I accept." She leaped into his arms and kissed him passionately. Finally able to squeeze his hands between him and her, he pushed her backwards. "Slow down there," he said taking a deep breath. "Let's get this over with so we don't have to stop doing this." He turned his face and rubbed his burning lips.

With a deep intake of air and pleased smile, she said, "Better hurry up. Don't think I will last much longer."

He didn't know if that meant her transformation or her lust. "One more thing. I'm sorry I don't have a ring for you. The one I gave Ember would have been perfect."

"Don't you worry. I have a surprise for you, but to your grand-parents house we must go."

"I think we'll take the quick way. They rose in the air and arrived at the king and queen's castle in minutes. It was planned in advance that an army of gallant soldiers would remain in hiding. Ari was informed that the end result was a presage to Addley's demise, not to mention lead them to Ember. There was no other way, and death was part of the transformation.

"Prince Ari, Addley, do you come with news?" King Berthold asked.

"No. I come with other news."

His parents and Ember's parents enclosed them in a circle.

"Please, elaborate."

"I don't want to be prince. I won't be prince, and I am going to marry Addley. I love her."

Yelling and arguing took hold. Lectures and warnings followed.

"It's final. I am going to marry Addley ere long." He grabbed her hand, and they left the castle as cries and disbelief prevailed. They were back at her place in a jiff.

King Dillon stood silently in thought. *Ari's performance was so convincing; almost too convincing. Dear God, let his acting be real and not betoken of his acceptance to King Eryn. Dear, dear God. I beg of you.*

"That was magnificent," Addley remarked with a sensual tone, pushing herself up to him.

Think fast. "Now, I have to figure out a way to find out if Ember is alive or dead before we can wed. Oh, and a ring. I have to find one."

"I have a surprise. Wait 'til you see this." She pointed her finger and the door flew open. Something swirled and shimmered coming directly to her. She grabbed it. Could he hide the fury inside of him? His fists tightened so hard that he had to extend the fingers out back and forth to get circulation going again. His emotions were everywhere after seeing Ember's ring. Angry. Excited. Sad. His mind felt like a game of ping pong.

"See. I knew you would want me to have this ring. Now you have to place it on my finger."

He took the ring, fingers a little shaky. *This is for Ember. I can do this. God, help me.*

"Ari?"

"Yes, the moment we've waited for all our lives. You and me, the way it should have been. But wait! How did you get this ring?"

"Never mind that. It's always belonged to me. Now, where were we?"

He placed it on her finger and gulped. Without looking at her prideful face, he stared at the ground. She tilted his head and kissed him, losing her balance at the thought of them. Moans of pure satisfaction made Ari want to retch.

She did it. Queen Malvoil will advance their positions to the highest level. She and Ari would reign in their kingdom. And she was foolish enough to believe that.

He pushed her back. Flora and Arwood seethed with scorn at having to watch her betrayal. King Dillon remained in a constant state of prayer. Even though they knew it was all an act, planned by all of them, just seeing him place Ember's ring on her finger was like sticking a knife in Ember's heart. But they had to hold it together.

"I can't marry you until I know for certain Ember is alive or dead. If she agrees to end the relationship, I am free. If she doesn't, she will have to die."

"Aah, that won't be so hard. She has no idea who she is, where she is or why she is there. No memory. She could be dead. I don't really know, but wouldn't that be swell if she were?"

Hiding the tears, he answered, "Yeah, swell," unenthusiastically.

"Let's get this over with. I would like to see the kingdom one last time." He had an army hidden behind him because that would be the safest way to keep them all together.

"You're a sentimental fool. I hope I can keep my body together until then."

His brows furrowed and then he caught on to what she meant. "Let's get going."

They walked and walked. The rest of the kingdom followed invisibly. Even Skyfire.

Chapter Forty-Seven

itting at the kitchen table, the whole household ate blueberry pie and drank milk while planning their attack.

Galaxas looked around, realizing Ember wasn't among them. She meandered out to the living room, but Ember wasn't there either. She softly walked up the stairs. Ember was sitting on the other side of the bed reading a book or staring at it deep in thought. So much so that she didn't hear Galaxas come in.

Ember had the page with Ari's picture lying in her hands. Galaxas touched her shoulder gently and said, "Follow your heart, even if love takes you to the stars in the heavens or down into the depths of the sea. Enter new realms if you have to. And that is what you must do. That is where your true love waits for you."

Using the index finger, Ember wiped a tear under her eye. "I just knew there was someone for me. What if I can't remember him or what he means to me?"

"I can't tell you why God gave me insight into your world. There is no doubt in my mind that He will make sure you get your memory back. You're too valuable to the kingdom and mankind, plus, I have a feeling you are extra-special to Him. I have no facts to back that up, just a gut feeling."

Ember listened intently to the battle Galaxas' planet endured and how they were sent to Earth to escape evil taking over their whole planet, and the tragedy of having to destroy her own father and grandfather. Galaxas explained it in detail. They bonded instantly.

"And did she mention how she couldn't avoid my charms?" Troid said smiling ear to ear.

"You wish, dandelion boy."

Ember looked at them with astonishment, waiting for an explanation, which Galaxas willingly provided.

"Ember, it's time. You need to be brave. We have to get to the portal location."

Nervously, she nodded.

Everyone came to that spot. Raiden and Troid set up an area where the rest of them could watch and be safe.

~

Ari and Addley arrived at the portal. Little did she know that a whole army was hiding behind them. Addley forgot one tiny detail. She was never to cross into another realm without Queen Malvoil's permission. Too unfocused because of Ari's declaration to her, logical thinking went right out the door.

"I have no way of knowing exactly where she is right now, but I will show you where we left her."

"Who's 'we'?"

"Treelin and I were given instructions from Queen Malvoil."

His body twitched at this new information. Queen Malvoil was the depiction of evil, and her husband, King Eryn, was even more diabolical.

Ari knew in the back of his mind that Skyfire was tuned in to Ember's being and would find her immediately. Being in different realms, he didn't have that ability, but once they are in the same realm, that will change.

~

Facing a case of the jitters, Galaxas watched as an area in front of them began to swirl like a horizontal funnel cloud. She had the ability to shield everyone with invisibility. Actually, Ember did too, but she wasn't aware of it because of the memory loss. Sharley didn't have time to explain much of it to her.

As they held their breath, Ari and Addley fell out of the funnel. They pulled themselves up and looked around. Not expecting this outcome, Galaxas and Sharley were surprised to see Ari with Addley. That caused Sharley to stop them from going forward until they could figure out what was going on. Ember stared in silence at Ari, heart racing, fear rising, and not understanding any of the situation going on around them.

"We can't waste time. Show me where you left her."

Addley walked to that location, but the army appeared from behind her. Galaxas and everyone watched in awe. They were in their kingdom forms and the horses were magnificent, just as she described in her book. Suddenly, Skyfire broke away and pawed at the shield. He was whining and snorting, standing up on two legs scratching at the invisible shield.

Addley turned around and Ari grabbed her hands to keep her from using any of her powers. Galaxas realized it was a trick to get her to bring him into Earth's realm. She watched as Addley wiggled and fought against Ari, screaming at him for being a traitor.

"Okay, I'm releasing the shield. Prepare for anything."

Now the army could see them, but they kept Ember hidden until they felt she would be safe. Sharley ran out in front of Galaxas. "We have Ember safe and sound. These people are here to help your people in battle."

By this time Skyfire was uncontrollable and pushed his way through to get to Ember. They backed away and watched the reunion. Ember still had no clue what was going on, but their bond was immediate, precious; so emotional, it brought tears to everyone's eyes.

"Take Addley, Ari demanded."

He ran over to Ember. They stared into each other's eyes for minutes. Everyone else remained silent, overjoyed, tears of gratitude and happy about this magical reunion of true love. A real fairy-tale ending. She stared at him, recognizing him because of

Aaron, but that was all she could manage. Her hand pressed down forcefully on her heart from a sudden burst of emotions running through her body as though she had been electrocuted.

"Prince Ari, she has no memory," Sharley yelled.

King Berthold and Queen Valeska walked up to Ari and Ember. Flora and Arwood were so happy that they couldn't contain their sobs. They all faced her. Tyrus and Virginia watched from the hideout, their eyes a blurry mess, too. They all were stunned at all the different forms the Ma Ozions took on. It was hard to focus on the seriousness of the moment.

"Ember, I am your grandfather, King Berthold. This is your grandmother, Queen Valeska. Your parents, Flora and Arwood are right here, also." Ari couldn't take his eyes off of her.

"Kingdom dwellers, her grief is great. It's time to restore her memory back," the king ordered.

"Only Queen Malvoil has that power," Addley mocked.

The king looked at her and grinned. "She doesn't have the Lord's power. We do." And with that, Ari faced Skyfire and picked up strands of his hair where the birthmark swirled and glimmered. He twisted what looked like a puzzle piece, realizing there must be a way to snap it off, and handed it to the king. It was as if a great force took over his mindset. King Berthold walked up to Ember and spoke softly. "This my dear, sweet granddaughter, will fix everything."

He snapped it against the mark on her face, but the glow vanished. Ember was still without memory.

Addley laughed wickedly.

"I don't understand why this isn't working," the king said worried.

Ari looked over at Addley as she laughed coldheartedly. Suddenly Ember's ring on Addley's finger started swirling and sparkling like the birthmark. The mark on Ember's face began swirling and sparkling in unison. All along, no one in the kingdom had any clue that it had the final power: powers of a love unification between her, Skyfire and Ari. The number three always held meaning of the greatest love, but the king had forgotten all about it since their kingdom had become so lackadaisical. Ari ran over and looked with disgust at Addley. Then he grabbed the ring and pulled.

Stench was filling the area and sweat formed into a sooty substance on Addley's body. He backed away and asked the king to place a force shield around her so she can't escape and contaminate them or the earth itself.

All eyes were on Addley. It looked like her face was liquefying and dripping down her body. How frightening to witness such vulgarness. Remembering their friendship at one time, it brought tears to Ari's eyes.

"Prince Ari, do you know how to get Ember's memory back?" the king asked with urgency.

Ari ran back to them. "I'm not sure, but let's give it a try." He held Ember's hand, and with warm eyes full of love, placed the ring on her finger. He backed up because immediately, sparkly lights started shooting out almost like fireworks and the birthmark began to swirl and glitter once again. When it came to a stop, Ember looked around at everyone. Hands covered her surprised mouth. The sparkly glow encompassed her, Ari and Skyfire in a powerful warmth. Leaning her head against Skyfire, Ari held her hands and they stared with loving eyes at each other for minutes. Sparkly bursts shot out from the three of them. All who watched were smitten by their true love.

Oddly, each and every person lifted their noses and sniffed. Smiles formed. They squeezed themselves as goosebumps spread head to toe. Whispering, each and every one said as if in a trance, "Warm cashmere woven with sunbeams and marshmallows."

King Berthold got excited. "Now, this is what true love smells like."

"I know who I am now." She looked at everyone. I know who you are. Skyfire! Ari! Mum! Papa!

Grandfather! Grandmother! Sharley!" Tears poured down her face and splashed with glittery pastel colors. Hugs and kisses went on for minutes.

Grabbing Sharley's hands, she broke out in shameful tears. "Sharley, can you ever forgive me for doubting you? I'm so sorry."

Sharley hugged her and confirmed, "Of course."

Ember turned to everyone. "Please meet the people who rescued me and who will help us defeat the Eryndomnites." She introduced everyone close to them, then asked Ari and her parents and grandparents to follow her. Tyrus and Virginia stood up, totally hypnotized by seeing everyone in their kingdom forms except Ember and Sharley. Ari decided it best to change his appearance for the moment.

"This man rescued me. He's been like a father to me. And Virginia has been like a mother to me. These guys here are just like brothers. Ember held Tyrus' hand and smiled up at him. "I can't ever repay your kindness. Forgive me for all the danger I put you through. I'll always love you. All of you." Nobody could have stopped the oncoming flood, even with magical powers.

Ember's parents couldn't quit crying but managed to show their gratitude. The king and queen, as well. Even Annalee and Mitchell were in tears. Ari pulled Ember to the side and held both of her hands. His eyes teared up and so did hers. "I love you so much," he declared as tears that glistened swirled down his cheek. In the back of his mind, he would never forget the state of doom he felt if Ember were never found. He had to shake the thoughts off.

Swallowing over and over she reacted. "My love for you reaches heavenly realms," she said while choking on her tears. They embraced and a flash of light beamed over them. Sparkling, twinkling and it spread a warmth over the crowd. There wasn't a dry eye around.

Stuttering, the king spoke to one and all. "The good Lord above is so pleased with this love reunion that he has joined them in a heavenly hug. Now this, dear friends, is truly a match made in heaven."

Galaxas looked at Troid. "How many couples are so blessed in their reunion that the good Lord above embraces them himself? Precious."

As her words ended, both of their hearts shot out light, and a warmth spread through them, including the sunset glow they had produced in the past. They hugged and stood for minutes not wanting this moment to end.

After the sentimental reunion, it was time to defend the Kingdom of Ma Oz and make plans.

Ember Leaned against Ari and Skyfire, and plans were being made to go back to Ma Oz and battle. A loud thud caused everyone to look over. Aaron scrambled to his feet. "Tania, he's a fraud. Please come with me." Prince Ari pushed her behind him. Everyone backed up.

"If you value your life, if that is what you can call it, you better back away. Guards, take him."

But Aaron flew at Ari. He tried to bite him, knowing the venom he carried would kill him, but Ari was too fast and too strong.

Addley yelled in fear for Treelin. "Treelin, stop before you get killed." Even though their lifestyle would be in the form of death, she denied the truth of it to register with her. Treelin had disguised himself as Ari to keep tabs on Ember. But, he certainly never planned to form feelings for her.

Everyone watching the fight didn't realize Addley had broken free and made her way to Ember. With evil eyes, she grit her teeth, soot dropping in globs, face disfigured, she pushed her hand out to use the abilities she still possessed in order to kill Ember.

Ember's heart of gold sank, trying to remember her as a friend and watching her transition to evil caused her not to react like she should have. How many long hours did she and Ari train in situations like this? Galaxas knew this would go badly. Before the king and queen intervened, her eyes shot right through Addley.

Addley fell to the ground. Her flesh started disintegrating. Ember covered her eyes. The guards held Treelin as he screamed for Addley. Ari rushed to Ember's side. He held her tight, and he, himself, became emotional over Addley's body fading away to embers with no way to stop it.

"I'm sorry. I couldn't allow her to kill Ember. Ember is too valuable to the animal kingdom and to mankind," Galaxas shared regrettably.

The king walked up to her and said, "Our kingdom owes you much gratitude. Thank you for saving my granddaughter. Thank you from all of us." His arm waved around the kingdom's inhabitants who had come through the portal with them.

By this time Addley's body was nothing but embers being blown in the wind and snow. Treelin had turned back to himself, exhausted with tormented agony.

The queen walked over to Ari and Ember. She grabbed both of their hands. "The life waiting for her in Brimstone Mountain is not a life. Inconsolably, neither is her afterlife, but it couldn't be helped. We, too, grieve for her."

Chapter Forty-Eight

T he next hour was hard. They had to go through the portal before it closed and wouldn't be able to return until the new moon rose in the kingdom.

Tyrus watched with sadness as Ember strode through the tunnel on Skyfire's back, Ari at arm's length. It was quiet after the final soldiers had gone through. Shortly, a suction sound filled the air and the opening vanished, leaving behind what looked like glitter shooting through the air. That, in itself, was magical to behold.

Treelin was placed in a prison chamber that included contamination safety measures. Galaxas was in awe at the enchanting and magical place of the kingdom. Oddly, it was exactly what she had imagined it to look like in her book. Being on high alert, battle preparations were scheduled before the guests were treated to a hospitality feast and shown to the kingdom's nature inspired, luxurious rooms. Thankfully, the odor that had drifted through the portal from Brimstone Mountain had dissipated, and pleasant, mild floral fragrances lulled peace in their hearts.

Galaxas looked around for Ember. She rested against Prince

Ari's chest. He stroked her hair. Then he tipped her face up and kissed her soft, scrumptious lips. Being in a magical place, glow covered them in an embrace. Galaxas sighed in romantic fulfillment watching their love reunite.

A guard ran in and interrupted the proceedings. "Your Highness, our most gracious and honorable visitor is back."

"You mean..."

"Yes, Your majesty. The highest realm."

The king bolted out the door. Galaxas had a sly smile on her face. She wrote the child's fairy tale, so she knew just who awaited his audience. Troid noticed her faraway look and saw the hair on her arms stand up. He squeezed her. She returned a look that said, *I'm too overwhelmed to speak.* He nodded that he understood.

After the preparations, they would all be given a tour. From what they had already witnessed, they would look at fairy tales in a whole new light.

Ari cupped Ember's face in his hand and looked at her with tenderness. "My heart is trying to leap out of my chest. I don't know if I could have gone on without you in my life. I hated pretending to be in love with Addley for the sake of finding you. At first, I was repulsed, and for the first time ever felt hatred towards her. That is a scary feeling. It felt like I was reaching for the sky trying to grab the embers of our love from scattering in the wind, lost forever, as if there was a physical presence of our love. I thought something happened to you and the thought of living without you wasn't worth living."

"With no memory, I felt the same thing but couldn't bring the memories back to understand these feelings. It felt like embers smoldering inside of my heart," she interjected. They clung to each other like they couldn't chance letting the other go. Then Addley popped up in Ari's thoughts.

"Once Addley started transitioning in front of my eyes, my memory came back to when we all hung out as friends. The sadness I feel towards her is for that friendship, but I still need God's help in forgiving her for what she attempted to do to you."

She placed his hand on her heart. Using a little romantic magic, she said, "Do you feel it?"

"I do. What is happening in there?"

Butterflies flew out and floated in the air. He looked around entranced and tried to do the same, except bumble bees flew out of his heart. He threw his arms out and folded down his lips. She laughed so hard; her arms supported her stomach. But to her surprise, the butterflies and bumble bees comingled in a friendly and beautiful display, then traveled out the window.

"You know, you weren't given the name Ember Pines by mistake, I came to find out."

"How so?"

"Hope of finding true love caused me inexplicable yearning, and love for you burned inside of me like cinders that smolder before going out. I was honestly losing faith in finding you. It was a frightening feeling."

Galaxas and Troid had been eavesdropping, not meaning to, but Galaxas couldn't get over seeing Ember, a fictional character, real, standing right in front of her. Her eyes kept wandering to wherever she was. They were blown away by the beautiful display of love. To be fair to their customs, their hearts would glow when their ordained true love was ready. So, they were used to a little magic themselves.

Chapter Forty-Nine

King Berthold appeared in front of everyone involved in battle preparations. Everyone stopped what they were doing and waited patiently for the message that was delivered to him. There was a heavenly glow about him, brighter and more ominous than their natural glow.

He described the meeting and formalized the final battle plan, reminding the team of the danger involved.

Treelin was interrogated, but realizing he had nothing to lose, he remained silent. Life as an Eryndomnite would be repulsive and lonely. There was no turning back and he knew it. With Addley gone now, he didn't want to live in dreary, frightful conditions the rest of his life by himself. From what he had witnessed, since his transformation wouldn't be complete for a couple more weeks, was that the creatures didn't know who they were or where they were. When commanded, they would kill, bow to the king and queen and do whatever they were instructed. Why didn't he listen to the warnings? He didn't want to live without Addley. The idiocy of thinking he had feelings for Ember faded away after the destruction of Addley.

He even contemplated if Addley and he were ordained to be together. He loved her no matter how much she claimed to be in love with Ari. If he wouldn't have accepted King Eryn's mark, maybe she wouldn't have either. At least he still had some of a conscience. If he disobeyed the king and queen, he would surely die and not have to live under their control.

"Guards! Guards, please let me speak to your king and queen and Prince Ari and Princess Ember. Tell them I have information that I am willing to share."

One of the king's royal guards walked in and handed the king a written message. "My queen, Ari, Ember, please I have news."

They all took turns reading it. "How can we be certain it's not a trap?" Prince Ari insisted.

"We will seek prayer, first and foremost. What does the lad have to lose? He was madly in love with Addley, and now that she has passed, all he has to live for is unholy commands and a lonely, sorrowful life. I have a suspicion Treelin wishes to die before his final transformation takes place. Can you blame him?" The king murmured sadly. "How goes funeral preparations for our dear Addley?"

"I agree with your assessment of Treelin. It twould be better to die, I suppose, but that isn't even a consoling idea. Ember has arranged services for Addley soon. Since she has not conformed to a complete Eryndomnite status, we agree it is fitting we should still celebrate her life as a dear friend," Prince Ari added. Ember nodded.

"Princess Ember, sweet candy of my soul, maybe we should wait a few days and combine the service with Treelin," Ari suggested.

"That does make sense. Certainly."

Ember turned her head to see Ari's finest, most loyal friend and senior guard walk in hand and hand with Sharley. Stars were twinkling in her eyes, and he couldn't take his eyes off of her.

As they approached, Sharley hugged Ember. "I found him. Isn't he just dreamy?"

"Oh, yeah. I would not have chosen anyone else for you. He

is brave, kind, devoted and one handsome guy. I am overjoyed for you both." She held Sharley's and Greyson's hand. Sharley cuddled up to him as strategies continued.

Chapter Fifty

Ari and King Berthold pulled chairs up to Treelin's cell made of glass. It was completely sealed off. Ari motioned for him to turn the speaker on.

"Treelin, you are aware Queen Malvoil will end your life for conspiring with us?" Ari began.

"Yes. I don't care."

"Death and life in Brimstone Mountain won't be all that different," the king spoke sorrowfully.

"At least I won't be transformed into one of the Eryndomnites." His body twitched. "It's repulsive. I have a suggestion for your kingdom."

"What might that be?" Ari asked curiously.

"Show all the kingdom what happens to someone who accepts the mark of King Eryn."

"That is a good point. Except for those who have witnessed it firsthand, our kingdom dwellers have no idea. Thank you and you can be assured we will do exactly that," the king said gratefully.

"Treelin, Addley's death has saddened the whole kingdom. Even though she betrayed us, she was a good friend and at one time, a true asset to the kingdom. From my experience, King Eryn is just as diabolical as Satan, himself. If your guard is down, he will deceive a person and trick them into believing his lies. So, for the good of our kingdom and avenging you and Addley, we must proceed with haste," Prince Ari added in order to offer some consolation.

The data provided was lifesaving. Plans were made to execute the strike at midnight. Treelin, dressed in a contamination suit, was escorted by guards wearing the same. He was pretty far gone, so the soot that dripped from him constantly was fatal to the Ma Oz Kingdom.

The king and queen, followed by Galaxas' crew and followed by everyone else in the kingdom, made their way secretly to Brimstone Mountain. Arriving not far away, the stench grew to repulsive heights. The sky took on a dreary gray haze and there was no breeze, just scorching heat. Moans of agony and sadness sprung from the crevices in its confines.

They rubbed their fearful arms, but the goosebumps kept growing and covering their whole bodies.

Galaxas was experienced in supernatural warfare but not going into its domain. She was a little freaked out. Troid remained at her side. Silence was almost overwhelming amongst them, but they pressed on. Treelin had to be at the front to get them in. They would have to take the suit off of him first. He led them into the secret entrance. There really should be no entrance or exit into Brimstone Mountain since the last battle, but Ma Oz kingdom allowed themselves to become complaisant. As for Treelin, shaking in his soot, knowing the evil outrage the queen will have towards him and the consequences of it, gulped the very little bit of saliva he had left.

"Get into position all." The king sent the message with several guards to relay to his army behind him. No yelling. They needed complete silence. He bowed his head before entering. Everyone around did the same. With a hand, he waved them onward while riding on top of his horse, Firestorm. His name was in reference to his fiery powers.

The whole army was cloaked in invisibility and a shield of protection, thanks to Galaxas and her gang. The place was filth, and the inhabitants were disturbing to the eye and ears. They, however, had no idea the army was atween them. Once they all made it to the center area, they would spread out. That was tricky because they would no longer be under the protection of invisibility or Galaxas' shield.

Each inhabitant of the kingdom of Ma Oz had their own special powers, and used together would be a force to be reckoned with. The king and queen, along with Galaxas and her team would enter King Eryn's chambers. They would remain invisible. Galaxas hoped their powers would work in this dark world of wickedness but was uncertain. If all goes as planned, it will be over and done within a twinkling of an eye due to the surprise element.

The evil king and queen slept in luxury, while their inhabitants lived in complete squalor. King Eryn jumped up in bed. Eyes searching the room. Galaxas had witnessed evilness plenty, but even his presence caused her body to shake. He was the description of evil and obviously, he loved and adored it.

He climbed out of bed and cast a wary eye. Just a tease of a crooked smile developed. Whoosh! He cast a lightning bolt in several directions. His eyes glowed a creepy, slimy green color. The iris taking on the form of a serpent. The shield and invisibility kept its form. He stared. Something was amiss but what?

King Berthold gave Galaxas the go-ahead nod. She nodded to Troid, Nebulane and Raiden. Their eyes of a sun drilled a sizzling hole through his slimy, maggot infested heart. He was paralyzed from shock and now unable to fight back. His eyes grew with fear. That mocking, grotesque smile faded to a thought that oddly came into his mind: *Every knee shall bow*. And he slipped down on his knees in agony as the life disintegrated away.

Queen Malvoil disappeared the second she heard the sizzling and smelled the vile odor of him being destroyed. The king and queen ran out to find her. That is when they heard battle cries from their own people. The Eryndomnites were taken by surprise. And here was Malvoil gritting her fanged teeth at Treelin.

"How dare you defy me," echoed through the hollows of the mountain. "Why did you bring them here?"

Words stuttering, he said, "Because I don't care anymore.

Addley's gone. Your lies of living happily and immersed in treasures have been revealed. There will never be happiness here or in the afterlife. Why live in the present when it is no different than after. My only consolation is seeing you destroyed so you can't lie or trick anyone else. That's why I did it!"

"Then, death you want; death you shall HAVE." With that, she blasted him to the afterlife. Ari and Ember ran up just as it happened.

The queen sensed their presence and turned with an amused smile. "Give it your best shot, kids." She was powerful and full of arrogant confidence.

Ari's face turned angry shades. Ember's eyes welled with tears from witnessing Treelin's death. They held hands and joined their powers. What Malvoil was unaware of is that the king and queen were behind her. They joined forces and with their extra superpowers, the evil queen faded to nothing but embers. Just before it was over, she yelled, "You were almost mine, Ember Pines," she could barely finish saying. Then she was nothing but scattering ash.

Her and King Eryn's ashes were swept up, placed in several containers and buried in the desert that was a part of the mountain. The rest of the battle went on for days. The most important part was to sneak up and surprise King Eryn and Queen Malvoil. If they were aware of their army, results would have been catastrophic. Treelin had saved their lives. Mourning his and Addley's loss, would be great amongst the kingdom.

The battle was finally over. Now to assess the damages to their army was emotionally draining. The king and queen, princes and princesses wandered to each section and each level with emotional guilt, shame and regret that it had come to this.

"Guard, please, provide the number of Ma Oz fatalities," King Berthold requested.

"Zero," Your Highness."

On and on they walked to hear the grateful tear-blinding emotional replies of "Zero, Your Highness."

Nebulane had accompanied them. Since their eyesight causes every area they look at to light up like daylight, she saw something of concern in the far distance. A hand went to the King's shoulder. Her face was serious. He looked over to see Queen of the Animal Kingdom, Melisande, and the king, Dillon, lying dead on the ground. Before Nebulane went to them to use her powers, a guard ran up. "King, your special visitor has an urgent message. No one is to touch King Dillon or Queen Melisande's bodies. Please follow me."

Nonstop tears flooded the area. Ari and Ember saw the crowd and walked over. They looked in the direction everyone was staring at. Ari was frozen like ice and Ember fell to her knees with gut-wrenching sobs. Ari began to walk over but Queen Valeska, with anguished words of cries, had held him back in an embrace. "No one is allowed to touch them."

King Berthold walked back, the back of his hand wiping his face continuously. He drew in a deep breath and placed a hand on Ari's shoulder. With tears dribbling down his face, he spoke. "The Lord is taking them home with Him. He understands your grief but wants you to know they are happier than ever. They love you so much. He said you and Ember will rule with His help and will be a blessing as were your parents. It is their time to come home, He said. Please know they believe in you both. This is why God allowed Ember to be transported to Earth, for her safety. Malvoil meant it as evil, but God turned it around.

"I am going to miss them so much," he said as his body fell to the ground, puddles forming grief-stricken tears beneath him. Valeska, Ari and Ember didn't have the strength to stand and fell to the ground themselves. The grief was unbearable.

A bright glow engulfed Dillon and Melisande's bodies and lifted them up in the air. The gasps caused the royal family to look up with disbelief. With all the magical things that happen around their kingdom, this was something they had never seen.

Everyone followed all the way back to Ma Oz. The Lord's angels sealed up any entrance to Brimstone Mountain. At Animalia, King Dillon and Queen Melisande's kingdom, the bodies were laid on the courtyard on top of a bountiful amount of flowers and fresh greens, still glowing. Animals far and wide came and encircled their bodies. Then their bodies rose up in the sky at the speed of sound and vanished. The kingdom heard the words, "Welcome home," and bittersweet tears were shed.

~

Tyrus and Virginia sat around a bonfire awaiting the outcome. The guys and Annalee joined them. Every animal far and wide began to howl, scream, and shriek in distress. Being around the unusual, they all knew it meant something. Fear rose in their hearts. They turned their heads and stared where the portal had opened previously.

All around the world, people stopped and listened to dogs wailing and all other animals wild and tame making sounds of distress. It was an eerie, almost saddening sound. News media would report on the phenomenon.

Chapter Fifty-One

Galaxas knew they needed to get back on earth soil. Their job was done. She looked reluctantly at Ember. "I have not seen your transformation into queen of the animal kingdom. I'm kind of curious to see if my illustrations look anything like it."

"My goodness. I've been this way for so long, I forgot all about it. I tell you what, Ari and I will come back with you. I have to say goodbye to Tyrus and Virginia. They treated me like a daughter." Her eyes blurred and she licked her tears. "Before we leave, I will perform the transition for all of you."

"Raiden's wife is actually from Earth, but she lives on our planet. I don't know what that has to do with anything, but it just came to my mind. This is really exciting, but they're waiting for us, worried about the battle outcome," Galaxas said.

Being in a different realm, they had no clue that only an hour had passed by on Earth, but in Ember's kingdom, it was a two-week battle.

"Let me get Ari, my grandparents and parents to thank you properly and tell you goodbye. I'll be right back."

The gathering was heartfelt. Even tearful. The whole kingdom expressed their gratitude. The king handed her one of the kingdom's scepters. They didn't need any scepters, to be honest, but it was a formality the loyal inhabitants welcomed. The scepter had a crystalized round top. He demonstrated to Galaxas how to use it in order to see them at any time. But, they were not allowed to reveal it to anyone else. If they did, it would disintegrate into embers. She was deeply touched.

They entered the portal and flew out as if they were thrown from a plane, it was so fast. Annalee and the gang watched things rolling at a fast pace and heard gravel clink in all directions. As their bodies tumbled to a rolling stop, Annalee and Tyrus jumped up from the bench surrounding the bonfire and ran to them. Dazed, rubbing their injuries, they sat up. Annalee almost tackled Raiden with welcoming kisses. He was recovering from the painful landing but welcomed her kisses.

Tyrus ran to Ember, breathless, not knowing what to say.

Ari lifted her up from the ground. By this time the whole gang stood around. Eyes were permanently affixed to Ari. He and Ember had changed their size to fit in with the people of Earth. He was one beautiful young man. What was so beguiling is that a mild glitter formed around him and Ember. It was a sight to behold.

With loving eyes, Tyrus addressed Ember. "I wasn't sure if I would ever see you again." He swallowed.

"After today, probably never again." Saddened at the realization, her head dropped, and her eyes teared up. She pulled herself together and spoke. "Our beloved queen and king, Ari's parents, of the animal kingdom, have gone home to be with the Lord. He said their work was complete and he brought them home." Tears fell between her and Ari. Sniffling she perpended, "They are extremely happy and loved there, but we miss them terribly. Ari and I have been training to take over their positions for years. I hope we make them proud." Sobs came expectantly. Galaxas wiped her face in the background.

Tyrus took her tiny hands. "There will only be success for you both. From what I've seen, you will make them proud." He tilted her tearstained face. "I am going to miss you so much. Just know that you are loved here. I pray God will have mercy and bring you two back to visit us one day. My life has been made complete because of you.

"Prince—King Ari, I mean—you are blessed among men. Take good care of her. She is very special. You are something special, too. I can already see that."

"Thank you, sir. And thank you for keeping her safe. After the celebration of life for my parents," he coughed to cover up his emotional tone, "we will be married and rule together."

"Virginia, I just remembered something about the photo of Tyrus' wife," Ember mentioned with an elevated voice.

"What might that be?"

"When we are sent to Earth to help with the animal kingdom, we are invisible. She was tending to an injured fox pup. She didn't know it, but it was going to die. I invisibly used my healing power, and the pup was renewed. This happened a few times with different animals. I always had a soft spot for her. She would have made a fine protector of the animal kingdom."

Virginia teared up and squeezed Tyrus' hand. "She was an amazing human being."

"We must depart now," Ember said with glittery teardrops.

Everyone hugged. "Could I have a picture with you before you leave, please?" Tyrus begged.

"Ari, for me as well," Ember pleaded. Of course, their pictures were done in some magical way. Photographs completed, all that was left to do was transform their bodies and leave. "You must never tell a living soul what you witness today, or we will have to erase it from your memory. I never want any of you to forget us," Ember admitted affectionately.

In seconds, she and Ari transformed into their heavenly given body forms. They were part animal and part human and all magnificent. Gasps of awe were heard. Tears streamed down Galaxas' face. She was the spitting image of her own illustrations that she had drawn of Ember in her book.

"Goodbye all. Never forget us and we will never forget you."

As they were sucked through the horizontal vortex, the portal closed permanently.

Nobody could speak for minutes.

Tyrus and Virginia invited their guests in for dinner. Conversation was lively and Galaxas signed her book for Tyrus, which he will treasure for the rest of his life. He looked down at Ember's picture and she magically waved. He quit breathing for a moment and wiped a tear in her honor.

"Hey all, I had a dream that we joined forces with—get this —a mermaid army. We made good friends with a Hagan and Chantara. It was so amazing, as if mermaids were real," Annalee just remembered dreaming and couldn't resist sharing.

Tyrus looked over at her. "From what we have witnessed these past few months, don't be surprised about anything. They're real. You watch and see and remember my words." He sighed as if looney tunes were taking over his body. Everyone busted up.

"Hold on there. I had the strangest dream myself," Virginia shouted out. "I dreamt this beautiful couple named Talia and Chatwin came to visit us. Sitting in a big room was Galaxas and her family. Talia had an enchanting sparkle about her, as if the Lord was showing her off, and then there was Ember and Ari and Hagan and Chantara. Altogether in one room. We had the best time. That is just so strange how we dreamt of the same characters that we have never met, apart from Ember and Ari."

The way everything was going and from what everyone witnessed, they all looked up to the ceiling in thought. It was going to happen one day. When and where, no one knew.

Thankfully the love that scattered in the wind was reunited. The spark has been reignited, and King Ari and Queen Ember will reign until the good Lord above brings them home.

It was bedtime and a mother read her daughter's favorite story, *Ember Pines*. She closed the book and laid it on a nightstand.

"So sweet girl, fairy tales do come true."

"And they lived happily ever after; right Mommy?"

"Yes, they did."

She handed her daughter a fluffy horse named Skyfire along

with Ember and Ari figurines. The girl cuddled them and lied down on the pillow. Mom kissed the top of her head, tucked her in, turned on a nite light and left the room, making sure the door stayed cracked open.

Outside the girl's window, the moon beamed, and happy stars twinkled in the sky.

THANK YOU FOR READING

~

Did you enjoy this book?

We invite you to leave a review at your favorite book site, such as Goodreads, Amazon, Barnes & Noble, etc.

DID YOU KNOW THAT LEAVING A REVIEW...

- Helps other readers find books they may enjoy.
- Gives you a chance to let your voice be heard.
- Gives authors recognition for their hard work.
- Doesn't have to be long. A sentence or two about why you liked the book will do.

About the Author

Linda Phillips lives in S.W. Florida with her two cats, Sprinkle and Skittle. Imagination is an essential component in reading and writing. Life can be hard, but a little imagination can give us wings and determination. Three children and eight grandchildren is a gift from God. Because she loves the color pink, she drives a firefighter pink Mini Cooper that keeps her late husband's thoughts with her everywhere she drives, and plenty of pink accents are found in her house. Writing first began as a way of therapy. Now, God keeps filling her imagination with more stories, and His influence is in each story. So, be on the lookout for other stories in the near future.

lindalouphillips.com

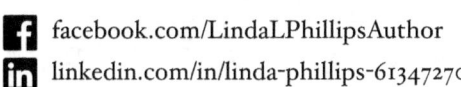

facebook.com/LindaLPhillipsAuthor

linkedin.com/in/linda-phillips-61347270

Also by Linda Phillips

WITH SATIN ROMANCE

Novels

Marry Christmas

Chocolate, Chimpanzees & Court Reporter at Chute Pond

Follow Your Heart

(A Stand Alone Fantasy Romance Series)

Moon Water

Dew of Heaven

Sunsets & Dandelion Kisses

Love Scattered in the Wind